THESILA PROPHECY
The Journey Home

ROBERT RUMBLE

ISBN 978-1-957781-38-9 (softcover)
ISBN 978-1-958128-72-5 (hardcover)
ISBN 978-1-957781-39-6 (ebook)
Library of Congress Control Number: 2022903682

Book Vine Press
2516 Highland Dr.
Palatine, IL 60067

Acknowledgments

I would like to thank Keni Aryani for creating the cover Also, I would like to thank Tom Antion for his invaluable education in internet marketing. Even if he focuses on how-to books, a lot of what I learned from him crossed over to fiction. Last but not the least, I would like to thank Jan Rumble for being my mom, for her love and support.

THE CAVE

http://www.thesilaprophecy.com/

A YOUNG MAN WEARING AN iridescent green bespoken outfit creeps through the forest like a cat. He has a fancy recurve bow in one hand with an arrow nocked but relaxed. Not even the birds realize his presence as he skirts the edge of the forest meadow. Stalks of waist-high amber grass stretch to a thick wall of morning fog, hanging over the grass about a bow shot from the tree line. *The fog in this place and time of day is unnatural,* he thinks as he moves closer one silent step at a time. From the mist, dozens of ice shards fly toward him like arrows. He drops to the ground as the shards pass over, shattering on the nearby trees. He scans the field seeing an ice ball rolling towards him, growing larger as it approaches. He doges to the side into the mist avoiding being crush.

He finds himself in a town square laying on a wood platform, holding two curved swords. Across the platform is a short, stocky man wearing scale armor and wielding a massive double bit battle-ax. Around the platform are scores of people wearing furs of different colors and styles, all laughing and pointing at him. He stands up and shakes his head trying to figure out what happened, when the ax swings back in his direction. He gets a sword up to block the blow but is staggered back to the edge. He ducks and weaves, avoiding the mighty ax. Using the swords to guard is fruitless as the ax plows through them sending him flying across the platform. When a quick double-handed swing connects, it sends his swords flying in different directions. He hits hard, sliding across the platform to the edge, and over into a forked tree branch.

Pinned between several tree branches, he scans the surroundings bewildered. He is tangled up in an uprooted tree rolling, spinning and bouncing in a turbulent river. His wet clothes have changed to flat green and brown with rips sewn close. The icy water sucks his energy, as his feet and hands turn blue and stiff, passed any sensation of pain, only numbness. The force of the water jams him into the branches as he fights to untangle himself from the branches climbing out of the water, only to have the tree roll sending him under. Fighting the cold, he scrambles through the branches poking his head above the surface for some air. The water steals his strength with exponential speed as the tree spins and bounces about in the raging river. He takes a gulp of air before the tree spins again forcing him into the dark water once more.

He opens his eyes gasping for air as two men on horseback barrel down on him out of the darkness. Glancing around, he is on the edge of a mixed forest of conifer and deciduous trees. Drawing the two slender curved swords, he runs deeper into the wood for cover. Hiding behind a tree, he does not want to do what he must—dismount the riders any way he can. The horsemen split into a search pattern, weaving around the trees with the swords ready to strike. With his back to a tree, he listens for the riders. His heart pounds as his chest rises and falls. With a steady ringing in his ears, he takes a couple of deep breaths to collect his thoughts. A branch breaks on the tree next to him and he swings his sword around, sending the horse and rider to the ground. The rider tumbles and lands on his feet, sword, and shield, ready for the inevitable fight. The other horse rider also moves in for the kill. The swordsman on the ground advances, swinging his sword in deliberate arcs. The shield knocks his swords aside as the unhorsed man brings the sword down.

Mashaun jerks awake springing to an upright position in bed, sweat pouring down his brow and his pillow soaking wet. Shaking his head, he scans the room. It is dark, except for a dull glow of light radiating from the ceiling. He thinks this is strange since his bedroom in Tianjin doesn't have a skylight. The bed is hard even harder than his bed in China, more like a stone slab. His satin sheets have changed to heavy, coarse animal fur. He sits up swinging his feet over the side of a rectangular pedestal about the size of a king-size bed. Trying to absorb his new surroundings, he wipes the sleep from his turquoise eyes scanning a room, but, obviously not his bedroom. Except for the distant echo of a waterfall, silence replaces the usual city sounds heard in the morning. As the room comes into focus, it appears to be a cavernous domed room with an orange glow at the end of a long passage. As the fog of sleep dissipates, he realize the room is inside a huge rock igloo.

Four empty stone pedestals projecting up about two feet from the floor along the back edge of the room, each with a different colored fur blanket. At the end is a table also grown from the rock floor. In the center of the domed ceiling is a circular opening which allows light into the room. On one side is a dark, shadowy doorway with the sound of falling water echoing from the darkness. He slowly stands, goose bumps cover his body from the cool, moist air on his naked body as he steps onto a smooth tile-like rock floor beneath his feet. The combination of the cold floor and the still air untouched by any heat cuts like a knife to the bone. Looking around for something to wear, he settles for the brown fur blanket on his bed. Wrapping it like an oversized toga, it warms him and gives him a sense of security. Even alone, he is more comfortable wearing something.

The room brightens like the rising sun of morning, chasing the darkness away revealing the smooth coffee-colored obsidian-like walls. It appears clean. No rocks, loose dirt, or even dust anywhere. The flat floor gently slopes down to a shallow bowl in the center of the room, directly below the hole in the ceiling. The long passage has a similar slope, from the walls to the center, extending from the bowl to the orange glow, which has become more yellow, a shallow trough leading into the shadowy doorway, creating a natural drainage system. Not far to the right of the darkened door is a colored map embedded on the wall, showing mountains, rivers, castles of different sizes and many symbols resembling caves.

The sound of the falling water becomes louder as Mashaun approaches the nearby, darkened doorway. As he nears the shadow door, his fur collects the warm mist lingering in the air, not cold as he expected. The nearby wall covered with condensation from the warm mist meeting the cool rock. Water runs down the wall in micro streams to the floor, into the depression, and back into the room. He touches the wall, and to his surprise, it is wet but not slippery like the floor beneath his feet. No moss or slime grew on the surfaces, which he expected from the constant moisture. Stepping through the shadow door, he enters another room. His silhouette disappears in the swirling mist. On the far side of the room, a couple of spheres emit light no brighter than a candle. With each step, the balls brighten until they fill the room with an eerie white light.

To his right, a waterfall about 12-feet high crashes down onto a course flat rock. Before emptying into a stream flowing the length of the room then disappears under the wall on his left. Along the left wall, above where the water disappears under a stone shelf with an oval hole over the middle the stream. Halfway between the falls and the shelf is a pool of bubbling, steaming water, separated from the stream by rocks of various shapes and sizes. The consistent splashing of the waterfall and the subtle bubbling from the pool echoes in the rectangular room, calming the senses, as a wave of peacefulness washes over him. Three paths lead from the door, one to the shelf over the stream, one down to the pool, and one to the falls. The pool water is murky, reminding him of a natural hot spring without the odor. With the caution of stepping into a steaming tub, he sticks his toe into the water and finds it's a little warmer than bath water. Laying his fur on the rocks, inch by inch he slides into the Jacuzzi-like pool, letting the bubbling water chase the chill away. Minutes feel like hours as his hand slips into the cold stream, startling him as he drifts into calm rest. Enjoying the dream, he thinks all he needs now is a beautiful girl to join him.

Mai awakens groggily and is oblivious to her surroundings siting up hoping she is ready for a medical midterm. She spent the previous night cramming for the test with a few friends, and it was well after midnight before she got to bed. Mai searches for her robe on the foot of her bed, but it's not there. She brushes it off, thinking she misplaced it again. Following the sound of falling water, she shuffles into the bathroom for a morning shower. Assuming her roommate is already in the shower as she enters the room filled with mist. Asking her roommate Christel how much longer? Maybe it is her nightgown sticking to her skin, or the stranger napping in a tub, except, they don't have one, or the cold, wet floor beneath her feet. Her senses come rushing back like a freight train as she suddenly realizes this is not her dorm room. Her mind races as she remembers the previous night. She stands in shock, frozen like a mannequin in a store window, trying to comprehend her surroundings, not sure if the person in the tub is real or a dream.

Jerking his head up and looking toward the door, Mashaun eyes a young woman in her late teens or early twenties wearing a long, sheer purple nightgown damp by the mist clinging to her lovely body. He stares at her in disbelief, this vision of beauty frozen like a rock. Several times, he motions for her to come down to the pool, telling her it's warm and will help against the chill. She stands like a statue, frozen in time, with only the raising and lowering of her chest with every breath.

Mashaun climbs out of the pool wrapping himself in the fur at the same time. She has goose bumps all over and stares blankly straight ahead. The mist further saturates her nightgown, revealing every curve. She appears Asian with almond-shaped green eyes and waist-long pomegranate color hair. He stands for a moment, admiring her smooth, flawless skin and the soft flowing lines of her body in almost disbelief. He wonders if she is part of his dream, or if she is a dream within a dream.

He waves his hand in front of her face, but she does not flinch. He gently touches her shoulder, which is cold and clammy; again, she does not move.

"Don't move," he foolishly says and retrieves one of the other furs to wrap around her. Slowly, her face relaxes, losing its stunned expression. A moment later, she slowly turns her head and stares at him. Still glassy-eyed and confused, she allows Mashaun to gently take her arm, leading her down the path to the pool.

"Get in. You'll feel much better," he says and then turns to leave.

Mai hates being alone, almost to the point of having a mild phobia. Growing up in a large family, someone was always around, and she was popular in school with lots of friends. In her dream, this stranger is kind and gentle, offering to give her space she doesn't want. Mai mulls over her options in an instance, deciding it is better to share the pool with this stranger than to be by herself. She lightly grabs his arm.

"Don't leave," she pleads in a soft, frightened voice.

Mashaun agrees, and then he helps her take off the fur and places it on a nearby rock. Mai slides into the warm water. While she is moving to the other side of the pool, he quickly gets into the water. She, at least, has a nightgown, which is more than he is wearing, making him a little uncomfortable.

This has to be a dream, he thinks. Sitting across him is this picture of his dream girl. As the water warms her up, she becomes more relaxed as the goose bumps disappear. The murky water prevents him from seeing anything below the surface; only a couple of purple straps over her shoulders are visible. He has always been a little shy, and this moment is no exception as he sits admiring her, not knowing what to say. Mashaun starts a sentence a dozen times, in his head, but no words come out. Trying not to stare, he avert her gaze, time and time again.

Mai eyes him over, thinking he is not exactly what she will call handsome, but he's not bad-looking either. He is a gentleman, almost too kind, which worries her. He wonders about his ulterior motives. She eventually realizes he isn't going to say anything as the water touches the bottom of his chin, staring at her, trying not to be obvious. A nervous smile creeps across her face as she introduces herself as Mai from Quezon City, Philippines.

Shyly, he introduces himself as Mashaun, telling her he lives in China but is originally from the United States.

"Where did you learn to speak Filipino?" She asks.

"Filipino? You're speaking English," he replies, surprised.

"No, I speak Filipino. My English is no good."

"How can we understand each other if we speak different languages?" he questions, perplexed.

In an uncomfortable silence, they sit in the pool, pondering this revelation, both feeling a little uneasy while at the same time safer in each other's company. Relaxed, Mai begins to talk nonstop about her home.

"I'm going to check out the rest of the cave. Will you be okay here?" Mashaun asks before turning to his fur, getting it wet as he gets out of the pool, wrapping it around.

"Wait," she says. "I'll come with you. Will you hand me my fur?" She does not want to be alone.

Mashaun holds the fur up so she can wrap herself. Holding their fur skins in place, they go through the door into the dome-room. It is well lit, showing everything clearly now. Five pedestal beds line the semicircle wall to the left, each with five geometric symbols embedded in the rock. Four identical shapes flank an irregular one in the middle. The symbols are dark on the two they woke up on, while the other three have a slight red glow within the symbols themselves. The map to their left reveals a lot more detail in the light, as strange symbols become visable next to the pictures. Directly across them is the small pedestal about the height of a dining table, full of dried meats and fruits with some drinks in stone cups.

After looking at each other and realizing they're hungry, they devour some meat and fruit, washing them down with some juice from the never emptying cups. The meat has the flavor of mild venison while the fruits Smell and feel like apples, oranges and pears, but they have a different flavor. Three differently colored jade-like mugs, each with a liquid tasting a little like pineapple, orange and cranberry juice.

The walls of the arched passageway are smooth and polished instead of rough like a dug tunnel, surprising both of them. The wall of orange glow is now white. Mashaun believes it is the cave entrance leading to the outside world. They step out of the cave into the warm sunshine beneath a cloudless sky and scan the scenery. The entrance is several yards up a cliff face, with loose rocks angling down from them to a grassy meadow full of wildflowers filling the air with their fragrance. They listen for any sounds of civilization but only the buzzing of insects and birds in the trees fill the air. He takes a deep breath, enjoying the clean air and fragrances from the meadow while Mai nervously scans the openness, taking a few steps back behind him.

Mashaun loves the outdoors, having spent years hiking, backpacking and hunting in the western States. Those were some of his happiest times, and this is even better. Glad he spent the time learning some survival skills in case something happened should he be stuck in the wilderness longer than expected, but this is beyond wildest dreams.

"Listen…What do you hear?" he asks Mai.

"Nothing, I don't hear a thing," she answers uncomfortably, peeking out from behind him.

"Exactly. No traffic, no horns blaring, no cell phones, just the sounds of nature in its purest form," with a calm factual tone, as grin stretches from ear to ear.

"You actually like this?" She asks, shaking her head while looking at him as though he were crazy.

"Absolutely." He responds.

A pair of wagon ruts coming out of pine-like trees on the left, crossing in front of the cave, and disappearing into the forest again to their right. On the other side of the ruts, tall trees with thick underbrush surround the medium-sized meadow. Off to the right, by the fringe and next to the trail, are a couple of rock circles with black centers looking like used fire pits.

Mashaun hunts around for some rocks to make a knife when he comes across the only shiny black rock in a pile of common rocks and boulders. The shiny rock already has the shape of a knife and needs a little sharpening for his purpose. Not thinking much of it, he chooses an oval rock and returns to Mai.

"What are you going to do?" She asks curiously with a tremor in her voice.

"Watch," he tells her and sits down to chip the obsidian rock so one edge is razor-sharp. He proceeds to cut parts from a section of fur to wrap around his feet before cutting a long narrow section to tie around his waist to keep the toga closed without constantly having to hold it. She observes intently before asking if he will do the same for her, handing him her fur. She sits next to him in her semi-dry nightgown, which isn't as revealing when dry, as he makes the robes.

They trade stories about the homes they knew before. Well, mostly Mai talks and he listens. He sometimes wishes she would stop chattering. During the conversation, he spots two pierce earrings in each of her ears. They appear to be tiny diamonds and emeralds. He thinks those may come in handy should they need some money.

It takes the rest of the morning to finish both outfits. By the time he's done, the sun has moved behind them, casting a shadow over the cliff wall. He tells her they should gather some firewood for the night in case it gets cold. She agrees, and they head down the rocky slope to the meadow. Turning around to help her off the rocks, he doesn't see the cave.

"Look!" He says, pointing where the cave entrance should be. Mai scans the cliff for the cave entrance.

"Where's the cave?" She asks nervously.

"I don't know," Mashaun replies.

He goes back up the rocks to where he thinks it is and reaches out to touch the wall, and his hand disappears into the cliff face. Stepping forward, he is back in the cave. Turning around, as Mai scrambles up the rocks, yelling for him. He steps out of the cave, and she stops.

"Where did you go?" She asks.

"Back into the cave. The wall, it's not real, it's an illusion!" He says excitedly.

"A what?" She replies.

"An illusion, something appearing different than it's true form. I have seen magicians create illusions. I have even seen three-dimensional holograms, but nothing even close to this," he admits a little excitedly.

"A hologram?" She inquires.

"Never mind. I'll tell you later."

Both of them stare at the rock wall then gaze at each other as though each wants to say something, but chooses not to. Mashaun stacks up a few rocks into a small cairn to mark the entrance before going to gather some firewood and dried grasses from the meadow. He tells her to stay away from the forest edge, not knowing wildlife inhabits this area. After several trips to the entrance with armloads of wood, Mai goes into the cave and proceeds to shuttle the wood to the back of the cave. Mashaun continues to gather more wood and some dry grasses along with some rocks to make a fire ring. He plans to use the hot rocks to help stay warm by putting some under the furs.

"Okay, how are we going to start the fire?" She asks curiously with a tone of skepticism.

"Watch," he says, scrapping two rocks together creating a spark. It takes some time, but he gets a small fire going and slowly nurses it up to where it is putting out enough heat for both of them. With the coming of night, the light gives way to the darkness as the flickering flames keep the shadows of the night at bay along with the chilly air. The perfectly designed room amplifies both the light and heat to the center. Warming the room faster than expected, they have to remove some of the wood from the fire to cool it down.

"The walls are changing," she says, startled.

Chapter 2

DALISTRA

http://thesilaprophecy.com/glossary

PARTS OF THE WALL HAVE pictographs a couple of shades lighter than the surface. They don't appear drawn or carved but actually part of the wall. In the flickering light of the fire, they appear to change from one scene to the next, like a flipbook. Running their hands over the pictures, they are smooth as a thin veneer covers the pictures. They continue jumping from one scene to the next, telling different stories. One depicts the life and death of humans hunting animals; some are familiar and some are not. Others show people dancing around campfires, with ruined castles in the background. The scenes continue, never repeating itself.

The most unsettling show is one of two people sitting around a fire with five bed-like pedestals arcing around them in a semicircle along the back wall. The first two are empty and missing the furs, while the other three show each with a different color of fur on the beds. They stare at the images, then glance at the room and back at the images. The flipping pictures show what they did earlier, including them looking at the wall, continuing to where the three people—two men, and a woman—

are being forced to walk with their hands bound behind their backs, surrounded by armed figures with swords, while a man and a woman dressed in furs appear to be hiding behind a flat wall. They scan the room in unison before rushing to the only flat wall in the room—the map. Mashaun reaches out and warily touches the map, running his fingers down the roads and rivers, but realizes it is solid.

Remembering how the cliff face looked real but wasn't, Mai picks up one of the sticks by the fire and yells at Mashaun to move as she lobs it at the wall, hoping it doesn't bounce back. He sidesteps as it flies past him and through the wall. His perception of the map changed, and they step through the illusionary wall. Standing in a dark, narrow hall about seven-feet tall and four-feet wide. The illusion prevents the fire light from illuminating the hall, but reveals the backside of the map, which has more details—more cities, caves, colors and symbols resembling a form of writing. On the left side of the map, are logographs, which is different from the upper right and lower right.

He tells her to wait and leaves the room grabbing a couple of burning sticks. He has no problem going back through the map with the torches, realizing it is only an illusion. The hall is short, only about 15-feet long with an arched ceiling before opening into a square room about 20 by 15 foot room. Following the wall, they come upon an ornate metal torch with a softball-sized sphere on the end. When Mai touches it, the sphere begins to glow, illuminating a section of the room. They find a sphere in each corner, lighting up the entire room in a soft light.

"Way to go, Mai! Let's see what's here."

Several racks with different weapons and shields fill the room. Swords and spears of various sizes line the first two rows, while round, square and oblong shields are on the third row. Along the sidewalls are various pole arms and hanging on the back wall are bows of different sizes.

"Wow! A weapons cache," Mashaun exclaims.

Mai stairs at him with sad, almost teary, eyes.

"What's wrong?" He asks her with some concern.

"I thought this is a dream, but I would never dream of something like this," she says, pointing to the weapons.

"You thought I am part of your dream. I thought you were part of my dream," Mashaun replies as he scans the room.

"This has to be a dream, but it must be yours," she softly says.

"Maybe it is, but I hope not," he replies.

"What?" she says surprised.

"Never mind," he replies.

"This has to be a dream," she mutters as she slides down the wall to a sitting position with her head in her hands. "I'm a third-year medical student. I'm a good student getting excellent grades. I have always lived in a city. I don't like the country, and I abhor violence of any kind," she says, almost crying.

Looking at Mashaun through her watery eyes, she continues. "How old are you? Twenty-five? I thought the man of my dreams would be... older and not so average, no offense," she offers.

"None taken," he replies, after he has the same view of himself.

"This is not a dream...It's a nightmare," she says at last.

"Yes, I am 25 years old," he says. "But you fit the girl in my dreams. Long red hair, green eyes, but Asian. The three don't exactly go together if you know what I mean," Mashaun curiously states.

"Don't worry. The red hair is from a box. My mother is Irish, and my father is Filipino. So I must be part of your dream," she tells him.

"I don't know," he replies. She detects the uncertainty in his voice. He was secretly hoping her red hair was real.

"We better do something about the fire before someone else finds this room," he says after remembering the wall.

They both rush out of the room to snuff the fire before scattering the wood and rocks outside the cave entrance, also kicking over the cairn. He enters the cave, as the creaking of metal and wood over shadows the natural sounds. Under the light of a yellow and blue moons, a wagon with a dozen or so warriors on foot marches from the forest to the clearing. Like the pictures on the wall, the soldiers wear leather armor, brandishing small round shields, with short swords and bows. The two lead horses carry a man wearing a metal armor clink as he rides, and a woman in a red cloak, carrying a staff. As the cage on wheels with two humans clothes in rags, curl up on the floor, pass beneath the cave.

He runs back and quickly starts throwing the remaining wood into the stream. Mai wonders what all the excitment is about.

"They're here!" he tells her, running to the stream with an armload of wood.

With all wood thrown in the stream, all they can hope is they don't spot black spot on the floor. "Maybe they won't spot the black spot in the dark." Using a small shield, they gather some water and try to clean it up, hoping whoever they are will not notice. Returning to the passage behind the map, they feel safer in their hidden room, watching the entrance until sleep finally overtakes them. During the night, Mashaun dreams of a woman in red next to a man holding a rope attached to a disheveled teenage girl on her hands and knees. He wakes up as the man is about to slit her throat. He shakes his head, trying to clear the image. It seemed so real, it scares him, especially after the wall showed them the room and the armed men. He does not fall back asleep during the rest of the night. Anytime he closes his eyes, the scene plays over again in his mind. Each time, he witness more of the abuse before her demise.

Hearing a commotion out in the dome room, he crawls to the backside of the map, remembering the pictures. He does not feel it necessary to grab a weapon. Mai wakes as he starts to leave. Putting his finger to her lips, Mashaun crawls up the hallway, confident they will not notice him. Not making a sound, Mai peeks around the corner observing everything as the wall predicted. A tall muscular man, a small, dark-skinned one-arm man, and a tall, slender teenage girl probably the youngest of the three. Mashaun reconizes the girl from his vision escorted out by a group of soldiers, along with the other two. Mashaun stands next to the backside of the map as soldier and mistress from his vision converse. He shakes his head in disbelief. He listens to them talking, but their words are foreign, which doesn't make any sense. He understands Mai, and she can understand him. So why can't he understand them?

The muscular warrior is wearing a chain tunic and coif, carrying a sword and standing a head taller than the woman. He says something, pointing to the two empty beds without furs. The woman wearing a blood-red leather pantsuit with a matching bustier and cloak is holding a red stone staff carved out of a single piece of stone. The top splits into six prongs curving up, creating an oval birdcage with two prongs missing on one side. Everything plays out like the pictures on the wall, and their appearance reminds him of the dream. She says something, looking scornfully at the man as he bows his head. Her sharp words send the man backing away as he answers her in a trembling voice. Mashaun perceives real worry and anger on her face as the warrior hurries down the hall. She turns to faces him, barking a few words making the man sprint down the hallway.

Scraping the burned spot with her shoe, she heads to the wall where the pictures are and starts attacking the wall with her dagger. The clanging of metal on stone echos in the cave as she furiously stabs and strikes the wall until the blade finally snaps in half before storming out of the cave. Mashaun can tell something is seriously wrong and it greatly upsets her.

"What did they say?" Mai asks when he returns.

"I couldn't understand what they were saying. However, the one in red is upset about the two missing furs. Then she went and attacked the wall. I want to see" as he turns to leave. By the time she asks him not to go, he is already heading down the hall.

The wall shows no marks where he thinks she was standing. It takes a moment for him to notice the pictures are different, not of a map, but of a cage on wheels surrounded by many figures lying on the ground with arrows sticking out of them. The other pictures are unchanged, but this one section has changed and the other sections are blank. Shaking his head, he hurries back to the safety behind the map.

"What did you see?" He briefly describes the picture to her.

"Oh, what are we going to do?" She asks, trembling.

"First thing is to find some weapons. I advise you to do the same. Something tells me, wherever we are, it is dangerous, so you might want some protection," he says as he goes to browse the bows. His thoughts flashed back to being on the school's varsity archery team and the times he went bow-hunting. But it was a long time ago.

It takes a while for Mai to come to grips with what he said. She reluntently realizes he is probably right, but she just wants to wake up from this nightmare. Wiping the tears from her eyes, she starts the task of hunting for a suitable weapon.

Long bows and short bows and straight bows and curved bows hanging in neat rows with a quiver of arrows by each one. After examining several bows, one catches Mashaun's eyes. The tips curl back toward each other as the limbs change hues in the dim light as he moves towards it. White bone is running from tip to tip and down through the middle, sandwiched between two pieces of dark wood, ending at the beginning of the curled bone tips. he has seen it before, but doesn't remember where. He gently removes the bow from the wall to examine it more closely. Attached is a bow string made of silk and mohair, in excellent condition.

bending the bow around his leg to string it, he readies to draw it.

"*TSAO KUVJ QOVB!*" a female voice says in a commanding tone. Startled, He drops the bows and it bounces and clatters on the floor, turning to scan the room, only to eye Mai looking at some daggers.

"What?" he asks.

"I didn't say anything," she says, glaring at him.

"Are you sure?"

"Yes, I'm sure," she replies, a little annoyed.

He picks up the bow and again, "*TSAO KUVJ QOVB!*" Again, he drops the bow and turns around.

"Did you hear that?"

"What? You dropping things, again?"

"Someone said something. You didn't hear it?"

"No, I think you're hearing things," she answers. *He's losing it already,* she thinks, shaking her head.

Looking mystified, he picks up the bow. Again, "*TSAO KUVJ QOVB!*" This time, he holds on to the bow and glances around.

"What? Who said that?" he asks.

"*KUVJ tywb uaz lamw.*"

"What? I don't understand?" with a confused voice.

The seconds slowly tick away as he continually scanning the room. "Where are you?" he says, getting a little irritated.

"*Nioby rua hvaju txisah.* I mean, in your hand, idiot," the voice says vehemently.

"WHAT!" he exclaims as he almost drops the bow again.

"Did you say something?" Mai asks, looking up from the row of daggers and short swords.

"Uh, no," he mutters.

He examines the bow and whispers, "What, how?"

"You have not heard of a spirit weapon before?" she says, a little condescending.

"Uh, no! Why, are they common?"

"Well put me back on the wall and be on your way. You obviously do not know how to handle such majestic beauty, artistry, and talent. So Put me back and be ou your way," she commands authoritatively.

"I know how to shoot a bow. Give me a chance to prove it," Mashaun whispers in his defense, but not knowing why.

"Well, you do have a gentle grip, and I sense honesty, a survivor...but a bit insecure. Um. Okay, I will give you one shot...literally. If you survive, then I will decide if you can remain in my company."

"If I survive?"

"You heard right, If you survive."

He takes the quiver of arrows off the wall and straps it to his belt.

"Okay, what do you want me to do?" Mashaun whispers.

"For starters, take me out of this room," she commands.

"My name is Mashaun. What is yours?"

"If you must know, it is Dalistra," she says with a pompous tone.

Mashaun tells Mai he is going to make sure it is safe and will be right back. "Besides, I want to try out this bow." She glances up concerned, asking about the armed men.

"Don't worry, I'll be careful, and I'll only be gone for a minute or two," he tells her as he leaves.

Mashaun walks down the hall to the map and stops, looking around making sure the cave is empty, before passing through into the dome cavern. Checking out the water room, he asks Dalistra about the test.

"Go to the mouth of the cave," Dalistra tells him. Stopping short of the entrance, The wagon with several people in the cage sits park by the fire ring. Several swordsmen are searching the tree line while a few more are on guard.

Dalistra let outs a long sigh when he scans past the wagon. When Mashaun asks what's wrong, she tells him she has been in the room too long.

Mai meanders around the room and listens to the stillness as the fear of being alone creeps into her head. She rushes out of the room, until she glimpses Mashaun and calms down as she runs to catch up.

Hearing footsteps behind him, he turns as Mai runs down the hall. Putting his hand up, to stop before turning his attention back to the meadow.

"By the way, how do you know my language?" he asks Dalistra.

"I speak many languages, including yours," she responds.

"Oh," he responds while standing at the cave entrance.

"Are they searching for you?" Dalistra asks.

He turns Dalistra around, looking for eyes or something on the bow, but finds a few faint symbols. "How can you see?"

"Not now. If you pass, I will tell you later," she states.

"Why are they looking for you?" she asks. Mashaun thinks about his answer for a moment.

"WHAT! YOU ARE A NAJ TEWB." Dalistra exclaims, trying to maintain her pompousness.

"Quiet, they'll hear you," Mashaun whispers, glancing about to see if anyone turns toward them.

"They will not hear me. If you survive, there is lot you need to know and comprehend."

"If I survive, quit saying if I survive. You said I am a survivor. By the way, what did you call me? A naj tewb? What's naj tewb?"

"You are an off worlder…not from Hauv Pem, I mean here."

Their conversation stops when the leader comes around the cage, looking at her prize catch. The scene plays out like in his dream and Dalistra senses it. Mashaun is too far to what she says to a man in chain armor, but he barks a command. Several of the remaining men head to the forest line to join the search. One of the guards yanks a young girl out of the cage. He can tell they are asking her something, but the young girl keeps shaking her head. The woman slaps her to the ground then the guard yanks her back up to her knees. The girl continues to shake her head, only to receive a slap again.

"Okay, what do you want me to do?" asks Mashaun.

"You know what will happen. So pick your target and shoot," Dalistra tells him. Without a second thought, Mashaun focuses on the woman

holding the staff and the man holding the girl's chain. He considers the options and decides the best course of action is to shoot the woman. It is a long shot, about 75 yards, but she's the closest. And with her being the leader, he thinks maybe he can change the known outcome.

This should be interesting he thinks. *I don't know what the drop will be, and I have not had any time to sight in the bow,* he mutters to himself.

"Don't worry. Visualize where you want to hit her," she tells him. It dawns on Mashaun, he has not mentioned shooting her. She knows what he is planning on doing. After all, it's the only reasonable shot available.

"Okay," he replies after a short hesitation. Cradling the bow in his palm and gently wraps his forefinger around the grip, he slowly draws the string back, it as the string kisses his lips and nose, he thinks it's a little light to make the shot, but Dalistra tells hm to focus on the target. She loves flexing her limbs again, like waking up in the morning, and his soft but firm grip around her body. It has been a long time since anybody held her with such tenderness. She is lost in her own soothing thoughts before snapping back to reality. Dalistra tells him to shoot for the forehead, showing him where to aim.

He releases the string, launching the arrow through the air like a missile as Dalistra lurches forward in his hand, catching him by surprise with her force. The arrow flies true, piercing the mage's upper chest, leaving only the fletching exposed. After seeing the arrow hit its mark, he reaches for a second arrow, which jumps into his hand. The woman stands for a second, looking at the fletching in disbelief before collapsing on the ground. The guard with the rope stares at the arrow then glances at the cave. Mashaun launches a second arrow at the armed man holding the woman, hitting him in the shoulder, forcing him to release the girl. The female prisoner scrambles under the wagon and curls up into a fetal position, hiding her head.

Several archers release their arrows toward the cave and Mashaun leans back against the wall as their arrows fall short. He manages to drop one of the archers before they advance toward the cave. With Dalistra's range and power, Mashaun realizes he has the advantage, picking them off before they move within range of their bows. Some of the swordsmen charge the cave, falling victim to Dalistra's well-placed arrows before they make it to the rock-slide. A few archers use the wagon as cover, sending arrows into the cave, bouncing off the interior wall as they whiz past.

Mai jumps in surprise, seeing arrows bouncing off the walls, almost hitting her, freezing in disbelief and fear. She flees to the safety in the back of the cave, crouching behind the table of food with her hands over her ears, trying in vain to block out the sound of bouncing arrows.

"It's not real, I need to wake up," she mutters over and over.

Chapter 3

THE PRISONERS

THE ARROWS CONTINUE TO FLY until the wagon guards run away or lay dead in the meadow. The one wearing the chain must have fled the battle. He assumes one got away along with the horses. Nearly a dozen bodies and pools of blood litter the once pristine meadow. Mashaun scans the distant tree line, looking for any movement. His string fingers are numb and sore at the same time with a layer of skin missing from the fingertips. The meadow is silent, even the birds have disappeared. Raised on a farm and being a hunter, death is not new to him; he even killed animals for food, but never a human. Yet in a matter of minutes, he has killed several. It troubles him even as he tries to think of them as animals, but it doesn't help.

"*Oh, your first human kill. Get used to it,*" Dalistra says mockingly.

"There is that, but I have never been shot at either," he answers with a tremor.

"*Welcome to my world.*"

"Great!" he replies.

"*It was much too easy for a mage. Let go check her out and don't talk to me. Think about what you want to say,*" she tells him. He doesn't understand how it is possible, but then neither does a talking bow. Still, a little confused, Mashaun agrees.

He steps through the illusion and out of the cave. In addition to the people taken from the cave, a couple of girls are cowering in the corner of the caged wagon.

"*A mage? Like a real magic user? Like fireballs and such?*"

"*Yes, a real magic user. You do not have magic where you are from?*"

"No, we use technology instead of magic where I'm from," he replies, already getting a little tired of her pompous attitude. He thinks if she would turn down her mightier-than-thou attitude, they can make a great team.

"Oh, you think so," she snaps.

"Quit reading my thoughts."

"Maybe. Remember to think when talking to me," she retorts. She doesn't want to push him too hard. He might put her back in the cave for another eon. Now she is out in the world again, she wants to remain here. So for now, she'll try to tone it down a little.

As Mashaun crosses the meadow toward the mage, he thinks about how he did.

"Are you thinking for me?" she says sarcastically.

"Yes," he replies, perturbed.

"Okay, you have used a bow before," she says with an egotistical slur. She admittedly likes the way he handles her, but pride prevents her from being honest with him. After all, she is royalty, and he is an off-world commoner. They do have their advanages.

"Yes, I was on the school's archery team, and I hunted with a bow for several years," Mashaun tells her.

"That explains your different style. But it works, so I will allow you to remain with me for a while," she says in her usual demeanor.

"Thanks...I think," he says out loud.

The mage is lying on her side, resting on the arrow protruding through her cape and above the bustier. After removing the arrow, he rolls her over. Mashaun removes the clothes from the mage as Dalistra tells him to keep the clone's eyes covered at all times. He also needs to collect some clothes from one of the dead soldiers for himself. He unties the bustier after some verbal mocking from Dalistra, then removes her clothes trying not to stare.

"Hurry up. Have you never undressed a woman before?" she snaps.

"No, they usually take their own clothes off, and in the dark," he says, taking the keys off her belt and tossing them to the prisoners.

"You cannot lie to me, so do not even try. Remember to think, don't speak to me." Dalistra tells him.

What? He thinks.

As he opens the front of the bustier, he is surprised to find no belly button.

She is a clone! I thought Fa—the king signed a proclamation forbidding the creation of clones," she tells him. Mashaun catches the pause but chooses not to ask her about it.

"A what?" he asks.

"A clone, cover her face, NOW." Something in her voice tells him not to question or delay; using the cape, he covers the clone's face. *"That is why she was so easy to kill. I'll explain later. Right now we need to burn all the bodies,* especially this one, and keep the eyes covered, it may already be too late." He senses real worry in her tone.

Mashaun tells the prisoners to strip the dead then throw them in the wagon. He grabs the clothes from the mage and quickly takes some from one of the dead guards. Mashaun finds the girl still cowering under the wagon, offering his hand. The girl extends her hand with caution and some coaxing.

"Leave her, she is a drudge," Dalistra tells him. Mashaun ignores her, gently taking the young girl's hand.

She gazes at him with teary brown eyes as he helps her out from under the wagon, giving him a hug. She is a tall, thin young women with matted black hair wearing a rough cotton poncho slit up the sides. She clutches a torn nightgown, as Mashaun brushes her hair aside, asking her name. The girl quietly breathes, "Abigail." Mashaun takes her back to the cave with Dalistra in one hand, carrying clothes in one arm and Abigail tightly clasping his other arm.

"How dare you ignore me?" Dalistra barks.

Mai runs from behind one of the beds when Mashaun returns. She asks who the girl is and what happened. As Mai approaches, she spots a terrified and distraught young girl. Mai reaches for her hand, but Abigail refuses to let go until Mashaun nods and gently tells her it's okay as Mai leads her to the pool.

Mashaun glances around, making sure nobody witnesses, him slipping into the weapons room. Draping the clone's outfit over some swords, he puts on the guard's outfit. The pants are too short and the waist too big. The shirt is two sizes too large, and the shoes don't fit at all. He keeps the fur wrapped on his feet. He checks the wall only to find the scene replaced by images of them walking through the forest along a stream. Without looking into the room, Mashaun tells Mai he is going to check outside and will be back shortly.

When he exits the cave, the once captives are trying on clothes. A pair of petite girls with dirty, knotted blond hair hanging to their shoulders. The muscular man with a black flat top and tattoos on his arms. A dark-skinned short older man with short curly hair—all of them wearing the same dirty poncho style outfits. Mashaun leaves them to their business and searches the wagon for anything useful. He finds a flint and steel, jade marbles—five green, two yellow and one blue—and several documents encased in a clay tub. Each document has the letters MSS in a fragmented triangle in the upper left and some kind of wax stamp in the shape of an oval cage atop a staff in the bottom right-hand corner.

Seeing Abigail calmer, Mai reassures her before leaving to go to the central room. Scanning the room for her clothes, she checks the weapons room. The outfit is too tall for her, and the bustier would have to be taken in to fit. Looking at the outfit, she figures she could make it fit with a few minor adjustments, but it will have to wait. Returning to the water room, she finds Abigail asleep in the pool. She thinks about waking her but decides to let her sleep and leaves the cave to be with Mashaun. For the first time she witnesses the aftermath of the battle. A meadow littered with dead bodies, and Mashaun is rummaging through the wagon, like nothing ever happened. She has never seen death before, as she almost throws up as she runs back into the cave, both nauseous and weeping, somehow finding her way into the weapons room. It doesn't take long for her to regain enough composure to go sit with Abigail in the pool, which, for some reason, is always soothing.

As the afternoon shadows begin to creep across the battlefield, Mashaun calls everyone to the center of the cavern. He starts by introducing himself, followed by Mai. Abigail tells everyone she is 18 and lives outside Lima, Peru. Next, Kazimir tells them he is from Perm, Russia. He has a round face, looking like a body builder in his mid-thirties. On one bicep is a tattoo of a red hammer, crossed with a sickle, and boxing gloves hanging from a four-leaf clover on the other. He ripped the sleeves off one of the shirts allowing his arms to fit, and the pants are small around the waist, needing some rope to hold them up.

Then, there are the twins, probably in their late-teens, looking like a couple of dirty models with long blond hair and baby blue eyes. Each wears small leather bands around their necks, wrists and ankles with the same symbol on the documents. They each have a tunic tied around their waist, leaving the sides open. Bowing their heads with soft, melodic voices, they say a few words, but the group can only make out the words Magdalenia, Elina, Ericka and Tenskie. Everyone stares at them, surprised and confused. Mashaun recognizes the language and asks Dalistra to translate, and she tells them, *"They are Magdalenia's house slaves, Elina, and Ericka, from Tenskie."* Last is a short, dark-skinned man probably in his early to mid-forties. He carries himself as a person of standing while speaking with clear and deliberate diction with words of someone educated, introducing himself as Berg from Cameroon.

Mai offers Elina and Ericka a couple of shirts to put on, which they do without a sound and without modesty, to the thrill and embarrassment of the others. The group is surprised when they can understand one another but not the twins until Mai suggest they probably can't comprehend anybody who did not wake up on one of the beds as she points to the back of the room. Berg rubs his chin as he is the intrigued by Mai's comments as the others fail to make the connection, and move on.

With all the soldiers' weapons and clothes in the laid out on the beds, they take stock of their spoils. They do some clothes trading for best possible fits, except for Mai who keeps the red outfit even though the twins try to take it off her, shaking their heads side to side with fear and tears in their eyes.

Mashaun tells them "Hvaju taju, Hvaju taju" before they stop and hide behind Kazimir.

Peeking out from behind Kazimir, ones asks Mashaun, "Kooj psua taru twua?"

"Did you kill them?" Dalistra tells Mashaun. He thinks about telling her about the bow, but before he could change his mind, Dalistra tells him *"TZSJS, I mean no!"* in no uncertain terms.

He thinks for a moment before shaking his head, no, saying "Tzsjs." Mai stares at him wondering how he knew the question, before accepting his answer. Mashaun points to the bands. She tells him "Lavw qhov tvrag gron tutsv svest" translated by Dalistra as *"They are the slaves' band with the owner's mark."* He tries not to show his surprise as she asks him, "Lawv puas muaj qhev, nws qhov twg los?" Again, Dalistra translates, *"Do you have slaves where you are from?"* and Mashaun shakes his head. She sadly says, "Uas suazoo ib liib qhov chwaz." Dalistra translates, *"Sounds like a nice place."* She sadly says before walking away.

"Where are we and how did we get here? More importantly, how do we get home?" Mai inquiries.

They stare at each with bewilderment.

Berg approaches the map noticing the writing is logographic. Pointing at the characters located above the landmass, he asks the twins what it says. They focus on him, cocking their heads to one side. He circles the land mass and starts naming countries. After a few minutes, Elina says Hauv Pem. Berg, repeats it pointing to the map. Elina nods. She then points to a city, Tenskie. Ericka circles a cove, and she says Shen Sherin. They take turns pointing to Khusari Hitvx, Cinsej Mej, Teroma Mej in the upper left part of the map. When Berg asks about places somewhere on the map, the girls shake their heads.

"We are in Hauv Pem," Berg tells them.

"Where?" Everybody asks in unison.

"Hauv Pem, wherever that is."

"Who woke up first?" Berg asks.

Mai points to Mashaun standing in the corner. Berg asks him if he likes this place and Mashaun mulls over his answer before nodding his head. Everybody starts asking him why and then asking him to send them back. Holding his hands up, he tells them he is also baffled and doesn't know how or why. Maybe we are part of one of your dreams or I am part of your imagination. They stop pondering on it could be anybody's dream or nightmare. Abigail suggests it could even be a collective dream. The group glances back and fourth, muttering I am not a dream. Dalistra tells him she is not a figment of his imagination.

"What about an alternate world? Or astral travel?" asks Abigail.

A hush fall on the group before Kazimir says "What?" looking at Berg. Abigail explains the theory of parallel worlds and how they may be on a parallel world. At the same time, they ask how and why they got here before looking at the twins. Abigail continues telling them their souls may have left their bodies back on Earth and traveled to this world.

"What? we're dead?" Mai Shriek. "No, not dead." Abigail responds.

Berg recognizes the blank stares from everyone—they are like his students when they still cannot understand a topic he just covered.

"Okay, so we can be in another world, in anyone or a mutual dream, all of us might have performed astral travel to this place or a combination of three, or something different. It means we are in Hauv Pem, but don't how we got here and most of all, how to return home." Everybody nods in agreement.

Berg regards each one before asking Mashaun what he was doing the night before. After thinking for a moment, he tells them he was watching an outdoor show, reminiscing the good times he had hiking in a distant forest.

"So you missed hiking in the outdoors, like here," Berg questions.

Mashaun nods. "I used to live where the trees were tall and buildings were short. Then I moved to where the buildings were tall and trees are short. I miss the tall trees."

Mai was living on energy drinks while studying for a test and felt overwhelmed, afraid for the first time she would fail a test. Abigail chimes in, telling everybody her friends all left for college. She didn't even apply and wished she had went with them. Kazimir tells them he got into drugs and gambling after losing his last fight, forcing him into retirement, leaving him devastated. They all stare at Berg, waiting for his answer. Lowering his head, he tells them after spending 12 to 15 hours a day at work for the last few months, all his girls wanted to do was to spend time with him and he barked at them, sending them crying to their mother. A tear runs down his face.

Abigail gives Berg a hug, telling him he will return to see his wife and kids. Mai acknowledges in a low voice, telling them all of them were yearning for better times. Berg snaps his heard around, Glancing at the symbols on the map. "I recognize those symbols, I was given a rock with similar pictographs yesterday. I think it was yesterday." The others nod in agreement, saying each one has also held a similar rock given to them. Mashaun tells them he bought one of those rocks. It was a green jasper stone about palm size. Again they nodded in agreement.

"You were the first one here what do you suggest?" somebody asks Mashaun, as they stare at him.

"Why are you staring at me? I don't know any more than you do!"

Berg suggests since he is the most comfortable in this environment, then he should take the lead. Kazimir stands in the back with his arms crossed, shaking his head. He will wait—learning, sizing up his opponent before making a move like in the ring.

Mashaun tells them they won't learn anything staying here; besides, this place is a trap. He suggests they spend the night in the cave for warmth and protection then leave in the morning before the owner of the wagon comes looking for it.

Mai and Abigail shake their heads in unison. "You mean leave the cave and go out into the wilderness? There's no telling what creatures roam these lands. I would rather stay here."

Mashaun studies them for a moment before telling the group he is leaving in the morning, though he doesn't know where, but this place is not safe. They can come with him or stay. He turns and walks to the entrance where he scans the outside from the safety behind the illusionary wall. Dalistra can tell he is not used to leading, never having the responsibility for the safety of someone else before, and it terrifies him. She cannot let him know, she admires his concern.

After an uneasy silence, Mai suggests everybody takes a bath since it may take a while before they have another chance, and get a good night sleep. They all promptly agree and head to the water room. The girls are to the pool first while the guys examine the weapons. Mashaun considers showing them the weapons room, but Dalistra suggests he shouldn't, asking him how well he know any of them.

"No more than I you, but you're right."

Mashaun slips into the weapon room unnoticed searching the chamber, trying different weapons. Finally, he settles on a couple of short, slightly curved swords to Dalistra's amazement.

"Two swords? You have me. What do you need with them?" she inquires with her usual pompous tone.

Mashaun tells her he used the method before in a live action game, he used to play back home, and they will be in use in case someone gets too close.

"You are full of surprises." she states, not fully able to hide her amazement.

Mashaun exits the room to find Kazimir joining the twins in the pool. Since no one minds, he goes outside to check the wagon and witness the day fade into night on this strange new world. As the darkness overtakes the sky and the first stars pierce the sky, a smile creeps across his face.

Berg joins Abigail at the food table, engaging Abigail in a light conversation as she enjoys the fruits and nuts, never touching the meat. He starts to reach for some jerky but grabs an apple-like fruit instead. While still munching on the fruit, Berg steps close to the wall and squints, running his hand down the wall. He turns and asks if anybody else has studied the walls as Abigail moves closer. In the faint light, she spots the color pictographs. Abigail calls Mai over to show her the new images. She gets Mashaun, showing him the new pictures on the wall as they examine the wall for some time, looking for the pictures from before but they are gone; they are replaced with new ones. Berg traces a pictograph with his finger, and it begins to glow.

Three evenly spaced circles—red, blue and yellow—rotate around a larger green square in the center. Each of the smaller circles connects to the center of the green square by a slim line. The three rotate at different speeds until they align at the top where the lines fall straight down to the bottom where they stay hanging while the circles continue to orbit. A second image appears with the circles aligned at the bottom, and they become one again with the circles. All of them study the movement, not saying a word until Abigail asks what it means. They glance at each other, puzzled, until Berg suggests it could be a planet with three moons. The lines represent some kind of connection between them and the planet, but he's only guessing.

"Follow me." Mashaun rushes to the map, and they follow. After studying it for a while, Berg points out the three cave pictures are larger than the others. The caves are equal distances apart, and if you draw three lines connecting these, the mountains south of the lake in the center of the triangle. Next, he points out each cave has a color staff next to it with a symbol similar to one of the cave walls. Mashaun tells them not to go anywhere and rushes out the cave to retrieve the mage's staff. Even though it is made of solid stone, it weighs about the same as Dalistra. The staff has a column of symbols, and he hurries back to Abigail, Mai and Berg at the map. Mashaun shows them the markings on the staff, and it doesn't take long for them to match the symbols to one of the caves. However, it doesn't make any sense. It shows the cave on the west side of the mountains, but the afternoon shadow covers the cave entrance, and the morning sun shines on the cave entrance.

"If I only had some paper and a pencil to copy the map," Berg says with a sigh.

Everyone is trying to figure out the sleeping arrangements when the twins exit from the water room, with Kazimir following close behind. They only have five pedestals and three fur blankets to divide among the three girls and two guys. Mai and Mashaun will use the skins they cut up for warmth. Mashaun suggests the twins share one. Kazimir will need one because of his size, leaving one for Abigail and Berg. Berg offers the last one to Abigail, telling her he will lie down by the fire. Mai gives the fur back to Berg. She will share hers with Abigail before asking Mashaun where he plans to sleep.

"By the door," he tells them.

She doesn't like him so far away. He is the only one she is comfortable being around, but Mashaun puts forth a successful argument about watching the meadow in case any more unwanted visitors. Eventually, everybody agrees to the sleeping arrangements and settles in for the night. Berg and Abigail sit on one bed talking—like father and daughter—about where each is from and what they did in their other lives, trying to forget their current isolation from all they know and love.

Mashaun finds some oil and uses it to turn the wagon into a funeral pyre, watching the flames lick the night sky. He wonders if what he did was smart. The flames pierce the night, revealing their position for a long way. The smell of burning bodies fill the night air. *What if it catches the forest on fire?* From some rocks along the cliff face not far from the burning wagon, he keeps a eye out, making sure the fire doesn't spread. A few times it tries, but he snuffs the embers out quickly.

Kazimir joins him, watching the dying flames from the burning wagon. Mashaun can tell something is troubling him. He is not good at hiding his emotions. After some prying, Kazimir asks him if he searched the wagon before torching it. Mashaun tells him all he found was a metal box with eight colored flatten marbles and pieces of paper; he will have them translated later. Kazimir's face sinks with the news about the papers. He asks about the documents, but Mashaun only tells him they are safe. The two discuss the papers for a few minutes before Kazimir returns to the cave for the night. He isn't going to tell the twins—not just yet. He may still be able to retrieve them down the road though he doesn't know how. After the wagon's flames die down, Mashaun returns to the cave entrance and gazes into the night sky filled with millions of stars reminding him of tiny pinholes in the veil of night. Since moving to the city, Mashaun stare up at the stars, wondering abut the last time he has seen so many. *Too long,* he thinks. Dalistra senses a tinge of sadness—not at being here, but more about not being here, and it puzzles her. Mashaun tries to find a recognizable constellation but doesn't. He believes it's because he has lived in a city for the last few years and he had forgotten how to find them in the night sky, or maybe they are on a different world.

Mai joins him at the entrance. After a bit of small talk, she asks how he understood Ericka.

"I have no idea what was being said," he says without even looking at her. She accept the answer, with a questioning gaze, but waits a bit before returning to the safety of the cave.

Mashaun asks Dalistra what she means about how easy it was to kill the mage.

"Most mages have a variety of protections, and clones don't. When a mage creates their clone, they have to spend time teaching them. Most use

magic to prevent the clones from learning any magic. After all, who wants a servant more capable than the master? The wizards give a few clones limited magical abilities, such as scrying or some protection spell. An extraordinary bond exist between the mage and their clone. Every action a clone does can be dictated by the wizard. Most allow the mage to scry through the clones' eyes, much the same way I use your eyes to view the world."

"Why don't the mages create several clones of themselves?" Mashaun asks.

She tells him making a clone is time-consuming and dangerous, leaving the mage weak and vulnerable for some time. She relates a story about a mage's clone going out of control and killing the mage before going on a rampage, killing several others before the city guards took it down. Many mages won't create a clone because of the dangers, and will shun any known clones. Mashaun sits, thinking about how different the two worlds are. He ponders on all the new information while staring into the night sky.

The blue moon begins to peek over the trees, lighting up the ground with a faint blue light, creating eerie shadows across the meadow.

Rising above the trees, the moon is slightly smaller than he is used to seeing. Dalistra admires the moon also. It has been a long time since seeing the moons. She tell Mashaun, it is only one of the three colorful moons. It is smaller with a slightly blue hue, not what he's used seeing. Some plants have different hues of blue with some sparkling with a bioluminesance.

Oh look, the moon Dasjin in its Life stage, and the moon Flalib is in its fire stage. It has been many years since I have witness the moons rising. Many plants and animals will turn to varying shades of blues, reds, and purples. Wait until three moons fill the night sky, the landscape is beautiful with yellow, blue, red, orange, purple and even green hues cover the landscape twinkling like the stars above. The darker the color, the more magical the plant or creature. Alchemist and artificers go out on full moons to harvest the dark hues and sparkling plants for their magical crafts, like potions, armor, weapons and other items. The more potent magic is used during the full moon, making the best magical item. You have arrived on a most auspicious evening with life and fire being full and a chaos crescent moon." Ending Dalistra lesson on the moons.

The meadow and surrounding trees display shades of blue, reds and purples sparkles like glitter around the clearing. Curious, he strolls to the closest one and tenderly runs his fingers over the sparkle. It attaches to his skin and fade.

"You are not from here, and can not use the magic."

He tries to comprehend the discovery but quickly gives up and decides he should hide the staff. Slipping into the weapons room, removing several swords on the back row, laying the staff down then replacing the swords, making sure everybody is busty elsewhere as he slinks back to the cave entrance and starts to unstring Dalistra, when she asks him not to. It has been such a long time. He agrees and drifts off to sleep.

Chapter 4

FOLLOW THE ROAD

THE MORNING SUN BEGINS TO climb into the sky, chasing the stars away as Mashaun awakes. He sits watching the first streaks of the morning sun peek over the trees, basking the cave entrance, noticing the light barely piercing the darkness of the cave when it should have lit up the pedestals in the back. This puzzles him. He walks out into the meadow, looking around. The sun's rays streak over the trees, squarely hitting the cliff face sparkles and shimmers as light reflexes off the rock face except for the cave entrance. He realizes the sun rays reflect off the cliff face but not the illusionary wall hiding the cave entrance. He examines the cliff to his left and right but only the reflection of the cliff. However, the light vanishes like the cave about halfway up the cliff face. He scours the wall for a path but shortly loses it as the sun climbs into the sky.

The golden rays of the sun warming the early morning air create a low ground fog as the forest comes alive with the morning light. Enjoying the early morning sounds for a few more minutes, he goes to wake the others. Berg is at the map, holding a parchment and ink for writing. When Mashaun asks him about it, Berg thinks Mashaun found it on the wagon and left it for him. They looked at each other, confused for a moment before continuing.

Even though the sun is fully above the trees, the cave is still gray, and it takes a moment for his eyes to adjust before touching Mai on the shoulder. She stirs, looking up at him with her sleep-filled eyes.

"Is it that time already?" she asks groggily.

Mashaun nods as she slowly rolls out of bed. During the night, she took in the outfit so it fits much better. Abigail must have heard them because she sits up blinking and rubbing her eyes as she scans the area. Abigail follows Mai to the water room to wash up before they head down the road. Shortly, Kazimir and the twins roll out of bed and head into the water room. Mashaun uses the waterfall to wipe his face and clean up a bit before going to the food table. He turns one of the extra outfits into a knapsack, filling it with dried meats and fruits, suggesting everyone else do the same. He goes into the water room and fills one of the water skins they took off the soldiers. Kazimir and the twins are sitting in the pool with their clothes on the rocks.

Mashaun tells them they are leaving, and if they want to come along, they better hurry. Kazimir stands, telling him they are staying. Everyone in the room stares with trepidation, as Kazimir stands naked waist-deep in the pool, walking up the path until he is inches from Mashaun. He is a head taller and almost twice Mashaun's size. The group waits for Mashaun's reaction. Even with the bubbling pool and the falling water, a stillness fills the room.

Mashaun studies Kazimir for a silent moment. "Fine, do what you want, but I'm leaving in five minutes." He turns and heads out of the room. Elina and Ericka glance at each other then back at the two, realizing it did not go as expected. Kazimir stand almost dumbfounded as Mashaun walks out the door followed by Mai, Abigail and Berg.

Mashaun makes a couple of holes with a dagger in his fur turning it into a cloak. Mai, Abigail and Berg follow and finish filling their knapsacks before heading down the cave as Kazimir and the twins exit the room. Kazimir and the twins quickly grab some food before hurrying to catch up with everyone else. The sun is well over the treetops, climbing into a cloudless sky, warming the morning air. The meadow is full of butterflies and the music of songbirds, bringing a smile to Mashaun's face. Something he has not seen or heard in some time, how much he misses it. Putting the sun on the left, they head up to the meandering dirt road with Mai walking on his right, followed by Berg and Abigail. Kazimir, Ericka and Elina follow a few paces behind.

The road quickly exits the meadow, entering the forest. On the right is water and mist bubble up out of some rocks, forming a stream next to the road. It's still a bit chilly in the shadows of trees as the tall conifer trees filter the sunlight, except for a few beams providing little pockets of warmth. The undergrowth is sparse with patches of ferns, wildflowers and mushrooms growing on the fallen deadwood crisscrossing the landscape. Even in the warmest of days, it probably remains cool and damp in the forest as evidence by the the moss-laden trees.

From the back, quiet complaining from the twins carry across the air. For the most part, the two girls mainly complain to Kazimir. Their complaints are falling on deaf ears not because he's not listening but because he doesn't understand, frustrating the three of them.

Kazimir figures out they're cold and goes forward to Abigail to steal her fur, but she resists, and when Berg tries to intervene, he pushes him aside as if he's a leaf in the wind. Mashaun takes a few steps back, telling Kazimir, if he wasn't so busy flirting with the twins, he could have done the same thing and not leave one of the cloaks at the cave. Kazimir says he will go back, as Mashaun says they aren't waiting.

Kazimir stands dumbfounded again, not knowing what to say or do. Everyone wait nervously as this is the second time this morning the two have faced off. Kazimir wants to take a swing at Mashaun, and for a moment, the two stare at each other, waiting for the other to blink. Mashaun waits for Kazimir to take a swing at him, but Kazimir steps back to Mashaun's relief. Having won the battle, he gives his fur to Kazimir. Tells him he needs to pay attention if he wants to survive, before heading back to the front. The twins stare in amazement, hoping to witness their champion in action, but are saddened when Kazimir backs down. They are, however, happy when he returns with a fur.

Mai asks Mashaun why he gave Kazimir the fur. He shrugs and tells her he is too hot with it, and Kazimir needs it more to please his new girlfriends. She grins and gaze at him, as they continue down the road. Dalistra likes the strength and compassion in him. After several hours of walking, everybody starts dragging, and Mashaun stops the group by the stream for a break. They eat some fruit and wash it down with some fresh, cold water while sitting under the trees in silence. At first, they are hesitant to drink the stream water until Mashaun does, resting for about 30 minutes before continuing down the road. Kazimir and the twins complain the rest is too short, but they stand up and follow anyway, not wanting to be left behind.

It's already late afternoon when they arrive at a level open area with the stream running through it. The trees' shadows are long, and the air is beginning to cool. They gather some firewood, and with the flint and steel, Mashaun quickly starts a fire, impressing Berg and Abigail. Everybody sits around warming themselves, as Mashaun disappears into the forest without anyone noticing.

In the forest, Mashaun and Dalistra talk about the day's events which will become a daily routine for them. She can help with the aim against threats, but not for food. Mashaun asks how she is able to do the things she can do.

"I can read the mind of anyone who holds me," she says.

No kidding, he thinks.

Quiet, and do not interrupt me, and think your question." She snaps. *"It also allows me to use your eyes and ears as my own. After a while, we can sense each other and speak to each other over distances."*

"Oh, I like that," he replies with enthusiasm.

Taking out the papers, he asks her, "What are these?"

"These are papers of ownership for the two slaves. They are your slaves now. You are a slave owner, giving you stature," she says with a somewhat cheerful tone.

Kazimir must have realized what they are and why he wanted them. Dalistra also tells him the marbles are a form of money used in the Khusari region.

He returns to help set up camp before disappearing into the forest again. He returns a short while later carrying a deer over his shoulders. Everyone except for Abigail congratulates him, welcoming fresh meat for dinner.

Abigail glares at him, saying "You killed it, a poor, defenseless animal? you are a monster." as she stands to leave.

"Yes, for food. You don't have to eat it if you don't want, but I would advise you do to keep your strength up," Mashaun responds nonchalantly before plopping the deer on the ground. He starts skinning and cutting it up, handing pieces of meat to everybody to cook. He finishes cooking the meat for their journey while everybody eats their fill and settles down for the night. Berg spreads his map to study the writing, asking the twins to translate. It is a slow process. Abigail passes on the meat, but after a few day she ends up eating some. Over the next few days, Berg learns some of their language and they learn some of his.

The twins' skin turn from a alabaster to faded lilac as the red and blue moon move away from full. When asked about it, they shrug their shoulders because they do not know the reason behind it. Dalistra tells Mashaun "they are Nstlev khaum neaj or purple magician." It appears, nobody has told them they are part Thesilan. Only Thesilans' have the ability to use the moon magics. Somebody decided not to tell them, or maybe this is their first change. Without proper training, the magic could kill them.

Every night he starts to unstring her, and she tells him not to. He carefully leans Dalistra against a tree and lies down, looking up at the trees when a long shadow covers him. Mai is standing over him with her fur, asking if she can join him. She doesn't like the forest at night and will feel safer with him. He agrees, welcoming the company and added warmth. Mashaun scans the campsite as Mai spreads the fur over them. Abigail is not far from Berg. The twins are on one side of Kazimir, sharing a single fur. Mai curls up close, putting one arm across his chest, and quickly goes to sleep. Dalistra venomously tell him "You got a friend already" as he slips into the peaceful bliss of sleep.

"No touch!" Dalistra commands.

Startled, Mashaun awakes as the Dalistra hits the ground. Grabbing her, he jumps in a flash knocking an arrow, not knowing what is happening. Kazimir stand not two feet from him white as a sheet, with bug eyes, shaking his hands.

"What are you doing?" Mashaun growls.

"I…I just wanted to see your bow," Kazimir says sheepishly.

"In the middle of the night?"

"Uh, I couldn't sleep."

"I don't care if you couldn't sleep. You do not touch my stuff again. Understand!" Mashaun is appalled, but not surprised, Kazimir would even try such a thing, let alone lie to his face.

"I…I am sorry," Kazimir replies and goes back to the twins.

I don't believe him, Mashaun thinks to which Dalistra agrees.

"Are you okay?" he asks her with concern.

"Yes, " she replies, a little touched.

Mai asks Mashaun who he is talking to. It dawns on Mashaun everybody is awake and is watching. He casually blows off Mai's question by telling her he often talks to himself, and she accepts his answer.

I bet the twins somehow put him up to it. But why and how? They don't speak the same language. But one thing's for certain, we will have to be more vigilant, Mashaun thinks while stirring the embers and adding some more wood to the fire, knowing the morning will be chilly in more ways than one.

Mashaun wakes as the sun's first rays pierce the light fog covering the ground. Seeing the fire is nothing but a bed of embers, he adds some wood to the coals and stokes it back to life. Mai, then Abigail and Berg, join him by the fire and start to discuss the plans for the day. Somewhere in the middle of the conversation, Kazimir slips in, trying to be unnoticed. An uneasy silence fill the area before they ask him about his thoughts on their plan. Kazimir smile in a stoic way, when included in the decision-making, which has been missing from his life. They all agree to continue down the road. They know what's behind them, and none of them wants to go back. Kazimir informs the twins of the decision as best as he can, trying to make it sound like it's his idea. After a quick breakfast, they pack up the camp and head down the road.

By mid-morning, the stream turns sharply away from the trail, and they break to fill their water-skins. The morning fog dissipates, leaving the foliage damp, giving a rainbow of colors as the sun reflects off the water droplets. Through the day, Mashaun points to different tracks on the road, informing Mai and anybody else who is interested. Most of the tracks he knew from his days of hunting. A few are unfamiliar and some are foreign. Mai is not interested in track identification and falls back to talk with Abigail. The two talk up a storm, giving Berg a sad smile, reminding him of home and his two daughters who he misses.

Frequently during the day, Mashaun appears to be lost in thought. Sometimes he talks to Dalistra about everything—from directions to local politics, learning her language or anything else he thinks about and sometimes remembering other places and times. He learns, while spirit weapons are rare, others do exist. Most of the time, they can sense others when they are close, and sometimes they can even speak to each other.

He gets a history lesson about the world from Dalistra, at least from her era. He tries to remember the important names and dates, but nothing is recent, and her memory is a little fuzzy and out-of-date.

During the journey, Kazimir and the twins work on learning each other's language while everybody spends the evening learning the twins' language. Using Dalistra, Mashaun manages to put enough words together to ask the twins a few questions. He asks them about the year, they shrug their shoulders, they don't tell slaves about the years. If the master wants a slave to know the year, they will tell the slave. He asks them about being a slave.

They wait on their master, and have been slaves for many turns of the seasons. They tell the story—how their father sold them to pay off a gambling debt when they were about eight years old. They have been slaves ever since. Mai is surprised with Mashaun's ability to speak their language but doesn't say anything, figuring he is a quick learner. During the night, they set up rotating watches, so everyone has the middle watch about every third night.

The journey is quiet until the fourth day when they run out of fruit. Abigail becomes distraught about having to eat meat, wishing they would find some fruit. Around noon, they round a corner are a couple of fruit trees including apples, pears, oranges and some wild berries, along with a few other vegetables. They spend the whole afternoon picking fruits and vegetables, eating their fill.

Ericka and Elina observe with wonder as the rest pick from the air and eat. The only fruit they see are the wild blackberries. The next morning, when they leave, Abigail goes grabs an apple for the road, but it is all gone, except for the wild berries. Confused, she rifles through their rucksacks and the fruit is gone. A little mystified, she accepts it is part of their dream and continues down the road. Every few days, they would find wild fruits and vegetables to fill the rucksacks as the twins stare in amazement, not understanding the group's actions. All of them are getting weaker, but Abigail to be suffering the most. After examining her, Mai says she is suffering from malnutrition, as is everybody. The only difference is she is eating less meat than everybody else.

Kazimir was telling the twins about a stew when they come across an old garden with potatoes, corn, carrots and herbs. They set up camp next to it complete with a makeshift stove and cooking pots. The twins have gotten used to them getting excited over nothing, but this time, they run around the meadow, pulling and digging. Kazimir makes his goulash for the evening meal. The twins gaze into an empty bowl but act as if they are eating a bowl of stew out of fear of angering their temporary master. The vegetables found on the trail satisfy their hunger but leaves them still hungry. Their pace slow during the day as everybody feel the pains of hunger.

The nights are steadly colder, forcing them to keep the fire going both for warmth and safety, but there is some concern it might attract some unwanted guests even though they haven't seen any signs of bandits since they left the cave. The fire burns out one night, and they awake to a cold, damp dawn with frost on the ground. Rubbing their arms and huddling under the furs in the predawn, they agree not to let it happen again.

Mashaun turns out to be a successful hunter, and the group always has fresh meat, which is the only real food the twins see, except for the occasional mushrooms or wild berries growing along the road. Around the evening fire, they often swap stories about their lives. Mashaun listens more and over the week. Kazimir and Berg manage to learn a little of the native language, and when the twins realize the group are naj tewb, they shake their heads in disbelief, not knowing what to think. At first, they shy away from the group, knowing naj tewbs are needed to have babies, but don't understand how. They decide Kazimir is big and strong, and they are used to having protection so they stay with him, with a different demeanor.

Chapter 5

THE MERCHANT

http://thesilaprophecy.com/people

FOR NEARLY TWO WEEKS, THEY follow the abandoned road. The days are quiet. Mashaun teaches Kazimir about different edible plants and how to build a fire. The only sword fight he has seen is on TV, and in LARP, but they practice in slow motion, and the group learns a few phrases of the native language. The twins skin is a deep daffodil.

One morning they wake to the clanging of metal on metal somewhere up ahead. Mashaun and Kazimir jump up and run ahead to check out the commotion. Mai briefly hesitates but soon realizes they are the only two fighters among the group and chooses to go with them while the rest remain behind. Mashaun's group closes in on the sound until the road opens into a clearing connecting to a well-traveled road. A caravan with five wagons and a group of armed men fighting off a larger group of attackers. Moving off to the side, they take cover in some bushes along the tree line. Mashaun stares in amazement for a moment as the attack plays out like his dream a few nights ago. Dalistra says "you know what to do, so do it."

Mashaun suggests it is in their best interest to help the caravan from the cover of the forest with their bows, spreading out to choose their targets. Closing her eyes, Mai fires first. Her arrow goes way over the caravan and into the forest on the other side. Kazimir hits his target, wounding the attacker, causing him to hesitate and allowing the caravan guard to finish the job. Mashaun spots a person on a horse across the road, successfully fighting several of the caravan guards. Mashaun draws back and lets the arrow fly, hitting the rider in the shoulder with a loud clink, taking everyone by surprise. He rears his horse, getting the attention of everybody, stopping the combat for a split second before turning and heading into the forest with his men close behind him. The guards do not follow. Some go to work making sure all the bandits on the ground are dead while scavenging what they can. Others tend to the wounded.

One of the guards comes across one of the group's arrows, sounding the alarm. The three remain motionless as the guards scan the tree line, looking for a clue as to who shot the arrows. Slowly, several of the men move toward the three. Mashaun motions for them to slowly back away, but Kazimir's massive frame and inexperience give them away as a sudden snap comes from his direction as he steps on a branch. Seeing the guards homing in on Kazimir, Mashaun steps out of hiding yelling "Stop!" with Dalistra across his back and his hands up in plain view. Mai quickly follows suit, not knowing why. She stands a little behind Mashaun, shaking like she is drench in ice water. The guards stop their pursuit, turning toward them as Kazimir disappears in the forest. The pair slowly walks toward the guards. Several additional guards run out and surround them, taking them to the wagons covered with tarps.

The first wagon is different from the rest, looking more like a covered carriage than a wagon. A portly man, probably in his fifties, exits, wearing a blue robe of fine linen trimmed in gold. Each of his fingers has an ornate ring. From inside the coach, a young girl asks if it is safe, making specific hand gestures. Her words are coarse and choppy. He tells her to be quiet and to stay put with a firm but gentle voice while facing her, performing hand gestures.

No one says a word as he studies Mashaun and Mai for a long time, while Mashaun sizes up the situation. Dalistra tells Mashaun she does not like it and he needs to be careful with his words. Mashaun agrees.

Mai thinks she must be a mess after days on the trail without a comb or a bath. They probably stink, too. She tries to straighten out her tangled hair to make herself presentable before one of the guards glares at her, shaking his head for her to stop.

Finally, the man asks them who they are and what they are doing out here. His English is superb and Mashaun is not sure if it has to do with his station or if he might also be from the cave. In any case, Dalistra doesn't need to translate. He speaks with the clarity of a native Filipino surprising Mai, and it shows on her face for an instant. The man catches her expression but remains stoic.

Mashaun speaks in a low, firm, but respectful tone, introducing the two of them. He tells the man they are travelers, and when they heard the noise, they came to investigate. Seeing the battle, they could either sit by or help, and they chose to help. The man listens to Mashaun intently, analyzing every word to determine if this person is a friend or foe, occasionally looking at one of the guards. After Mashaun finishes his story, he shuts up.

The merchant speaks with one of the guards. After a long pause, the man welcomes them and offers them some food and drink. They try to be polite while eating, but it has been a long time since either of them had something other than meat and berries. He introduces himself as Pavvo and his granddaughter Toni as she steps down from the carriage, wearing a long dark-blue tunic trimmed in gold. She's in her early twenties with daffodil skin and medium length caramel hair tied back in a waterfall. "She is a nydaj khaum neaj or a yellow mage." Dalistra tell Mashaun. During the introductions, they move their arms and hands in a stylized rhythm.

Pavvo also introduces the captain of the guards, Wilmer, and his lieutenant, Axtel, both wearing full chain armor, carrying long swords and bows. Mashaun finds it interesting as Pavvo converses with Axtel instead of his captain, Wilmer.

Pavvo asks where they are heading. Mashaun shrugs and tells him they are not sure. Pavvo offers them a job, telling them a couple more guards are a welcome addition to help replace the ones they lost on the route this time. Mashaun tells him they will have to think about. He offers them a place to bed down but they respectfully decline.

Mashaun asks Pavvo if he has ever heard of the city Thesila. Pavvo tells him it used to be magic capital eons ago. It is somewhere east of the Dragon Mountains, but not to waste his time searching for it. Many have searched for the ancient city of Thesila, but it remains hidden, and he will say no more. When he asks Mashaun why, he thought it might be someplace to explore. Why not. Mashaun thanks him, and with Mai, they head back to camp. Mai tells Mashaun she is surprised how well he speaks Filipino. Surprised, Mashaun tells her he was speaking English.

"Maybe he is also from the cave," they say in unison.

Dalistra tells Mashaun she doesn't trust Pavvo and they should take a roundabout way back to camp. Mashaun discusses the situation with Mai, who also is uneasy, but agrees they should take a long way around. They turn off the road onto an animal trail, taking them away from the rest of the group. A few times, they catch a glimpse of two figures following them and decide to split up. He ducks behind a tree, and she continues hoping they will follow her. The plan works as two soldiers following her pass by, oblivious to him. The soldiers come around a leafy clump of bushes, and Mai sits on a log with her back to them. They chuckle, seeing her in such a vulnerable position when they remember there were two of them, only to detect Mashaun behind them. The soldiers quickly turn around becoming face to face with Mashaun with his hands on his sword's hilts. They know they've been caught, and sit down without saying a word. Mai is glad they chose not to fight because she can't fight. She also doesn't want Mashaun to know.

Mashaun asks the soldiers why they are following only to find out Pavvo has ordered the soldiers to follow them back to camp. Pretending to understand, Mai sits and listens. Mashaun tells Mai they are just foot soldiers and are following orders. Mashaun suggests they escort the soldiers back and have another talk with Pavvo to which she agrees. They march the guards back to the edge of the road to let the two guards go, telling them they want to speak with Pavvo at the forest edge. Pavvo and Axtel meet with Mashaun and Mai at the edge of the forest a short time later.

After a lengthy conversation, Pavvo agrees to go with them, providing Axtel and one of the guards go with them. Mai and Mashaun agree. The five head through the forest to the old road and arrive at the place where they left the group, only to find it vacant. After a few short moments and some calming words from Mai, the others slowly appear from the bushes. First is Kazimir, followed by Berg, Abigail, and eventually the twins. Pavvo and Axtel study's them for a while before Axtel nods his head, and Pavvo sits down by the cold fire pit, joined by Mashaun and everybody, except the twins, who remain standing by the bushes, not saying a word.

Pavvo and the twins stare at each other for a long time as though they recognize each other. Pavvo tells the group they are smart, not trusting anyone at first sight, but at the same time, they need to know whom they can trust. They talk for some time before parting ways, and Pavvo tells them his offer still stands. After he leaves, the group asks about the offer and Mashaun tells them, asking for their opinions. Kazimir doesn't trust him, and the twins say "Tzsjs" with a tinge of fear. Berg and Abigail are unsure about him but believe it will be safer in a larger group, especially since bandits are in the area. Dalistra commands Mashaun to take the group and join the caravan. After all, Pavvo is correct as to the location of Thesila. After some discussion, they will join up with them in the morning. However, they need to cover each others backs and sleep as a group at night with their own nightly patrols.

During the night, Mashaun overhears Mai sniffling, as the tears land on his chest. He picks her head up and gazes into her watery eyes, asking what's wrong as he wipes the tears from her cheek. She tells him that's the first time she shot a bow, let alone killed anything, let alone a person. Mashaun tells her she missed, and she hangs her head apologizing. She closed her eyes, released the arrow, and then saw an attacker with an arrow in his shoulder. He tells her it was Kazimir's arrow, not hers, and she doesn't need to apologize. She lets out a sigh of relief while being a little ashamed at letting him down. He never should have put her in a contrary to her beliefs, telling her it he will not do it again.

"She can not shoot or fight, what benefit is she? Leave her, I say," Dalistra spits.

"No, she has other skills. You are too quick to judge," he snaps back. Dalistra holds her tongue, waiting for the right time and place to teach Mashaun who the boss is. Mashaun can already feel the better connection along with an increased tension with Dalistra. During the last few weeks,

the bond between Mashaun and Dalistra has strengthened, giving him the ability to occasionally notice her emotions. At the same time, he can sometimes block her from reading his mind. Several times, her contemptuousness is too much, and he would put her down and walk away until he could no longer sense her. Each time, he had to go a little further to not sense her. He is curious at how far they can be apart and for how long can they have a strong bond, but he doesn't want to test it.

Kazimir is sure Mai missed on purpose; after all, no one can be that bad of a shot. Nevertheless, he is unsure what to do about it. If Mashaun does not know, it can be dangerous for the group. Maybe the twins are right. He should be the leader. Mai has Mashaun's ear, and if he tries to bring it up, it can cause more tension between the two which will affect the entire group. He senses Mashaun doesn't trust him, and the incident with the bow does not help matters and it weighs heavily his mind, he slowly drifts to restless sleep.

The next morning—like every morning—the fog is thick, making everything wet and cold. Mashaun has the fire stoked up when the others slowly join him for a quick breakfast before heading out for the day. Breaking camp, they head out in the usual manner—Mashaun and Mai in the lead followed by Berg and Abigail. Kazimir and the twins are further behind than normal, partly because the twins are pulling on Kazimir's shirt, trying to hold him back. They don't want to join the caravan, and they are trying to make him to do something. He keeps telling them he won't let anything happen to them and he will find a way to free them, even though he has no idea how. They don't fully comprehand what he is telling them, but he likes to think they do.

When they break out of the forest, the caravan is in the final stages of packing, hitching the horses to the wagons and putting the campfires out. The drivers are mounting the wagons while Pavvo oversees everything. Axtel greets them as they approach the wagons. One of the guards tell Pavvo they've arrived as he accompanies them to him. Mashaun tells Pavvo of their decisions and wants to know if they are acceptable.

After some thought, he tells Mashaun they are more than acceptable and asks them to stay on the right side of the road. Mashaun glances at the group and receives a positive nod, and so it is settled. Before taking their place, Mashaun gives Pavvo Mai's bow, telling them it will do better in someone else's hands. At first, he is a little surprised but remembers the arrow they found in the forest and nods, giving the bow to Axtel to distribute. Kazimir stares in disbelief, feeling foolish for his previous thoughts, thinking he may have underestimated Mashaun.

The caravan heads up the road with Pavvo's carriage in front, followed by the three buckboard wagons full of merchandise, with the camp wagon bringing up the rear. The camp wagon is similar to the lead carriage except it has no windows. It also has cooking utensils and dried food hanging from the sides. Wilmer rides on the top of the lead wagon, and Axtel is on the last wagon with 10 guards on each side, walking with irregular spacing between them. Mashaun and the group walk on the outside in single file with Mashaun in the front and Kazimir in the rear. Around noon, they take a break, and the caravan stops for a short time, giving everybody a break including the horses.

Pavvo invites Mai and Abigail to ride on the middle wagon. He tells Mashaun the twins cannot because they wear the slave collars. The two gladly take the invitation and quickly climb onto the wagon, taking their seats, relieved to be able to sit after all the walking the past few days. The caravan continues to travel the long road at a snail's pace, allowing Mashaun to disappear into the forest long stretches at a time, leaving Kazimir to keep them together, which he does, believing Mashaun is starting to trust him. Mashaun is generally looking for signs but mainly wants to avoid the dust, prefering the forest than the road anyway. He is more comfortable walking in the woods. The extra cover will give him the element of surprise if the bandits return. He can also spy on the caravan, making sure Mai and the group stay safe.

"You are a sly dog." Dalistra taunts. Mashaun ignores the comment, not wanting to banter with her. *"Ignore me for now, but you won't for long."*

The caravan stops shortly before sunset. The wagons park in a loose half circle with the horses tethered by the cook wagon. The main camp is on the inside of the circle with a guard on each wagon. Mashaun's group sets up camp slightly inside of the open end of the wagons. A couple of guards set up Pavvo's pavilion by his carriage with a smaller one to the right of him. Five four-man tents set up around the area for the guards. Each tent has a small fire pit with a larger one in front of Pavvo's pavilion.

Mashaun's group lays their furs on the ground around the fire pit and is getting ready to have some dried meat and fruit when the cook's helper brings over some hot stew and some bowls which they accept enthusiastically. Abigail hungrily eats the soup, leaving the meat, which Kazimir is more than happy to take off her hands. The twins are reluctant to eat with the rest of the group like during the first few days on the trail.

After some time of eating and relaxation, one of the guards informs Mashaun, Pavvo requests his presence. Two guards stand outside Pavvo's pavilion when Mashaun arrives, and they step aside as he passes. The pavilion has one central room with a curtain separating the second section. A low circular table with a three-legged iron pot with burning embers is placed at the center of the room. Pavvo sits across the table, flanked by Axtel and Wilmer on each side. Their weapon belts are lying on the floor with the bows hanging on one of the poles used to hold up the pavilion.

Pavvo greets him and motions him have a seat. Mashaun follows suit, hanging Dalistra nearby and gently laying his weapons on the ground beside him. Pavvo's granddaughter offers him some wine. He graciously accepts, and she fills his silver chalice. He tries to speak with Dalistra, but she is afraid to speak or chooses not to—he's not sure which.

After a brief moment, Pavvo asks Mashaun where he acquired the twins. Pavvo does not beat around the bush, so he tells them most of the story, leaving out the part about the cave and killing the probable owner. When they ask him where they are all from, Mashaun thinks for a moment about the conversations with Dalistra and considers using one of the places she told him of, but if Thesila has been in ruins for a thousand years, then so have the others. He tells Pavvo he's from Tianjin, and when Pavvo asks about its location, he says it's a long way away. He can tell from their faces they know he is not telling them the whole story, but Pavvo nods his head and grins, letting the matter drop.

Pavvo recognize the collars and find it is strange he is in possession of them, so he asks Mashaun about the owner's certificate or a bill of sale.

"The city takes a dim view people in possession of stolen slaves... even if they are indentured servants," Pavvo says.

Hesitantly, Mashaun tells them yes, and Pavvo has one of the guards retrieve Mashaun's pack. Mashaun shows the documents to him. Pavvo studies them handing them back.

Pavvo says, "They're authentic owner certificates, but the owner will not be happy you have those documents."

Mashaun asks about the difference between a slave and an indentured servant. Pavvo explains, indentured servants can become slaves and are never able to pay off their debt. Mashaun gets a quick education of how the world works from the three. They talk for several hours before Pavvo offers them the extra guard tent, taking his leave for the night. Mashaun graciously accepts the tent and goes back to the group where they anxiously await his return, bombarding him with questions about what they want. He is telling them a summary of the conversation when a couple of guards brings a tent and set it up for them. Mashaun tells the group they can use the tent. It only sleeps four, and since they have rotating shifts, it will work for now.

The Harmony or yellow Moon rises above the trees casting a yellow hue across the land, as Mashaun takes fist watch.

"Being able to use two moons magic is rare. Magdalenia will want them back, and you stand in her way," she tells Mashaun during their night patrol as he ponders this new information.

The night passes quietly, and the mornings have gotten colder with a few clouds lingering about. While they are breaking camp, one of the drivers offers to carry their supplies on the wagon with the girls. They follow the same routine as they did the day before, stopping for lunch before continuing until almost dusk. Pavvo invites the group to join him for the evening meal, alone with Toni, Wilmer and Axtel. They feast on some kind of fowl with some potatoes and vegetables. The light conversation is mostly about the day and everybody's experiences. Pavvo is the only one who understands them. The group keeps quiet and listens for the most part, answering questions with careful thought, not totally trusting anyone outside the group. Pavvo asks the twins about how they came to be with the group.

In a subdued voice, Ericka does most of the talking with her eyes looking down, telling them the sale was supposed to be temporary but they were indentured for another five years in Tenskie. They were on their way back to Shen Sherin when the wagon was ambushed. Axtel nods and Pavvo lets the story drop and the conversation becomes more casual. Dalistra asks Mashaun if he has noticed Pavvo looking at Axtel after each story as if he were an aura reader, Axtel apparently has an innate ability to tell if someone is telling the truth.

The next morning, they continue on their northward journey with the usual positions. Mashaun spends a lot of time in the forest, and since the wagons are slow, he has no problem keeping up. Shortly after lunch, two guards approach the twins. After a brief exchange of words, Elina slaps the guard, and the two of them quickly run to Kazimir, hiding behind him. The two guards return to their positions, and the twins remain close to Kazimir for the rest of the day.

During the evening meal, Mashaun overhear Kazimir and Mai discussing the incident. He asks the twins about it before talking to Wilmer. They both know it is not over. Shortly before they have the evening meal, the two guards approach Kazimir and tell him they want to rent the twins for the evening. At first, he doesn't understand but listens to the twins muttering, "Thyve tsiiwv hyais tzsjs." He recognizes *tzsjs* and refuses. Confused and upset by his comments, the guards tell him they're sharing the camp so he should share his slaves. He has no idea what they said as the twins affirmatively nod their heads while looking down. The two guards realize Kazimir doesn't understand them, so they try to push it a little harder, but he holds his ground, and the guards don't want to lose any pay for fighting in camp. The guards leave after making some incomprehensible comment the twins understand too well.

Chapter 6

THE ATTACK

THE NEXT EVENING, THE TWO guards approach Kazimir with a different approach, but receives the same results. Mai gets Mashaun, and they return as the discussion becomes heated and is about to break out into a fight. Wilmer and Axtel are close behind, joining Mashaun in the middle to break up the argument. Unless the disagreement is settled, it can affect their survival. Mashaun whispers to Kazimir if he can take them one at a time without weapons. He answers with an astounding yes. Asking the twins if they trusts Kazimir to fight for their honor. They stare at each other with confusion, thinking for a moment, Mashaun tries to ask a second time to pronounce the words right. They agree, though nobody has ever fought for them before. Dalistra is looking forward to a fistfight—she hasn't seen one since being put into the bow. Mashaun proposes a friendly fight. Kazimir will fight one of the guards, and if the guard wins, the twins will spend the night with them. If Kazimir wins, however, they will leave the twins alone. He tells them, no weapons or armor. The two guards chuckle and make some comment about the old man before agreeing.

Everybody forms a circle with Kazimir on one side and the guard calls Max, the one Elina slapped earlier, on the other side. He is about 20 years younger than Kazimir, who stands a full head taller and easily outweighs him. Before the fight starts, someone shouts he has a yellow on Max, followed by several more. Soon a lot of betting is going on, and Mashaun takes all the bets with the confidence Kazimir will win. If he loses, Mashaun has no idea what he is covering. Only it is a lot of money.

Early in the fight, it is obvious Max has speed, agility and youth on his side, but Kazimir has strength, stamina and experience. Watching the two reminds Mashaun of a cougar and a bear fighting. Max connects several times for every punch blown by Kazimir, but Max goes flying back each time. Max learns how to read his opponent and soon realizes speed alone will not work. Every time Max connects, he shakes his hand, as if he hit a stonewall. He changes his strategy. Kazimir lands face down in the dirt, and Max jumps on his back, only to fall off as Kazimir stands. Max attacks low again, but this time, Kazimir reads his move perfectly, not only stopping the attack but also throwing Max into the crowd. Max gets up and puts his hand up as Kazimir advances. Max stands up and approaches Kazimir to shake his hand and, in one last feeble attempt, tries a surprise attack. Kazimir jerks him around and flings him back into the crowd like a rag doll. Max starts to stand but can't or chooses not to with Kazimir towering over him, shaking his finger at him. Wilmer calls Kazimir the winner and their funds increase, thanks to Kazimir. The caravan guards know the twins are off-limits.

Mai and Mashaun go to see how Max is after the bout. He is a little sore but will survive and humbly tells them, he will make amends in the morning. Mai examines his wounds with the diligence of a mother to her child, applying some wraps around the larger wounds before their healer shows up. Aside from the healer, several other men show up admiring her work, and when she is done, they all have tiny cuts they want her to attend to them, while their healer shakes his head and grins as he leaves. She examines them and kisses their wounds before they leave with a smile, feeling much better.

Useless...apparently she will be useful after all, Mashaun thinks sarcastically. He can tell it does not please Dalistra. Axtel stops by their camp later in the evening to congratulate Kazimir and to tell them if anybody gives them problems, they should let Axtel know. After his display of hand-to-hand, no sane person would argue with Kazimir. He also gives Mashaun a small kit and tells him it will make the bows last longer. They invite Axtel to join them, and he does for a little while. Axtel explains the kit and walks Mashaun through each item for cleaning and protecting. Mashaun senses Dalistra cooing as he soothingly rubs the wax onto her limbs. *Oh, you like that,* he thinks. But all he senses from Dalistra is soft purring. Mai observes Mashaun with affection and jealousy as he rubs the waxy oil into the limbs of the bow the same way he caresses her at night.

The next few days pass by quietly. Kazimir and Max make amends, and it appears a friendship is developing between them. Often, the two spar with each other using different weapons. Kazimir works on his weapons skill while Max improves his hand-to-hand. Max becomes more cordial to the twins and even intervenes when an argument about them develops between several other guards. The twins even relax a little around Max, sometimes sharing a meal with him to the jealousy and envy of others. During the next week, they pass by several small ruins next to the road. Old roadhouses for travelers, one of the guards tells them. About 10 years ago, other races stepped up the attacks on anybody in the wilds, and owners turned up missing. The city guards patrol the road between the city and outpost about a day's travel out, but people still turn up missing. It has gotten treacherous for travelers, and many merchants don't travel outside the city anymore, making the caravan more profitable and more dangerous.

After about a week on the road, Berg and Abigail sit on a wagon during their early morning watch. The moons are starting to sink behind the mountains, casting long, dark shadows across the landscape. Abigail quietly points at a shadow moving along the edge of the forest, but only makes out the fuzzy outlines of the trees. Earlier in the week, he told Abigail his night vision is terrible and he is nearsighted. She keeps his secret, making sure she is always on guard duty with him. They have an agreement should anything happen, Berg will wake Mashaun, acting as if he is waking him for his shift, while Abigail keeps watching the figure. Berg does as they had discussed and tells Mashaun about the shadow. He nods, telling him to wake Kazimir and the guards as quietly as possible. Staying in the shadows, Berg makes his way to Kazimir and the other guards, telling them what Abigail saw. Moving among the shadows, they wake the guards.

Mashaun joins Abigail on the cart, where she quietly describes the locations of the shadows. It doesn't take long for him to catch a glimpse of them stealthily moving along the tree line. joined by several other shadows, he tells Abigail to inform Axtel while he keeps an eye on the shadows. Shortly Axtel is on his side, asking about the commotion. Mashaun describes the shadows' locations and their movements. Axtel studies them for some time before whispering they are setting up for an attack from two sides. Mashaun listens and then quietly suggests they move up their timetable by starting the attack before the enemy is ready. Axtel agrees. When the men are awake and ready they will have a surprise waiting for the guest.

They quietly agree on their chosen targets. Their arrows fly through the darkness, striking their intended victims with deadly accuracy. One of the targets releases a loud cry of pain. The fight is on. A rain of arrows flies in both directions, with a couple of guards launching flame arrows into the forest, hitting different trees. The fire arrows cast enough light to silhouette a number of figures lurking in the forest and the caravan. The attackers try to run, but another volley of arrows flies in both directions. The sound of arrows whizzing through the air pierces the silence of the night with the occasional cries when the arrows hit their targets.

Mai and Abigail stumble across the caravan's healer, only to find him as a casualty from the volley of arrows. He is the first dead person Abigail has seen up close, and it makes her sick to her stomach, losing what is left of dinner. Mai grabs Abigail's head and turns it toward her close enough to smell her vomit breath, telling her they need a medic and they are it. Now, they have work to do. They cover their heads as another volley of the enemies' arrows lands around them. Mai grabs the healer's equipment, thinking how archaic it is, and goes around helping the wounded. Abigail shortly follows. She doesn't want to see any more blood but she doesn't want to be by herself either.

Kazimir first picks up the bow and sends a few arrows into the dark, dropping it to grab a sword and shield, dwarfing them in his hands. Seeing several enemy swordsmen breaching the parameter, he charges into the fray. The enemy finds he is a formidable warrior and the guards are glad he is on their side. His shield bash sends the opponent flying back into his comrades, knocking them down. Kazimir trades his sword for a larger one. Several of the guards take up a position behind him and to one side and use him as a tank while they use their bows with deadly accuracy before switching to swords. The three of them fight like a well-rehearsed team as they slowly make their way forward against the onslaught of bandits.

Pavvo and Toni stay in their carriage, each with a dagger and a repeating crossbow ready for any uninvited guests. Several small slits for arrows allow the passengers to shoot anyone driving the coach. Wilmer is a blur with a long-sword in one hand and a short sword in the other, cutting his way through the enemy while staying on one side of the coach. The long sword glows yellow before a flash of light as lightning streaks through the air with a thunderous boom. Startled, many glance his way, only to witness a line of burnt grass and dead bandits. Axtel protects the other side with his flail and spiked shield, with every strike on the shield, the attacker winches in pain.

Berg and the twins hide under a wagon. He has a short sword for protection but quietly prays he will not have to use it. He offers the girls a dagger, and they both refuse. The twins know slaves with weapons end up in the arena or death. The arena games are violent and deadly. They will not survive and will rather be someone's pleasure slaves than fight in the arena. The three remain quiet under a wagon, between the wheels, throughout the battle. Once, one of the guards falls not far from them, still alive. They quickly drag him under the wagon and stanch the bleeding.

The black of night gives way to the faint orange glow of the early morning light bringing the battle more into focus. From Mashaun's vantage point on a wagon the bandits outnumber the caravan guards and their only real advantage is the defensive position of the wagons. With the clashing of steel behind him, Mashaun realizes the enemy is in the camp, but he is busy with several archers hiding past the tree line. He takes cover beside the wagon and continues to fire at the archers in the forest. Every so often, a muffled scream escapes the forest. The body count continues to climb on both sides as the battle wears on into the early dawn.

Mashaun scans the battlefield seeing bodies littering the camp and surrounding area, realizing it is only a matter of time before the enemy overwhelms them. He scrambles up on the cook wagon for a better view, looking for the leader. From the distance, is the man whom Mashaun shot the last time they attacked the caravan. He takes aim and lets the arrow straight toward the man's chest. Mashaun launches a second arrow before the first one reaches its intended target. The bandit leader knocks the first arrow aside with a small arm shield but doesn't anticipate the second one hitting him in the shoulder again. The two glare at each other for a long moment before Mashaun shoots the third arrow, only for him to move out of the way, but enough for someone to sound the retreat.

The moans of the wounded and dying fill the peacefulness of the early morning. Mashaun scans the surroundings, seeing dozens of bodies lying on the ground. Mai and Abigail are busy helping the wounded. The landscape, caravan and its guards have a fresh painting of blood. Wilmer and Axtel check on the carriage, making sure Pavvo and Toni are okay while several of the guards go around making sure no enemy survives and scavenge anything worth keeping. Mashaun goes into the forest to check the ones he heard cry during the battle, finding only a few dead and several blood trails. He starts to follow a trail of blood when he jerks around hearing a noise behind him. With a quick sidestep he turns with Dalistra drawn, Axtel stands, shaking his head. When he asks him about it, Axtel says nothing. Instead, he turns around and heads back to the caravan. Mashaun hesitantly follows, figuring it probably isn't safe to track them alone anyway. The caravan is busy putting the wounded on the wagons and piling their own dead for a funeral pyre upon their return.

Mai's and Abigail's clothes are soaked in blood. They receive some of the extra clothes from the dead men and burn theirs so they won't attract wild animals. Mai likes her outfit but understands they have to burn all the bloody clothes. The guards are glad to have them around during the fighting—Mai has managed to save quite a few lives with her medical skills which increased the guards' morale. Mai's knowledge in medicine is far superior, giving her a definite edge over the previous healer. The guards will miss the old healer, but are glad Mai is an excellent healer and she is on their side.

Several guards stand on the wagons as lookouts. Others hitch the horses to the wagons and the caravan begins to rumble up the road. Mashaun takes a quick count and finds they are down to less than a dozen guards who are still in fighting condition. If the bandits attack again tonight, they will not be able to hold them back. He speaks to Wilmer who nods in agreement and tells him they are still several days from Shen Sherin. Mashaun asks him if they can make it to the city should they push. Wilmer shakes his head and advises against such action because it will leave the wagon less defensible during the night.

Mashaun decides to disappear into the forest, dropping back to monitor the trail behind the caravan. He waits in the bushes until the caravan disappears around the bend in the road before stealthily moving through the foliage along the forest edge, being ever vigilant about his surroundings and the forest on the other side of the road. After several hours, when he decides they are not being followed when a distant dust trail catches his eye. He heads back to the caravan moving through the forest like a deer, staying inside the forest edge, noticing the dust cloud slowly closing the distance between them while watching for the movement of their scouts, which he is sure they have.

The caravan does not stop for lunch due to the late start, and they want to close the distance to the patrol area of Shen Sherin. It is late afternoon when a company of armed riders approaches the caravan. The leader says they are from Shen Sherin and need to speak with the owner. Each of them wears chain mail, carries both lances and swords, riding tall in the saddle like seasoned warriors. Pavvo stops the caravan and has a short private conversation with them before continuing up the road. The riders join the caravan, riding in pairs in flanking positions on the back end of the caravan while the leader rides in front with Pavvo's carriage. The sight of the city guards is a welcome sight indeed, and when the men take their positions, the morale of the caravan jumps.

The bandit leader drives his men at a quick pace to catch up with the caravan, if they don't attack the caravan tonight, it will be too late. The bandits slowly continue to gain on the caravan, and it could be a long night if Mashaun doesn't return before it gets dark. His plans change when he spots the bandit leader rise over a knoll at the edge of the forest on the other side of the road. The leader in front of the bandits is acting as a forward scout. *How unusual,* he thinks. He could take a shot now, but it could reveal his position, instead, he chooses to wait…for now.

This is the first time he is close enough to scrutinize the bandits' leader. He has black hair tied back into a short ponytail. He wears a metal breastplate, with a small round shield and long sword, which is why his first arrows were not fatal. He studies him for a long time from the shadows of the forest as the leader scans the area before disappearing back into the forest. At one point, the bandit leader stares in his direction, but takes no action as Mashaun freezes. Dalistra tells him to shoot. With over two dozen men coming up the road he can't avoid all of them for long, she agrees.

When Mashaun does not catch up with the caravan by early afternoon, he realizes they did not stop and he will have to be careful not to be mistaken as an enemy when he catches up with them. He eventually eyes the caravan in the distance and it is only a matter of time before the bandits reach them. Once the caravan stops and the dust settles, he spots extra horses on the road with them. The six well-armed strangers will make his return more dangerous than before.

Pavvo stops the caravan early to give the men and the animals some extra rest; it's still two dangerous days until they reach the city. He has the wagons set in a tight semicircle, with the city guards setting up camp on the open side. He request to see Wilmer, Axtel, Mashaun, Mai, and Tara in, the city guard captain. Mai searches for Mashaun, but he is not in camp. She frantically goes around the camp, asking everybody if they have seen him, but nobody has. Wilmer tells her they spoke in the morning but he had not seen him since. This troubles not only Mai but the rest of them as well.

Mai wants to go find Mashaun but Kazimir stops her, telling her he is capable at taking care of himself in the wilds, better than the rest of them together. She snaps back at him, implying the only reason he stops her is so he can take his place as the leader. This not only stuns him but also hurts him, and he lets go of her. She immediately feels ashamed at letting her emotions get the better of her and apologizes, wanting to take her words back. She realizes he is right, both in stopping her and Mashaun's capabilities. He accepts her apology, and the two of them go to the meeting together.

The bandit leader and Mashaun travel down the road. The leader, with his band, continue to follow the road while Mashaun mirrors him on the other side. The horseman is apparently unaware of Mashaun. As the long shadows stretch westward, one of leaders men comes out of the forest on the other side and speaks to him, at which point they stop and set up camp. Mashaun backs deeper into the woods and continues to the caravan. Shortly, he realizes the reason they stop is the caravan has made camp only about an hour up the road. He approaches the caravan from the road, so they have some time to make sure he is not the enemy. Two riders on horseback block his passage until one of Pavvo's guards tells them to let him pass. When Mashaun gets to camp, one of the guards tells him the meeting has already started without him. Surprised, Mashaun rush to Pavvo's tent.

He enters Pavvo's pavilion, asking for forgiveness, but he has some news about the bandits. Mai jumps up and gives him a warm welcome until Wilmer clears his throat. Mashaun can feel Dalistra's jealousy and envy as the two sit down. The conversation continues back to a strategy for the night.

"What news?" Pavvo asks him. Mashaun advises them on the bandits' numbers and camp location. They listen intently as Mashaun suggests they take the battle to them. Wilmer argues it will leave the camp unprotected should they attack. His counter offer is they send a squad of bowmen to harass them during the night, putting them off-balance and reducing their numbers.

Mashaun explains his idea, and not everyone agrees. But after some discussion, it gets the approval of the group. Axtel will take five of the best archers and meet Mashaun at the cook's wagon. Mai feverishly opposes the idea, but for every reason, she comes up to Mashaun to tell him not to go. Mashaun says he should go—he has seen their camp. She doesn't argue anymore. She wants to go with them in case someone gets hurt, but she does not need to be in the raiding party when there are still wounded people in the camp who need tending. She reluctantly agrees.

Shortly after sundown, the small group moves into the forest and heads for the enemy's camp, maximizing the darkness before the moon rises. About halfway, Mashaun suggests they rendezvous here before continuing to the bandit camp. Once within sight, Mashaun finds a hidden vantage spot within sight of the leader's tent while Axtel takes charge of the rest. They wait for most of them to bed down, leaving only a few sentries. The plan is to catch them off guard and keep them off balance as long as possible. As if on cue, arrows fly from different directions, taking down several of the sentries, with one falling into one of the fire pits, creating a loud ruckus.

The camp awakes to find as they stand up, some collapse to the ground with arrows in them. The whole scene reminds him of a dream. Mashaun waits for the leader to step out of his tent. The leader emerges, to find out what is happening, only to find one of Mashaun's arrows hitting him in the chest. Before the leader can react, several other arrows find their mark, like déjà vu Mashaun witnesses the carnage. Without his precious armor, the leader is vulnerable. The arrows drive deep into his chest, as he stares in disbelief at the arrows protruding from his body before collapsing to the ground in a heap. Most of the camp has gotten up and is blindly sending arrows back into the dark forest, not realizing the shooters have already moved to a new location.

The plan is to send two or three volleys of arrows into the camp then move to a different location, then launch another volley. They will keep up the attack until dawn, or if they're met with a serious threat, they will meet back at the rendezvous point. The next volley into the camp comes from different directions, and the camp takes up a defensive position, hiding behind shields while sending arrows wildly into the dark forest. The arrows will stop long enough for the camp to feel safe, and then another round would send them scurrying back behind their shields. After several hours of the random attacks, the bandits surround themselves with shields and refuse to leave their makeshift fort. They even stop shooting arrows and coware.

Seeing they no longer have any targets, Axtel decides it will be futile from this point on, taking his group to the rendezvous with Mashaun following before returning to the caravan. Axtel takes a body count. Over a half-dozen bandits killed or wounded, including the leader, while none of them even got a scratch. Nobody says a word as the archers keep close to the forest, remaining vigilant to make sure no one is following. They didn't stay all night as planned, however, the bandits will need a few days to lick their wounds and possibly find a new leader.

When Mashaun's group arrives back at the caravan, the camp rushes to greet them with curiosity and enthusiasm. Everybody wants to know how it went. Mashaun receives a hug and kiss from Mai. Mashaun tells Dalistra not to say a word before she even has a chance. Kazimir, the twins, Berg and Abigail are curious about the evening's event. Kazimir is a little upset he was not invited. Thinking fast, Mashaun tells him if anything happens to him, he will have to protect the group. Kazimir leaves with a grin on his face.

Pavvo summons Axtel and Mashaun for a status report. He is curious why they returned so early. He is pleased it is a success and their leader is dead. The enemy is only slightly injured, and it will not be long before they regain their senses. However, the death of their leader should buy them a few days. They double the guards anyway, but nothing happens. The convoy leaves before sunup the next morning. Pavvo still wants to put some distance between them and the bandits.

Chapter 7

SHEN SHERIN

http://thesilaprophecy.com/realm/shen-sherin/

THE NEXT DAY DAWNS WITH the cool, crisp air in the morning, warming up as the sunlight blankets the ground. The days are getting steadily cooler as they travel. Max tells Kazimir they are heading toward the land of the long night where it remains dark most of the time during the winter. They cover a lot of ground before they set up camp. The conversations are more about the city than the bandits, but the guards are still doubled. The city guards update the caravan guards about the events from Shen Sherin and the surrounding area, which isn't much except for Magdalenia. They tell them she has been furious the last few weeks, taking her anger out on anyone glancing at her wrong. Rumor has it someone has killed her clone which had her stone staff while transporting two of her prized slaves, and they have disappeared. In a hushed voice, one of them says rumor has it she doesn't know what has happened to her clone but the guard captain made it back, and then turned up dead a few days later.

Only Mashaun truly knows the real story, and having the owner's certificate for the twins, he hopes it will offer some safety for the group. Mai has asked a few times what had happened, but he refused to tell her for her safety. After hearing the story, he realizes the dangers to everyone if the secret was discovered.

After dinner, Mashaun leaves camp to practice with swords. After a short time, one of the city guards catches him and offers to spar. Introducing himself as Cyngir, Mashaun is grateful and the two begin with slow movements. Within seconds, Cyngir realizes Mashaun has no idea what he is doing. Wilmer studies Mashaun from a distance before offering him a demonstration on how to use two swords. Cyngir and Wilmer spar at full speed as a crowd gathers to enjoy the demostration. After each short burst of action, Wilmer asks Mashaun questions about what he saw. teaching him you don't block with two swords, but channel their force away, leaving your free hand to strike.

The next day, when the caravan stops for lunch, Wilmer points to a mesa on the horizon. He tells Mashaun it is Shen Sherin, but it is too far away to make it by night. Instead, they will have to spend the night at the Arnbor stronghold. It's a fortress for merchants, which is a short day's journey from Shen Sherin. It can hold and protect a dozen caravans if needed. Every merchant pays to help maintain the fortress and the garrison housed there. By early afternoon, a circular palisade comes into view, towering above the extensive clearing.

It has a 15-foot wood wall with a walkway along the top for guards. The fortification also has several wooden towers located around the perimeter, with a ballista in each. By a massive gate is a small wooden building with a short round man guarding the entrance. Pavvo and the city guard captain speak to him for a short time before showing him a metal disk. The wooden gate opens, and they enter into the protection of the fort. Inside stands a two-storey building next to the gate has a meal area and barracks for the guards. Wilmer tells Mashaun the city guards who patrol the road spend a month at a time here before rotating back to the city.

By nightfall, several other caravans enter the enclosure and set up camp. Most of the caravans are empty and use Arnbor during the winter to store their wagons. Several are heading south. The merchants have dinner with Pavvo. Wilmer tells them a few years ago, it overflowed with caravans, but had died down because of the increased attacks. After they set up camp, Mai helps the twins cover the leather bands with a cloth to hide their identity. They may not dress the part of a slave, but there is no hiding their slave-like mannerisms.

Some of the caravan guards are longtime friends, and they're laughter and merrymaking well into the night, something the group has not heard since they arrived in the cave. Even Mai, Berg, Abigail, Kazimir and the twins join in the festivities. A guard from another caravan grabs Ericka, and as she struggles to break free, Max intercedes, and she hides behind him. The two men talk for a while before Max points to Kazimir.

Seeing an opportunity, Max asks Ericka about when they first met. At first, she stares at him blankly, and then she understands and approvingly nods. Max arranges a friendly fight with Kazimir. Mai rushes to find Mashaun as the bets fly. Pavvo's guards see this as a chance to win their money back, increasing the stakes. Berg starts taking the bets before asking Mashaun about covering them, but Mashaun nods his head affirmatively while standing on the sidelines. There are lots of greens and yellows, with even a few blues thrown in to sweeten the pot. There isn't enough money in the pool, and if Kazimir loses, there can be problems again. Some of the merchants even bet on the bout, including Pavvo, bets several red Kuj on Kazimir, surprising many.

The two opponents square off in the circle, both looking determined to win. Kazimir's opponent is taller, has the same build, and is several years younger. Kazimir goes down early in the match, surprising him, and scaring Ericka. His opponent tries to stomp on Kazimir's head, missing, as Kazimir manages to roll back up on his feet. They go after each other like two juggernauts, each taking turns briefly being in the dirt. After a time, the two tired warriors circle, waiting for the other to make a move, when someone throws a dagger in the center of the circle, followed by a second dagger from the other side.

The two men circle the knives, each attempting to grab one, only to fail time and time again. Eventually, Kazimir's opponent gets one knife and kicks the other out of the circle, almost hitting someone. Feeling more confident with the knife, he attacks. Kazimir reads his move and blocks the knife with his arm while pivoting around, catching his opponent in the side of the face with his elbow, sending him stumbling across the circle. Before he can regain his bearings, Kazimir is on him. With a couple of fast blows to the midsection and a knee on the face, his opponent goes down. Everybody holds their breath to see what the guy on the ground is going to do next. Some yell at him to get up, others tell him to stay down. Eventually, he waves his hand to surrender.

Kazimir helps the man up, and they both hobble over to a makeshift table, leaving a trail of blood droplets behind them. Mai joins them at the table to patch them both up, shaking her head. She does not understand the need to fight, let alone for fun. Both love the feel of her soothing touch as she wipes the blood from their faces. The man reaches for her arm, but she pulls away before he can grab her. Kazimir shakes his finger and points to Mashaun, and the guy glances at her, then him, and nods. Someone brings both of them a mug of ale, and they sit there drinking long after Mai leaves.

During rest of the night, people walk up to them and thank them for making them some extra money or putting a good fight. Once, several drunks from the different caravans walk up to them and start harassing them. Kazimir still understands a little of what they are saying. The two start to stand as several of the guards intervene, sending the drunks on their way as they turn and give the two men a thumbs-up.

Berg takes the winnings and gives them to Mashaun since he has all the party's money. The money pouch is getting heavy, and he doesn't feel safe walking around with so many marbles. He finds Pavvo who is collecting his winnings, and asks if he will help keep the party funds safe. Pavvo is more than happy to help, except he only has one lockbox so the two of them count the money with Mai and Axtel watching. Mai's eyes becomes saucers when she realizes how much the party funds have grown from nothing in the cave even though she has no idea of the value of each. Pavvo fills out two receipts, and everybody there signs them. Pavvo says he will put one in the lock-box with the money, and Mashaun will keep the other one. On the way back to the group, he gives the receipt to Mai and asks her to keep it safe as he disappears into the darkness like usual.

Mashaun strolls the wall, staring at the silhouette of the city in the moonlight, wondering about the stories of Magdalenia. Mashaun considers the possibilities of dealing with the twins and Magdalenia in the city, knowing it is all speculation. He thinks back to his other life in the city and how life there was much simpler compared to the one here. He gazes into the night sky as he often does, pretending to scan for a familiar constellation, giving him time to ponder about his new life; he is still unsure whether it is a dream or if he is in another world. He has always been the quiet one, sitting in a room, observing while not being noticed. But it was different here. People follow his words, and his deeds affect others which is overwhelming Dalistra remains silent as she listens to his thoughts, feeling a little sad for him. She remembers her father saying leaders are not from birthrights but arise from chaos. She didn't understand what he meant until now.

Snapping back, he remembers Pavvo said this is the end of the season and he wouldn't leave again until the spring, offering him and Mai a position in his house. He hasn't told her yet, wondering if Kazimir and the others received a similar offer, and he hopes they did. He is tired of them looking up to him, but he enjoys it too.

He strolls the walls for hours and occasionally strikes up a short conversation with one of the guards, using Dalistra to translate. Mashaun keeps to himself most of the time, sometimes talking with Dalistra about the city and Pavvo's offer. Dalistra likes the offer but is open to going places.

"Anywhere is fine after being locked away in the vault for eons." What she doesn't tell Mashaun is she has a vendetta and is looking for someone. He is her only means of finding them and when she does, he will extract her revenge.

They leave by sun up the next morning even though most are not thrilled about it. Many are still feeling the buzz from too much alcohol. The Shen Sherin castle looms over the countryside atop a mesa, protected by the sea on two sides and a group of islands on one side. There is a river snakeing through the countryside between them and the castle. Log buildings rest on pillars three feet or so above the muck and the earth. The logs have two sides planned to fit flush next to each other on the smaller buildings, while the larger ones have a patchwork of log squares five feet across. They approach a stone bridge stretching across the river in multiple spans. A variety of shops and inns nestle among tall buildings of rocks and trees with thatched roofs line the road, extending into the cleared forest. The townsfolk scurry like ants as the caravan passes. Every so often, some townsfolk approach the guards, trying to sell their wares. The guards brush them aside like pesky flies. The buildings are rundown; the people have hopeless eyes watching the caravan rumble down the road past them, oblivious to their plight.

Growing up in a small village, Kazimir identifies with the situation, and Berg's childhood was worse than what he observes. Both of the men found a way out of the poor neighborhoods—one by strength, the other with his brain. Mashaun has seen similar scenes in and around different cities. He walks through town with heighten senses, as a crowd gathers around them, staring with hands out. Mai and Abigail have only seen people like this on television watching the people trudge through the mud with empty eyes. With heavy hearts tears in their eyes they sit on the wagon, creaking as it rolled pass the village. The sound of falling water grows louder as they approach the river. They ask one of the guards about it, who tells them it is low tide which doesn't make any sense.

In the middle of town is the only bridge across the river Sherin, reaching over fifty-feet from one side to the other. The arch-type rock bridge has two gatehouses, one on each end with a wooden section with a collapsible middle if needed. Across the bridge, the town spreads out haphazardly with a four-way intersection in the middle. The castle lies to the left. On the right, the Dragon Spine Mountain Range towers in the distance over the trees. Straight ahead, the road continues through the fields before disappearing into a forest of evergreens and deciduous trees.

The caravan turns toward the castle, which sits on the furthest island of a network of islands, each protected by a gatehouse and drawbridge in addition to a major guardhouse. They arrive at the city entrance in the afternoon. Across a sixty-foot stone bridge eight horses wide with three barbicans. The drawbridge to the first island is thirty feet to a gatehouse with a wall reaching skyward above normal high tide around the circumference of the island. Barnacles and moss covers twenty-feet below the island, a current flows upriver as the tidewater rises.

"I've never seen such a wall. It must be twenty to twenty-five meters tall," Mai says in awe looking up.

The gatehouse and the walls are solid stone, without any seams, brick or mortar looking like slabs polish marble grown from the earth. Passing through the first gate at one end of the island, they see a second slightly smaller gate about fifty feet ahead of them. When both gates are closed, it creates a box trap and whoever is in the middle is at the mercy of the archers.

The gate guards make everybody, except for the city guards, walk through two glowing multi-color crystal rock pillars about ten feet tall with runes written on them. The guard in chainmail covered by a blue tunic with a thirteen arm Kraken speaks to everybody as they approach the pillars. When Wilmer and Axtel go between the pillars, their weapons show a light green aura. When Pavvo goes through it, his tunic has a blue aura, his rings have a yellow aura, and his dagger has a salmon aura. Upon seeing this, Dalistra tries to talk Mashaun into staying in the village and not entering the city. She tells him the two columns detect magic, and every type of magic glows a different color. It is used so the guards can identify who has magic, its kind and potency, everybody around can also see.

The guard stops Mashaun before the pillars and asks about any magic. He is unsure how to answer, feeling everybody's eyes on him when he does not answer right away. Finally, he tells the guard he doesn't know and the guard tells him to walk between the crystals. Dalistra has a deep crimson aura as he passes between the pillars, and everybody stares at him, as time itself stand still. Most view with curiosity. Some with fright. Others back away. A red glow is rare; most have never see a blood red aura. Mashaun hears swords being partially sliding out of their scabbards and notched arrows aimed at him, frozen in time, and afraid to twitch, he waits for something to happen. Scanning the crowd, as they inch back, and Axel blocks Mai from charging in.

Another guard comes out of a door and asks if he is going to cause any trouble. Fortunately, Dalistra translates for him and Mashaun timidly shakes his head, telling them tzsjs. The guard tells the men to stand down and instructs Mashaun to follow him, which he does without hesitation. Pavvo tries to follow, but a couple of burly swordsmen stop him at the door. After a brief conversation with the captain and the exchange of jade, they allow him to enter. The room has four well-armed swordsmen, one in each corner. Their swords are in their hands, ready for a fight. In the middle of the room is a small table with two chairs. On the table lies a parchment which appears to be a registration form. It requires the owner's name, the type of magic item, its color, how long he has it, where he acquired it, intended purpose and length of stay in the city, along with some other information. The only reason he can understand the parchment is through Dalistra's translation.

Pavvo tells him they have not seen an unregistered red glow in ages, and most have never seen blood red.

"Only spirit weapons glow with deep red, and your answer to the city guard, err...didn't exactly help." Pavvo tells him in order to enter the city, he needs to fill out the form on the table. Mashaun does not want to give all the information out, so he decides to fill it out but plays ignorant on things like the weapon's name and is vague on the where and when he had acquired Dalistra. After he fills out the form, one of the guards exits and returns later with a woman. She has a square made of four smaller squares and places one of the smaller squares on the ground kitty-corner to the table. She moves counterclockwise, placing the second cube, creating a turquoise wall from cube to cube and to the ceiling. She continues until they are within a six by six by eight cube. She sits in the chair across him, wearing a guard outfit with a silhouette of cross swords over a hippogriff, above her left breast. Her face is soft but stern with piercing blue eyes with coal-black hair tied in a bun. Dalistra is unusually quiet. She takes some time to read the form before speaking with a soft, stern tone—one that commands attention.

"Just so you know they can't hear us. I have seen other spirit weapons, devil swords, ego weapons, soul swords, whatever you want to call them. I also know they won't remain with a person for long if the two beliefs are too different. They will always require a blood test before allowing the person to use them. They always have a name, and they make sure you know it."

Feeling trapped within the cubicle, he listens to her intently.

"I'm Katherine, Captain of Munthiv and responsible for the safety of Shen Sherin. Now let make this as painless as possible. First, what is your name?" She sternly says.

"Mashaun," he whispers as his voice trembles.

"See, that wasn't so hard. Now what is the bow's name?" she asks.

Dalistra tells Mashaun not to say a word, but both know it won't work.

"I don't know."

She repeats the part about spirit weapons' names and their ego makes sure the wielder knows it.

He says, "I can't say."

She stares at him for a short while before saying, "I don't care what he is telling you, but you are going to tell me who the bow is."

"It's not a he! It's a she," he blurts out before thinking. Dalistra gives him a disgusted feeling.

"OK, now we are getting somewhere."

"How can I address her properly if I don't know her name?" she asks.

"You can address her through me," Mashaun quietly answers.

"We'll come back for her name in a bit. So where did you acquire her?" she asks.

"Northeast of Tianjin," he tells her. She smiles and moves to the next question.

"Why are you in my city?" she asks sternly.

"I'm a scout for Pavvo's caravan, the gentleman standing over there..." Realizing he can't see out of the cube.

She continues to question Mashaun for over an hour, sometimes rephrasing the same questions, looking for any deviation in his story. Eventually, he slips muttering Dalistra, and Katherine puts it down as the bow's name. She makes him unstring Dalistra, telling him the bow must remain unstrung while in the city. When Dalistra is unstrung, Mashaun notices the connection is broken and can't feel her in his head. He understands why Dalistra did not want to be unstrung.

She picks up the four cubes and walks over to speak quietly to Pavvo, who nods affirmatively before saying something to one of the guards. While he is gone, Katherine asks Mashaun if she can hold the bow while they are waiting for his permit. Feeling it might be a trap, he agrees anyway, handing Dalistra to her. She examies the bow for some time, admiring the workmanship before gently handing it back, thanking Mashaun.

Mashaun and Dalistra. She tells him it is a rare treat to see, let alone hold such an item of beauty—fine craftsmanship from the Thesilan age.

The guard returns, giving her a small metal disk. She tells Mashaun, he must return it when he leaves the city. It allows him to enter the outer islands only, and he cannot take the bow to the inner islands. He can only take it to Pavvo's place if one of his people accompanies him. She hands the disk to him as he leaves the room. He understands a little of what she says. Pavvo fills him in on the rules of the city. Joined by a couple of his guards, they walk to the Red Wagon Inn.

The road passes between two thirty-foot walls with several towers and bridges and only two sets of double gates. Guards patrol along the top, watching the people below. The clashing of metal echos from the otherside. The second gatehouse stands on the far end of the island, with a bridge leading to a larger island. Two broken stone statues rest atop a six-foot square stone base. Pavvo tells Mashaun every bridge has a pair of mirror statues. The figures are the patron Gods for the island. Each sculpture used to hold a moon ball to light the gate, but few have survived the civil wars or the ravages of time. Unlike the walls, the statues were hand-carved by Thesilan artisans.

Pavvo tells him the city stands on a group of islands, separated by bridges. Each bridge is wide enough for two wagons, with a gatehouse on each island. Every island has a stick by the gates extending down into the river with hash marks to mark the delta level. He shows one to Mashaun and it downs three marks. Mashaun guesses it to be about three feet below the bridge with the current running toward the river. During times of high water, they close the gates to keep most of the water off the islands. Some of the bridges have two long ropes used to roll up the wooden bridge, while others use an oil trough down the middle.

There are 15 islands. Only a couple islands are natural, the rest are grown during the Thesilan era under the command of Khusari. All the islands have grown-rock walls around the perimeter to control the river and protection. The wall facing out are over fifteen feet thick with magic wards carved into them, the island edges facing another island nothing more than a watertight palisade. There is a single bridge connecting each island with a gatehouse and a metal gate.

Mashaun absorbs everything he is told and observes.

"A few years back, the water covered the bridge by over two shtem…I mean feet, during a triple new moon," Pavvo tells him. "Each island has several wells with a water desalination building and the more exclusive places have their own well. Under each island lies a network of stone tunnels used as a sewer system dropping garbage into the river under the islands then out into the channel. The market island, Synhom, contains open bazaars and shops carrying everything except for livestock or smiths, bowyers and fletchers."

They arrive at the Synhom gate. It is not what Mashaun expected. The major roads are made of cobblestone, complete with curbs. Roads crisscross each island from bridge to bridge with an open area at the major intersections marked by open markets and a nonworking fountain. Some still have a glass ball resting in a cradle on top. Pavvo tells him the balls used to light up, but the magic is gone, so it sits there as a reminder of what it was.

Grates placed in the curb allow water to flow into the sewer below. Each opening has an internal flap rises and closes off the hole when the water gets too high. Every island is its own district with its own specialty—to the right are livestock and weapon, to the left are the bakers, and down the middle are craftsmen and exotic goods. Every island has its taverns, and rooms for residents and guests while maintaining their own militia for order and protection.

Beyond the first set of islands are the wealthy and noble, which requires an invitation to enter. The bridges leading to those islands are narrow, allowing only a single carriage on the bridge, and the roads allow a carriage and horse to past, most walk or ride a horse. Many have estates outside the city wall, but the city offers better protection and they are willing to pay extra for the increase in safety. Most of the buildings are only two stories tall, with rooms in the back for horses and carriages. Each house displays the owner's crest, representing who they are and their station. Most have a private well and connection to the sewer system.

A major road goes from the island of Synhom to the city administration offices on the island of Tiswaj. The bridge from Tiswaj to the Castle Island Strasev is narrow with a major gatehouse on each end. Every island maintains their own government and the chancellors for each island have an office on Tiswaj. They keep careful count on the passage through each gatehouse on a daily basis. The interior islands are a little higher above the water line until Strasev is nearly ten feet above the water, and the castle is nearly twenty-five feet above the river.

Chapter 8

RED WAGON INN

Pavvo tells Mashaun thievery runs rampant on the outer islands, and they hunt new targets. Throughout the city are regularly spaced columns, some are broken or missing. The ones still standing have spheres the size of a basketball on top, or metal brackets supporting a bowl for burning oil attached on the side. Mashaun senses a tinge of sadness from Dalistra.

The city streets are busy with people hurrying to their respective destinations. A few times, someone approaches them only to be turned away by Pavvo's guards. Shortly they cross the bridge leading to Oralub Island. No one gives them a second glance as they make their way down the street to the Red Wagon Inn. Pavvo makes sure the wagons are around back before going inside to make arrangements for Mashaun and his group. Wilmer and Axtel stay in a semi-private room while the rest of the guards sleep in the common room. Everybody will take turns staying with the wagons, watching the merchandise until all the wagons are empty.

Pavvo returns a short time later with three metal cards with the same pattern of holes in them. He tells them the room is on the second floor and the water closet is at the end of the hall. There is a room for a hot bath on the bottom floor, and the food is not bad. He has paid for a week, but the group will have to pay for any extra days. All he asks in return is they help protect his goods for the week. They glance at one another and figure it sounds fair so they agree. One of the serving girls shows them to their room. It has six beds each with a chest at the foot. They drop off their gear and lay down on a straw-filled mattress—it's not much but it is still better than sleeping on the ground.

Before going downstairs, they decide to divide the money but realize none of them have any idea the value of the different colors except for the twins, and they still struggle communicating with them. But the twins show them it's 10 green to one yellow, 10 yellow to one blue and 10 blue to one red. Kazimir suggests Mashaun and him should receive a larger cut because they did most of the work which results to a multi-way argument over the division of money. Mai and Abigail believe they need a larger share for keeping the group healthy. Berg thinks everyone should have a share, and the twins slowly back away, not wanting to get involved.

After a few minutes, they agree to make eight equal piles of money, one for each of them and a party fund going into the general fund pile. They want Mashaun to handle the general fund, but he declines and asks Berg instead. Abigail stares at her share for a while before asking how much it is worth. They all turn in unison towards the twins. Using the items in the room and their clothes, they are given a quick lesson on the value of things like shirts, shoes, daggers and blankets, among other stuff.

The twins are excited about having some money they can call their own. Slaves' owners usually keep track of their money, reporting it to the city so they know when the debt is paid. They all go to the inn's common room for dinner and check the evening crowd. The place is already full when they arrive, and it takes several minutes to find a table for all of them. The twins' mannerism changes from being friendly to subservient. They remain silent unless they are asked. Their head always downturn to the floor, standing next to the table, never sitting down. Kazimir tries to talk them into look up or sitting down, but they shake their heads. Berg suggests he should allow them to assume the role for now so the group does not attract undue attention. Kazimir quietly tells him that's not right but deep inside, he knows Berg is right.

After a short time, Mashaun tells them the place is too noisy for him and excuses himself from the group. He goes to the caravan where he relieves a couple of grateful guards. Axtel soon joins him, telling Mashaun there should be at least two people visible on guard duty, and two more hidden. Mashaun apologizes, and then they talk about stuff until a strange sound catches Mashaun's attention.

The swooshing of high-pressure water hitting stones is moving down the road. Mashaun stands and gazes in amazement the wagons and the street. A horse with a 10-feet pole across its front with several tubes shooting spraying water on the street and on the front of the buildings. The water takes all the filth down the drains into the sewer. Axtel tells him every island used to have a couple of them, but many have stopped working. Now, they only have about one for every two islands. Some have pleaded with Magdalenia to fix them, but either she won't or can't.

"Like the sphere post and many other magical amenities, the magic is running out and nobody can recharge them. Many say Magdalenia could charge the globes since she's a purple mage, but her underlings prefer the dark if you get what I mean," Axtel says. Mashaun nods his head.

The rest of the group stays in the inn for a time, enjoying the drinks and the atmosphere. Mai and Abigail join some of the dances and have drinks bought for them. Berg studies the social interactions of the patrons and samples some of the different meals, while Kazimir relishes in the different drinks are being served by the twins. It is the first time they can relax since arriving in the cave over a month ago.

The next morning, they leave in different directions with their usual pairs and agree to meet back for lunch. All over the city, remnants of sculptures—still fountains, paintings on building walls and more—remind the citizens of a time when art and magic abound. Shen Sherin is a magnificent city, but is only a shadow of what it used to be eons ago.

Mashaun takes a bath and shaves before purchasing a few items so he can shave on the trail. Mai also takes a bath in a different room. When Mai purchases some shaving supplies, the clerk gives her a strange gaze but sells it to her anyway. As the two spend the morning wandering the streets, Mashaun is curious why some townspeople staring at him, whispering while pointing, and even crossing the street as they approach, only to cross back after they pass. They find a clothing store. They buy some better travel clothes, but Mai makes Mashaun wait outside while she also gets a dress for the inn.

After their baths, the twins wear their hoods up to hide their faces while taking Kazimir on a tour of the island. The twins know the islands well after living here for 10 years. They do not want to have any money on them while they are wearing their slave bands; they give their money to Kazimir to guard in case Magdalenia finds them. After the tour, they take him to an upscale clothing store where they all purchase some new clothes. At first, the clerk is not going to wait on them. But when Kazimir puts a blue on the counter, the owner smiles and changes his attitude. The twins don't buy anything nice. When returned to Magdalenia, she will be furious with them. She will take it away, and their punishment will be harsh.

Berg and Abigail set off to explore the city and find a different bathhouse. They find one with running water, although it is a little more expensive. Both buy some new clothes, with Abigail looking around for a short leather skirt to no avail. She settles with a tight black leather pants and a blouse to match which is against Berg's better judgment. Berg gets a simple shirt and pants before looking for a bookshop. Berg picks up a dictionary along with another map for comparison. Abigail finds a cloth bound book with blank pages and a pen set. Their next stop is a music shop. She hunts for a guitar but there was none. She settles with an ornate string instrument made of wood and bone resembling a small harp.

They enjoy a small lunch together, talking about what they have seen before Kazimir and Berg go to the wagons, relieving some of the guards. They are surprised to see one of the wagons is gone. One of the guards tells them Pavvo took it early in the morning. They give several guards the afternoon off, and the twins stay in the room for fear of being recognized. While rubbing Dalistra, Mashaun asks the twins about maps, and after thinking for a moment, they tell him of a place which is only a short distance away. They will not go with him, fearing they have already spent too much time in public. They know it is only a matter of time before the guards show up for them. Dalistra translates what the twins said, but her tone is more subdued as she is half-asleep.

In the afternoon, the twins decide Kazimir has treated them better than anyone else has. Everybody has treated them like people and not as property. They are both glad to have a chance to be free even though they are aware Magdalenia will soon find them. They will eventuality return to their old life and she will probably use the whip on them. Thinking this will be their last night of freedom, they decide to repay Kazimir tonight, the only way they know how.

Mai and Abigail go window-shopping as Mashaun goes to the
Gold Compass Cartography shop. In a dim room, an elderly couple sits
behind a desk, watching him. The woman has long white hair hanging
freely down to her waist, while the man has medium-length white hair
with a matching beard. They study Mashaun for a short time before
the man offers to assist Mashaun. Mashaun asks for a map of the local
area. After a while, the old man nods. Grinning, he shows him a wall of
maps. Carefully, Mashaun sifts through the maps, looking intently at
the different cities and any geographical features. The maps are crude
drawings at best, nothing like he is used to reading back home. After some
diligent searching, he decides on one of the older maps. Their characters
are similar to those on the map on the cave wall, and it has more details
than cities. However, it only covers the area around Shen Sherin, from
the mountains to the ocean and several hundred miles north and south.
When he exits, the girls are waiting for him, and they return to the inn as
a group of townsfolk follows them from a safe distance.

Kazimir and Berg are still watching the wagons when Pavvo,
Wilmer, Axtel and some guards return with an empty wagon and huge
smiles. They greet the two before Wilmer and Axtel release the guards
and join them watching the remaining wagons. Wilmer hands Pavvo a
book, and he disappears into the inn. The conversation stays light until
Kazimir asks about the wagon. Wilmer and Axtel, decide to tell them
about the sale and the split they each recieve. Seeing the blank stare on
their faces confuses Wilmer and Axtel until they realize the group is from
another region.

At first, Kazimir has a problem when they use big words, so Wilmer
and Axtel try to keep the words and concepts simple. Kazimir and Berg
have been spending their evenings with the twins, learning the local
language, hence they can understand simple sentences. After explaining
how everyone who helps with the caravan is paid, Wilmer and Axtel give
Berg and Kazimir a quick lesson on politics, money and social status.
They also them about Magdalenia, one of the ruling people in the city,
followed by Pavvo, and last is the king. They hesitate before telling them
no one has seen the king for years, and there are rumors, he may be dead.

Chapter 9

BRAVE OR FOOLISH

WILMER AND MASHAUN HAVE GUARD duty when a fog rolls in, starting with the mist rising up through the sewers. In less than an hour, the fog pours over the lower walls, filling the streets until a watery haze shrouds the entrance to the stables. Wilmer tells Mashaun to keep an eye out for the gangs roaming the city during the fog. About then, voices pierce the fog.

"Look, a wagon with only two guards. We can take them," says one of the voices.

"Don't be a fool. That wagon belongs to Pavvo. If you want to continue breathing, you will forget it and move one," an older voice replies.

As the voices move away, Mashaun asks what happened. Wilmer tells him he has never heard of Magdalenia's people ever attacking Pavvo's merchandise.

Several uneventful days later, Pavvo sells all his goods and makes a tidy profit after giving everybody their percentage. He even gives some to Mashaun, Mai, Kazimir, Berg and Abigail. When Kazimir asks about the twins, his response is straight and unemotional. Pavvo tells him everybody receives payment according to a contract at the beginning of the trip. "However, because of your contribution to the success of the sale, I am giving each you a guard's share for part of the trip." Mai receives a larger share for being the healer, and Mashaun gets a bonus for taking out the bandit leader. The two slave don't receive anything, because they are slaves.

As the moon begin rise, Magdalenia and several guards storm the inn. Everybody backs away as she accuses Kazimir of stealing her property, the twins, and murdering her clone.

He stares at her, not understanding much of what she is saying but her tone is undeniable. He manages to recognize a few words. The accusation catches him by surprise as he stammers for an answer. He takes a defensive stance, glancing at Pavvo shaking his head, letting the guards roughly escort him and the twins out of the bar. Pavvo witnesses the encounter, but remains quiet until after they leave, and then he sends one of his guards for Mashaun.

Mai and Mashaun return shortly, and Pavvo explains what has happened, telling Mashaun he will have to go to the magistrates in the morning with the certificate of ownership to keep Kazimir from becoming a slave or worst. He also tells him when he does, they will ask him all kinds of questions about how they came to be in his possession, and Magdalenia will conclude he killed her clone and will try to make him admit it. He will probably be charged with theft, assault on a citizen, and possibly land piracy for starters.

Mashaun nods and goes up to his room with Mai, where they discuss the plan for tomorrow. They decide he will go by himself to see the magistrates and argue his case. He prefers if Pavvo does it for him since he hates speaking to groups, especially when it is not in his native language.

The guards take Kazimir and the twins to an island at the base of the castle and enter a stone building. The first room is a small cubicle, barely enough space to hold them. One by one, the guards transfer them to a second room, where they turn over their clothes, and are given a small sheet with a hole on the top for the head. It hangs down in the front and back with each side open, similar to the outfits the twins were first wearing. Each is put into a different cell with stonewalls between them. Magdalenia ignores the twins, thinking it will be better to let them spend the night wondering about their punishment.

Magdalenia plans her assault for the next day. She is undecided whether she wants Kazimir executed or sent to the arena for some fun. Magdalenia understands it will be an uphill battle for the twins since she does not have their papers. She sent them back to Tenskie to have their contract renewed for another 10 years. It is easier there than in Shen Sherin. However, if it comes out they are on their way back from there, it will not sit well with the magistrates. In addition, her power and influence within the inner islands have been diminishing over the last few years, and with the well-known loss of the clone and the staff, her standing has eroded more quickly. On the bright side, her influence in the outer islands has grown, mainly because they still fear her. Her brother's influence within the city has grown, almost surpassing hers. He has the respect and the ear of the upper class, nobles and even the king, if he is not dead.

This case quickly gets the attention of the city. Neither of them have the proper documents proving ownership, even though everybody recognize the symbols on the collars. Also, it is unusual for ownership papers to leave the city except to skirt the laws within the city, and has drawn a lot of attention. Last is a rumor the king himself with his court will be watching, and he never involves himself in civil cases, leading to wild speculations.

The city is abuzz about the upcoming trial between the newcomer, a stranger, and Magdalenia over something as important as undocumented indentured servants. The stakes are high—should the newcomer win, it could set a precedent and reduce Magdalenia's prestige within the inner circle even more. This will be to the delight of many, but the city will face her wrath. If Magdalenia wins, the newcomer will become her slave, and most of the town expects her to use him in the arena where she can make some money from his humiliation and death.

The case has the city divided in many ways, and the chaos moon, (new yellow moon), doesn't help. Some want her to win because of who she is, and some don't for the same reason. Some disapprove of slavery and see this as a possibility of changing the laws while others like the current system. City guards stay busy breaking up more brawls than usual. The group is lucky to avoid a scuffle in the inn by making it up the stairs and staying in their rooms except for Mashaun, who wanders the city alone, thinking about the next day. He wants to visit Kazimir but decides it will be better not to tip his hand yet.

The guards awaken Kazimir early in the morning when a thin, wiry middle-aged man with short blond hair wearing a red robe arrives. When they let him in the cell, he introduces himself as Thom and he will represent him in front of the magistrates. Kazimir explains they do not have any papers for the girls. They came upon the wagon surrounded by dead bodies, and the girls locked inside. They let the girls out and burned the wagon with the bodies. Thom asks about the "we" and Kazimir realizes he slipped. He tells him about Mashaun but does not tell him about the cave. Thom wants to speak with Mashaun but unless he is at the hearing, it won't happen and he will have to try for a postponement. It will be tough as it is against Magdalenia's counselor. After a lengthy conversation, Thom decides on the defense. It's going to be a hard sell because the other side has one of the best barristers in town. Thom tries to speak with Ericka and Elina, but they will not allow it. The opposing counsel has already been there, and the guards will not allow them to speak with anyone else. The guards are well paid to make sure the twins are not allowed to see anyone. Slaves and indentured servants receive free counsel. Slave owners' and magistrates may visit them at any time while barristers need a document from the owner. Thom tries to argue they belong to Kazimir but the guards want to continue breathing, hence, won't cross Magdalenia.

Pavvo and Mashaun leave at dawn for the castle where the case is going to trial. On a normal day, it will take about an hour. But today, it takes them three hours to arrive at the castle courtroom. The few shops are open with one or more guards and all the side streets have extra guards. There is already a crowd at the last bridge and up the path to the door. Only the brave or foolish argue with Magdalenia, and many want to see the fireworks. Pavvo and Mashaun force their way through the crowd to the front door of the outer castle, where several well armed guards stop them. Pavvo tells them they have business dealing with the slave case. After Pavvo slips them some blue jade kuj, the guards step aside. Inside, there are armed soldiers wearing partial plate along the walls and archers on an elevated walkway. They make their way through the crowded courtyard to another door where he pays another guard to enter the courtroom. They stand in the back, waiting for the case to start.

At the far end of the room are three high-back chairs behind a half circle table sitting on a platform, allowing them to oversee the room. Along each wall are tables and chairs, and the three make an equilateral triangle with a stone circle in the middle. Like all major walls, the building appears grown, including the tables and the center circle. Symbols etched into the walls give off an eerie glow in a sequence of colors rotating around the room.

Mai tells Berg and Abigail they are moving to a different inn for safety reasons. Dalistra has a fit when Mai picks her up. But she should not reveal her abilities to Mai. She is furious at Mashaun for allowing this floozy take her away from him when she hates even being touched by her. The three gather their things and quietly slip out the back where Wilmer and Axtel sit on one of the wagons. Mai tells them it will be safer if they move before the court's decision. They need to move to a different location without telling anyone. Wilmer and Axtel tell them to wait in the wagon. They hitch the horse as Mai tells them where she wants to go. Wilmer tells her there is a safer place and they need to trust him. Without an answer he cover them with the tarp as the wagon rumbles down the street and over a couple of bridges.

There are several other cases of people with unpaid bills forced into servitude. Some have a specific time limit while others are indefinite, but all have a set amount for their release. Mashaun studies the proceedings hoping to understand little of what to expect. Pavvo whispers this is nothing and he shouldn't pay much attention to these cases.

After lunch, is the case of Kazimir versus Magdalenia over the property of Ericka and Elina. First, they bring in the twins, their hands manacled behind their back with a chain leading down to a cross chain connecting their ankles. They lead the twins to a wooden bench and attach their chains to the wall. Next, they bring Kazimir in, setting him on a chair next to Thom. Magdalenia and another woman sit across the aisle. Kazimir turns around scanning the crowd. Seeing Mashaun and Pavvo, he whispers something to Thom. Magdalenia also turns to study the crowd. She has never seen so many people in the courtroom. She glances at the royal balcony where the king calmly overlooks the room. His presence could affect the outcome. Taking one last quick glance at the crowd, she sees her brother. The two stare at each other for a moment before she quickly turns around, wondering what he is doing in the room.

Three magistrates walk in and take their seats behind a high table. As they eye the room, it becomes deathly quiet. The magistrates acknowledge the king, who motions for them to proceed, and they recognize each barrister and ask for a statement from the accuser, Magdalenia. She is the spitting image of her clone, wearing a long black robe with a blood-red leather bustier laced up the front, with brown hair in a french braid.

She accuses Kazimir of knowingly stealing her property, and she not only wants them returned but also wants him as her slave for restitution. Thom tells them his client did not knowingly steal them. Instead, he came across them in the wilds and has taken care of them, and they should belong to him as they were abandoned. He closes his statement by asking if she can provide the ownership certificates for the slaves. Magdalenia cannot produce the needed documents, and when the magistrates ask her why, she tells them the document were given to someone else to keep safe. For hours, they call people who vouch for her ownership of the twins. Magdalenia tells them she has owned them for many years, and is common knowledge. Thom's asks one question, "How do we know you didn't set them free?" Before she can answer, the magistrates tell her to stand in the question circle in the middle. One of the guards lifts a section, and Magdalenia steps in. Pavvo tells Mashaun the rocks veins will turn different colors, depending on whether the person is telling the truth or not. If it turns red, then they are lying.

The magistrate repeats the questions. Why were they out in the wilderness without travel papers? Who has their papers? Usually, when slaves travel, they bring their travel documents, and not the owner's certificate which stays with the owner in their home city.

Magdalenia says they were on loan to a friend in Tenskie and were on their way back. The courtroom becomes abuzz when she mentions the city of Tenskie. Everybody understands to skirt the slave laws in Shen Sherin, you send them to Tenskie. She tells the court she didn't worry about sending the papers with her clone with a company of guards. After all, who in their right mind will attack a mage unless they know she was a clone? She gets excited toward the end, feeling a little desperate. The railing color fluctuates during her answer but never becomes red. When the magistrates are finished with the questions, Magdalenia returns to her seat.

Kazimir tells the same story as before. When Thom asks about what he meant by we, Kazimir tells them Mashaun. Thom requests Mashaun to take the stand. Magdalenia glances at her barrister before looking back at the crowd and observes Mashaun making his way forward. She quickly recognizes him as the one with the red bow. Taking his place in the circle, placing his hands on the bar, he introduces himself as Mashaun from Tianjin. One of the judges asks him where, and he tells them it is far away. To his surprise, his speech is translated word for word. His answers are choppy, but he understands the questions in his language. Thom questions him at length about Kazimir and the twins. He tells them about seeing the wagon in the clearing with dead bodies around. He tells them he let Kazimir and the twins out of the cage and burned the dead in the wagon as a funeral pyre.

Later, he found a metal box in the ashes with the documents, and he gives them to Thom who hands them to the magistrates. Thom asks him how many documents were in the box, and Mashaun tells him two. Thom asks if Kazimir had slave collar on at the time, and when Mashaun says no, there is an audible silence from the crowd. Thom then follows by repeating Kazimir was caged with known slaves. The law is clear—slaves and non-slaves remain separated but this was not the case here. Thom asks Mashaun about Kazimir, and he tells them they have traveled together since then and he had permission to take the twins out. Mashaun chooses his words carefully, telling only a limited truth. He has rehearsed the story so many times in his head he almost believes it himself, although he is still apprehensive about being on the stand changing color.

Magdalenia's barrister gives Mashaun the arrow. One of the arrowspulled from the captain's body and asks if it belongs to him. He examines it for a short time and hands it back.

"No. Would you like to see my arrows?" he says. The railing does not change color. Mashaun is a little surprised when neither sides asks about the staff, or why he or the clone was in the forest and not on the road.

The judges move something on the table, and a light blue cube surrounds them for several moments before the cube disappears. The room is like a cemetery as they have Ericka and Elina taken over to the magistrates, and a guard pulls down the left back shoulder to expose a magical glyph about the size of a playing card face. It is a picture of the castle on a mesa with a number under the mesa. They compare the glyph and documents to determine if they are the same. They compare the tattoo and the documents with the documents kept by the city on all slaves. They find inconsistencies between the three, and they are suspicious when done in Tenskie. When the magistrates ask why the twins' internment was renewed, Magdalenia tells the court their father still owes her money, and the agreement was his daughters will work off his debt. The agreement is not common, it usually only happens when there is new debt.

They know the tags on the collars belong to Magdalenia, and they want to give the twins back to her to reduce her wrath. However, Mashaun has the legal certificate of ownership. According to the law, the twins belong to Mashaun. The magistrates realize if they try to give the twins back to Magdalenia, it will undermine their already tenuous credibility with the king and his court. With the room packed wall to wall and the king looking on, they have to follow the book, no letting Magdalenia off this time.

The magistrates are satisfied, Kazimir did nothing wrong and order him released. The courtroom explodes with excitement the guards have to calm them down. Magdalenia stands and protests while the magistrates tell her to sit down several times. According to the law, the twins are the legal property of Mashaun. Magdalenia is furious and starts to storm out of the courtroom when Mashaun tells the magistrates their service is paid in full, and he wants to release them from any further servitude. Magdalenia turns and stares at him, as he avoids her gaze as the seconds slowly tick by, as the room becomes still. She raises her hand and begins to speak in the language of magic, and the symbols on the wall become a solid color. She stops catching the symbols are now glowing brightly from the corner of her eye. In a huff, she turns around and continues out the door, as the crowd scramble out of her way. Stopping briefly she has words with Pavvo as she charges out of the room.

The magistrates nod and instruct the guards to remove the collars and the glyphs. Mashaun quietly tells Kazimir to watch their backs before asking him to go with the girls and to take them back to the inn when they are done, asking the magistrates if it's okay for Kazimir to stay with the girls. The courtroom is full of talk as the people file out into the city streets, spreading the news about the surprise in court. Soon, it's on every island of the city and beyond.

Pavvo tells Mashaun it was not the smartest thing to do. "You made a dangerous enemy, but her expression was worth it." Pavvo suggests they move to a different inn or better yet, leave the city tonight. Mashaun nods. They return to the inn where Axtel quietly tells Pavvo Wilmer took a wagon and went to the Golden Unicorn. Pavvo tells Mashaun the twins are safer at his place for the time being. He tells Mashaun, Magdalenia will not attack them while they are under his care. Mashaun is hesitant but finally agrees.

Shortly, Kazimir and the twins join them in the inn, each of the twins giving Mashaun a tight squeeze and kiss, thanking him for their freedom. Mashaun tells them he needs to leave town, and they will be staying with Pavvo for now. The twins nod their head in agreement. Pavvo quietly tells Mashaun Mai is not where he thinks she is and he should visit a friend of his, Llewellyn, who has a place up in the mountains. Mashaun nods.

Pavvo asks Kazimir if he has any plans before offering him a position at his manor. Kazimir will be a bodyguard, and the girls will learn usable skills. Elina enthusiastically says she wants to be a mage. Pavvo thinks about before telling her it might be possible. Before leaving, Pavvo points out two men sitting at a distant table, wearing red tunics with a red staff and a sphere in a basket, work for Magdalenia and are probably there to keep an eye on him. Mashaun studies them from the corner of his eye during the evening as they remain at the table. Once, someone with the same outfit stops to talk with them. He wonders how many others who work for her are there in disguise.

After a good meal and some brandy, he goes to his room for the night. Lying on the bed is a cryptic note from Axtel. After taking some time to decipher it, he burns the note, making sure not to leave anything but ashes he scatters out the window. The note tells him they went to the Golden Unicorn and they will wait for him there. It also says everything at the gate is arranged, all he has to do is leave the city.

After waiting for a few hours, he slips out the window by using the bed linen as a rope. He ties it in such a way when he reaches the ground, he can remove the linen so no one can tell from the outside. A thick fog fills the streets, extinguishing non magical light. A few guards have lights piercing the fog with a beam like a flashlight. A few blocks away, all the lights shine through the fog like normal. Night watchmen armor clink and clatter over the stillness as they make their rounds. Using the shadows for cover, he sneaks to the rock wall by the gate, climbs over and into the river. Hiding under the bridge, he uses the linen rope and creates a makeshift hammock, providing a dry place to rest in until morning. He has to make it across another island and bridge before exiting through the gatehouse, and with a little luck, they won't be looking for him until he is out of the city.

A cool breeze awakens in the early morning hours as he almost rolls out of the hammock. Over twenty feet below him, a fog rises from the sea-grass growing in a mud flat with a stream flowing through it. Barnacle crusted walls line the man-made canyon. About three-feet below the bridge is a six by eight opening with an arched top extending through the island. The creaking and moaning of footsteps on the bridge signals life has return to the city. Peeking out at a group of peasants going across the bridge toward from Synhom to Munthiv then the mainland for the day. Scampering out from under the bridge, he falls in behind them, walking across the next island and right through the next gate. He keeps his hood over his head like everybody else as he walks through the gate with the crowd. Before the sun reaches the top of the trees, Mashaun is on the road. With some vague information, he heads toward the mountains, hoping it is the right direction.

Late the following morning, the two men convince the innkeeper to check on Mashaun, only to find him already gone. The innkeeper is upset about the linen, but glad he disappeared in the night. Magdalenia will leave him alone now once her men report to her. The two men fume as they search the room, coming up empty-handed. Neither one wants to tell her he has slipped away unnoticed after what she did to the captain guarding her clone. They spend the morning looking all over the city only to end up empty-handed. But they have to tell her what happened, hoping for the best.

In the morning, Kazimir is introduced to his trainer, and the twins are given some test on their magic abilities. By noon, word reaches Pavvo Mashaun has disappeared in the night and has taken all the linen with him. Pavvo sends one of his guards with a yellow marble for the innkeeper. He has always given him a good price while his men are well-cared for, and he wants to keep the relationship.

When Mai, Abigail and Berg wake up, they vaguely remember arriving at a stone building in the evening, but they are too tired to pay much attention to where they are. Downstairs they find Wilmer already having breakfast at rectangle table as he motions them to join him. He explains the owner is a long time friend, an elf named Sivish and they can trust him. Their eyes light up with both amazement and wonder. Berg had heard of them back home, but they are a myth.

He tells them Mai needs to stay here for a while because they will be looking for her and Mashaun because they shared a room. When Berg and Abigail ask about returning to the city, he tells them they can return anytime they want. However, it will not take much to connect them to Mashaun. They didn't even talk it over. They eye each other briefly before inform him they will stay with Mai.

Mai and Abigail dislike the decor of the inn. Full animal mounts including a couple of bears, mountain cat, moose, and a few strange looking creatures with eyes scrutizing their every move as they cross the room. Over the bar is a full shoulder mount of a unicorn with golden fur. On the left is a lyre with gold inlay in the shape of a unicorn. On the right are two swords, a Bastard sword and a Flamberg hanging in an X.

Abigail sits facing the fire but she can still feel the eyes piercing her soul, so she takes her food upstairs, followed by Mai is also uncomfortable in the room.

The wooden tables and chairs are randomly scattered around the common room with an open area in front of the bar which has a mural carved into the wood. Upon closer inspection, Berg can see it is a story of a unicorn, a woman with a lyre, and a boy with a two-handed wavy sword fighting an invasions of some kind of short squat humanoids. When he asks Wilmer about it, he recites the story of the unicorn over the bar and how this place was founded.

Chapter 10

SPIRIT WEAPONS

http://www.thesilaprophecy.com/legends

Mashaun realizes how much he has come to depend on Dalistra, especially in the wilds. But he doesn't have much choice since Mai took her when they left the inn for safety. It takes him less than an hour to pass through the gate, the mainland town and into the farmlands. The river stays on the right of the road. The farms are on the left. The scenery doesn't change much except for an occasional farmhouse or a fishing shack.

By mid-afternoon, the farms become sparse. The scenery changes to trees with leaves in a kaleidoscope of colors. During his long trip without Dalistra, he begins to wonder if he perhaps trusts her too much. After all, he was one of the best on the school archery team. It is almost dark when a small, fortified manor house comes into view. It has a metal sign with an imprint of a unicorn inlaid with gold coins, with three Chinese-like characters written underneath. Mashaun assumes it is the Golden Unicorn.

A tall stonewall with heavy doors protects a courtyard. Inside is a two-story inn, stables and various other buildings built into the wall around an open area in the middle. By the stable is one of Pavvo's wagons. The inn is a modest cut-stone building with shuttered windows opening onto the courtyard. The walls have circles about chest high with ladders up to a walkway at the top. The heavy inn doors open with ease, revealing a bar in front with a shoulder mount golden unicorn on the wall overlooking the bar, reminding Mashaun of a hunting lodge with full mounts of bears, cougars and wolves randomly spaced along the walls. He finds it interesting they are all full mounts and the only partial mount is the unicorn.

There is a fire in the hearth built into one wall, which provides some light and warmth to the room. As he moves to the bar to ask about a room, he has the uneasy feeling someone or something is watching. However, none of the patrons are paying any attention to him. The innkeeper is lanky, with pointed ears and almond-shaped eyes. His forest-green hair is tied into a ponytail hanging down past his shoulders, which offsets by his lightly bronzed skin. Without saying a word, he points to a small table in a darkened corner and goes back to his work.

Two human girls scurry about the room, serving food and drinks to the patrons, moving in a smooth, rhythmic dance. In the corner, Berg and Wilmer are seated, enjoying a bowl of beef stew. He orders some from one of the serving girls and joins the two men. They greet him, wanting to know how he got out of the city. Mashaun asks about the girls, and they tell him they spent the day in their room. Mashaun starts to go up to see them, but Berg tells him they will be down in a moment. Berg and Wilmer are curious about what happened in court as they swap stories over the hot stew and drink. Berg has the mead while Mashaun and Wilmer enjoy some brandy after Wilmer declares it is the best in all the land.

Shortly, Mai glides down the stairs, wearing a long, peach silk off-shoulder dress with yellow flowers and a black bustier accentuates her figure. She has enough makeup to highlight her soft features. She is extremely overdressed for the inn—all eyes turn as she makes her way down the stairs and across the room to the three men. The room is abuzz with curiosity and questions as people move out of her way, as though she is noblity. Even the serving girls' attitude changes in Mai's presence. The three men bow, and she curtsies before Mashaun as he offers her a chair.

Mashaun wants to hug and kiss her but chooses not to. "My lady, it is an honor to have you at our table tonight."

Mai loves the attention she is getting from everyone, especially from Mashaun. Wondering how she paid for such a fancy dress, forgetting the money made since the cave. Whispers abound in the room, wondering who she is and where she's from.

Giving the room a time to settle, Abigail appears, wearing a skintight knee-length coal black leather skirt with a pair of pink heels clicking on the steps as she sashays down the stairs. The young men fall over one another attempting to reach to the bottom of the stairs first, each clamoring for her attention and company at their table. This is a new sensation for Abigail. She beams with joy at all the attention but with a nervous smile. She glances at Berg, who nods, realizing she can enjoy the evening. When she chooses a seat, many of the young men try to sit next to her and buy her ale, which she turns down for wine. Abigail has never had so much attention or alcohol before. After drinking a few glasses she sways in her chair and her speech is slurred.

Berg keeps a watchful eye on Abigail. It is obvious the wine is affecting her. Several young men offer to take her upstairs and put her to bed. She pulls away, but one man named Hauns leans over to whisper something, and she slaps him. He grabs her arm, turning to go upstairs as she struggles. Berg tells the table to wait, as he puts himself between Hauns and the stairs. He is a foot taller than Berg with arms the size of Berg's leg. Berg's hand is shaking and his voice shows nervousness. Mashaun and Wilmer stand a few steps behind him. Mashaun observes all the animals seem to be looking at them. Hauns pushes Berg back into a table.

"Mind your own business, old man," Hauns tells him. The animals have all moved to a crouch as if they are ready to attack. Berg says Abigail is his daughter and reaches for her hand. Hauns snickers, grabbing Berg's wrist, throwing him into another table. Everybody moves away as the cougar lands on Hauns, pinning him face down as the other animals circle the group. Berg cautiously reaches for Abigail's hand and escorts her over to the group's table. Mashaun turns back to survey the situation—Hauns is nowhere to be found and the animals are back in their usual places in their usual stance. Wilmer tells them the animals keep the peace, and all the locals know better than to start a fight in here. Hauns will wake up outside and will not be allowed in here ever again.

Mai takes Abigail to bed as the guys change the conversation. They need to purchase more food and equipment for their travels, especially warmer clothing with the evenings getting cooler. Mashaun understand weather and inform the others it will get cold in the mountains and it will probably snow. Berg and Mai have never experienced snow. Wilmer offers to pick up some supplies they need for the journey and will return in a few days. They thank and give him some money.

After dinner, in the privacy of a room, they discuss their plans. Mai tells Mashaun his bow hates her. He gazes at her as if she is crazy. Abigail, in a half-awake stupor, asks, "How can the bow not like her?" Mai tells them she tried to string it earlier in the day to practice, and she couldn't string his bow. In addition, she has a feeling the bow does not like her. Berg starts to ask how.

"Why did the bow glow red when entering the city?" Mai interrupts.

"The city is protected by the two stone pillars revealing all magic items when it passes between them. He was a stranger with magic, so they needed to question him, that's all," Wilmer interjects before anyone has a chance to say a word, knowing what the colors mean. They actually understand what Wilmer tells them.

"Fine, but you didn't answer the question. Your sword turned green, Pavvo's robe, blue, and his bow, red. What do the colors mean?" she asks rather insistently, also sparking Berg's interest.

"Green is minor magic, blue is defensive magic, and red is major magic," Wilmer tells her. She nods and lets the conversation change to something else. Berg thinks there is more to the story but also chooses to drop it.

After everybody goes to bed, Mashaun restrings Dalistra so he can talk with her but soon discovers it is a mistake.

"HOW DARE YOU LET THAT WENCH TOUCH ME!" Dalistra shouts at him.

"BESIDES HAVING THE TOUCH OF A TROLL AND THE MIND OF A SPITTED PIG, SHE HAS NO BUSINESS BEING ON THIS TRIP AND SHOULD HAVE STAYED IN THE CITY WHERE SHE COULD HAVE WORKED IN A BROTHEL," she continues.

"SHE IS NEVER TO TOUCH ME AGAIN!" she finishes.

"SHUT UP!" Mashaun shouts back to Dalistra's surprise. Mai stares at him, asking if he said something. He shakes his head.

"I could have left you there, and you would probably belong to someone else, like Magdalenia. Do you want that?" Mashaun asks. Dalistra becomes silent.

"Okay. Then put it behind and move on," he says as he leans her in the corner and goes to bed. He can tell she is still mad and wonders if he should even use her before she calms down.

The next morning, Wilmer heads back to the city with the wagon. Berg and Abigail decide to travel with Wilmer and help with the supplies before continuing into the mountains. Abigail's head is pounding, and the bumpy road makes it worst. But she is glad to be away from the inn and all the dead animals. Mashaun and Mai spend the morning exploring the inn and the courtyard. In one corner, Mai shows him the archery range which is about a hundred feet, and a small arena for handheld-weapon practice complete with an animated opponent.

When Mashaun asks Sivish about them, he finds out they are for anybody to use for a small fee. Mashaun thinks about it for a quick second. What else is he going to do while waiting for the others to return? He pays the fee for a day. He spends several hours practicing his swordsmanship, with the opponent who is always slightly better, before returning to his room for Dalistra. As Mashaun passes through the common room, Sivish is at the bar, cleaning. He calls him.

He is the first to pay any real, serious attention to Dalistra, noticing the bow curves more than normal bows do. Most of the bows are straight, but a few of the more expensive bows have a slight recurve to them. Dalistra has more than a quarter circle curve. Sivish asks if he can hold his bow for a minute.

Dalistra is exceptionally quiet around Sivish. It is obvious Sivish has experience with bows, and after a short time, he hands it back to

Mashaun. He follows Mashaun to the archery range to study his shooting technique. Mashaun tells Dalistra not to help him. Since he started using her, he can differentiate if she is helping or not. Mashaun places his first set of arrows around the center of the target. Sivish inquires as to where did he find such an exquisite bow. Without turning, Mashaun tells him he doesn't remember; only somewhere south of here.

"You found Dalistra hidden in a cave." with a factual voice.

Mashaun stops and slowly turns around to gaze at him with questioning eyes before asking him. How does he know her name? Dalistra also wonders but is a little nervous at the same time. Sivish smiles and asks Mashaun to join him inside. Dalistra warns him to be discreet as he already knows more than she likes.

The two go into the back where Sivish has a table for the employees. There are three barmaids getting ready for the evening. He asks them to leave. He offers Mashaun a chair and serves up a couple of mugs of his homemade elfin ale he gets from a locked cabinet at the back of the room. They both sit on opposite sides of a round table as Mashaun hangs Dalistra over the back of the chair so he can lean against her to receive her thoughts as they talk. Both men wonder what the other is aware of and how much they should divulge and where to start as they study each other.

Mashaun speaks first, asking Sivish, "How do you know Dalistra's name, and how long have you known?"

"I suspected when Mai first arrived but wasn't sure until I held her this morning," Sivish replies. There is a short pause. The two men take a drink.

"Does Magdalenia know you have the bow?" Sivish asks him.

"I don't think so. Why?" he asks.

"She will kill to get her hands on your bow. Dalistra is a young spirit weapon. In other words, she was a young woman when put into the weapon. She is also one of the last spirits placed into an item. Her spirit was forced into the bow against her will causing the banning of the spell use several thousand years ago." Sivish states plainly.

Mashaun stares at him, puzzled, and gets the same sense from Dalistra. However, she has a vague idea why Magdalenia is looking for her.

"However, it was the forcing of the spirit of the young princess into an item that brought the races together, realizing it could happen to one of their loved ones," he continues.

Princess?

"Yes, you didn't know?" Dalistra says.

"That explains it," Mashaun answers.

"Quiet, you two," Sivish tells them. Mashaun glances at him, surprised he can hear them.

Sivish continues, "The Thesila council of mages ruled any person caught using the spell would be put to death publicly as a deterrent to anyone using the spell for any reason."

"The elves used the spell to preserve the spirits of some of the young who were gravely ill or injured early in their life. However, it was always by their choice. The elves knew how potent the magic was and kept the secret for eons until the war between the elves and the humans. Somehow, humans managed to steal the spell and learned how to use it. Soon afterward, the war ended, but the knowledge had already gotten out. Even though casting the spell is taxing on the caster's mind and body, some still used the spell. Elves live a lot longer, so it does not affect us as much as humans. As the elves feared, many human mages lost their lives trying to cast the spell, but it didn't stop the most compenent mages from using the spell for their own nefarious reasons." Mashaun tries to figure out what all this had to do with Dalistra as he remains quiet, sipping on the elfin ale.

"Eventually, casting the spell became a business. Mages would charge substantial sums of money to cast the spell, and that is where Dalistra comes in. Mikolas Tenskie, one of Magdalenia's ancestors, fell in love with Dalistra."

"What? Mikolas is one of Magdalenia's ancestors. I'll kill her," Dalistra says furiously.

"However, she was already betrothed to another, Prince Karemon of Thesila," Sivish continues.

Mashaun asks, "Is there is any relationship to their last name and the city?"

"Yes," Sivish replies.

"Now, let me continue. Mikolas was drunk with power and decided he would put her spirit in a special bow so he could always keep her near.

Spirit weapons have a mind of their own and often will seek vengeance if forced into an item." Mashaun thinks; is how she can help hit targets. But for the first time, he wonders if she can force him to miss. Dalistra remains silent, realizing her secret was about to be revealed, and she can't stop it.

"One day, when Mikolas was out hunting with his sons, they were attacked, and he was killed. According to the story, he shot a dozen arrows and missed every one, which was unusual, for he was the best archer in the land. Each family member who used Dalistra would eventually befall a similar fate. The Tenskie family believed Dalistra had cursed them and sought to destroy her. Are you following me so far?" he asks Mashaun, who nods affirmatively.

"Prince Karemon became King Karemon and ordered his guards to bring Dalistra to him and all copies of the spell be destroyed. Shortly after, the council at Thesila agreed. Before Mikolas' family could destroy Dalistra to break the curse, King Karemon got Dalistra back and decided he would hide her. Some say she asked him, allowing her to seek revenge, some say an orcale told him she was a major part of a prophecy, and some say they didn't know the freeing spell back then. I doubt the last one.

King Karemon gave all of Tenskie's lands to Dalistra's father and banished Mikolas. King Karemon died a few years later, never revealing her whereabouts. Then how did you know where she was and why didn't you retrieve her? I was not the one destined to wield her, you are. Now let me finish.

The power of the magic was too enticing, and many mages were put to death. Many spirits return to the afterlife, while some remain trapped on this world. The mages stopped using the spell as many destroyed any reference to the spell. With each generation passing its knowledge disappeared from the world. A few ancient elves know the ritual but have not performed it for many Elvin generations. The Tenskie family has been searching for Dalistra to break the curse, and if Magdalenia learns of Dalistra, she would stop at nothing to destroy the bow before the bow destroys her."

"Take me back, it is my blood oath to wipe out Mikolas's bloodline," she vehemently tells Mashaun.

"No, there is a time and place for everything," he tells her, much to her chagrin.

Mashaun keeps receiving affirmative tones from Dalistra as he listens to the story. Realizing he understands Sivish without Dalistra but wonders why he is telling him so much information. Nevertheless, he is telling him the truth, so what does he want in return? He wonders how much of his story he should tell Sivish. Dalistra tells him to stick to the story.

Sivish continues. "While humans may have learned the spell, they were not as careful with the device to hold the spirit. Spirits placed into weapons, armor, devices and even clothing remain there until it loses its ability to hold the spirit. However, humans do not make long lasting items. Many of the spirit items eventually wore out or were destroyed without any thought given to the spirits within, trapping them between this world and the next. Without the proper ritual, they are trapped and unable to continue on their journey. I know the ritual if Dalistra would like to be free."

Catching Mashaun by surprise, and Sivish realizes it. Mashaun tells him the complete true story and catches Sivish off guard when he tells him he is from another world. Sivish grins before telling Mashaun that explains his lack of understanding of the world. Sivish asks about the others, and Mashaun tells him about Mai, Berg, Abigail, Kazimir and the twins, complete with the freeing of the twins.

Sivish grins when he hears how Mashaun is able to turn the tables on Magdalenia but is also worried she can be a deadly enemy and she will take her vengeance on the city folks. Mashaun asks Dalistra about being freed; after a while, she tells him no. Sivish is right about vengeance and she wants to see Magdalenia and the rest of the bloodline fall first. Only then will she allow Sivish to release her. Over the next few days, the two of them spend the afternoons talking about a variety of subjects.

Katrina pulls Wilmer into the interrogation room and sets up the cubes. They found several of the night watchmen, and several of her henchman killed the same night Mashaun disappeared. They were pierced by arrows with the same fletching they showed Mashaun in court. Even though he denied knowing the fletching, there is fervor to finding him. I don't think he killed them. Magdalenia is using the same tactic she used when Tera stopped her son, and the explosion from the broken staff killed him.

"There is a reward of one red for his capture, by Magdalenia. One red will have every bounty hunter looking for him."

"I will let him know," he says and thanks her.

They leave the gatehouse and Wilmer takes them straight to Pavvo's manor on one of the innermost islands, where everyone greets them. The next few days, Wilmer and Berg go into the city to pick up a few items at a time so as not to draw attention. Pavvo also has a few guards help with the list. They acquire warm clothes, food and few other items, but they never pickup more than a few items at any one place. The town folks are a bit jittery, and when Wilmer asks about it, they brush it off. It doesn't take long for Wilmer to notice a couple of peasants taking an interest in them, and when they move in their direction, the peasants disappear into the crowd, only to reappear later. Whispers of some of Magdalenia's people are turning up dead. Her people are actively searching for the bow glowed red at the gate a few days ago, and its owner reaches Wilmer ears.

Axtel teaches Abigail how to play her harp and he is impressed. She is a fast learner. She also spends time writing short stories about their travels and puts them to music. She asks Axtel not to tell anyone; she wants to surprise them.

During the evening, Berg asks Kazimir about his plans. He hopes he will stay with the group, but his disappointment shows when Kazimir tells him he has accepted employment with Pavvo. He wishes him the best before changing the topic. The twins have begun their testing, with showing promise at being a multi-moon mage. But still, they need more practice to see how much magic they can channel. Kazimir spends his days patrolling the grounds and watching the gate when he is not practicing. Since he is the newest member of Pavvo's house guards, he usually gets the jobs no one else wants and is on the receiving end of jokes. Most of the time. It doesn't take Kazimir long to join it and return the jokes or pranks.

Every day, he meets with the guard captain on the practice field for his lessons. He teaches Kazimir about the different styles of armed combat. Kazimir, in return, teaches unarmed combat. Eventually, Kazimir specializes in one style of fighting—the bastard sword and shield. He likes the extra protection of the shield, and with his size and strength, he one-handedly uses the sword with ease. Abigail stays in the manor, enjoying warm baths and talking with Toni, who helps her make short skirts and dresses for the two of them, much to the displeasure of Pavvo. Abigail is surprised at all the help Toni gives on the songs, especially after finding out she lost her hearing about 10 years ago.

After a week, Wilmer, Berg and Abigail arrive late in the evening with a wagon full of supplies—rucksacks, bedrolls, some food, and warm clothes for the group. The wagon has far more than they can possibly carry. Mashaun doesn't ask about the extra supplies, figuring it's for the inn. Wilmer apologizes for taking so long because Magdalenia's people were always watching. He doesn't see any of them on the road, but it won't take much for them to find out where he is. He suggests to leave in the morning as it will keep Magdalenia guessing for a little while. And even if she does figure out where they are, she won't follow them into the mountains. When Mashaun asks why, he is told it is a long story.

but agrees with the last part. For the most part, Dalistra has been silent, something Mashaun enjoys while at the same time finds unsettling.

Chapter 11

MYELIKKAN

DURING THERE USUAL EVENING HUNT, Mashaun has a long talk with Dalistra and her blood oath. He promises to help her deal with Magdalenia down the road. He wants to make sure there is not a problem with him choosing the time and place for her to seek her revenge. She assures him is not a problem for now, but he can tell she is not happy abut waiting. The next morning is cold as the four head downstairs for breakfast.

Wilmer and the teamster are waiting. Wilmer tells them to hurry, with a sense of urgency in his voice. Puzzled, they start to speak when He tells them Magdalenia has figured out where they are and they need to hit the road now. He explains the rest of the stuff is for Llewellyn and he is going to travel with them if they don't mind. Without a glance they quickly agree. Wilmer has been there many times and another sword arm is always good. They meet up with Mai and Abigail who are eating some fruit at the wagon, telling them the news. And like the rest, they are glad to have him along.

There is the shift from autumn to winter as some of the trees stand bear with multicolored leaves covering the road, which quickly turns into a a path and then two ruts. Soon the winter snow will block the pass, and the people in the west can rest as the snow prevents the denizens of the eastern forest from crossing. The leaves make a crunching sound as they travel up the road, taking time to enjoy the picturesque scenery as they walk next to the wagon. When night approaches, they find a small clearing off to the side of the road where they make camp for the night, each pair taking turns standing guard. The days are progressively colder as the group follows the road climbing into the mountains. At times, they wonder why they chose to travel this time of the year, but realize they didn't have a choice. Rounding one of the bends in the road, Mashaun glances back as several men on horseback quickly come up the road behind them and he tells Wilmer.

Putting the girls on the wagon, Wilmer and Mashaun hide in the trees and wait for the six horsemen wearing Magdalenia's crest to come into range. They fire their arrows. Mashaun misses, and four of the horses charge to him and Wilmer while two others speed up the road after the wagon. They charge, closing ground with lightning speed. Wilmer drops two of them before they close reach the forest. Mashaun fires a second shot and it misses. Flinging Dalistra aside, he yells at Wilmer to protect the wagon and draws his two swords as the riders charge. Realizing the wagon has no fighters, Wilmer charges through the forest, hoping to catch the wagon on one of the switchbacks. Mashaun quickly takes one of the horses with a low sword slice, throwing the man to the ground. But the man rolls with experience rising quickly with his sword in hand. Dalistra screams in his head, NO, in a panicked voice.

"This is not what I had planned. Wilmer was supposed to stay here."

The other man gets off his horse, and the two of them approach Mashaun. These are swordsmen of many battles. He starts on the defensive and keeps his back to a tree, hoping not to get struck by a sword. After one gets through his defense and nicks his arm, he decides the best defense is a good offense, as Dalistra shouts *"NO."* Waiting for one to charge, remembering his lessons, Mashaun slides the attack to the side. He takes another cut to his arm as he the plunges his other sword into his opponent's abdomen, forcing him to the ground in agony. Swinging around, Mashaun faces the other one as his other opponent takes advantage of the situation, landing a blow on Mashaun's shoulder, forcing him to drop a sword. His opponent's evil grin is enough to scare the most hardened fighters as he lunges toward Mashaun clumsily sidesteps the attack.

The two circle, waiting for the other to make a move. When his opponent drops with an arrow in his back, Mashaun collapses. The next thing he remembers is being on the wagon with his arm in a sling and Mai watching over him.

"Good, you're awake. So I can kill you with that stupid move," Mai says in a huff, Dalistra agreeing with her.

Too tired to argue, he stares at her with a smile and fades out. The next day, Mashaun thanks Wilmer for shooting the other one but is curious how he got back so fast. Wilmer and Mai tell him they were dead before they returned to him. Mashaun shakes his head, drifting back to sleep.

A couple of days and he is tired of riding the wagon and walks along the side for some time. Mai tells him he is a lousy patient and needs to stay on the wagon, but Mashaun glances a smirk.

"If you ever do that again, I will tie you to a rock and throw you in the river, do you understand?" Mashaun tersely tells Dalistra.

"It was not—" she starts to say, but he cuts her off.

"Yes, it was. I can tell when you are helping and when you are not, and you were deliberately missing, just like Mikolas," he says sternly.

"Okay, but don't you want to know why?" she responds awkwardly.

"I don't care why, you do that again, and you will slowly rot away at the bottom of a lake where no one will ever find you, ever. Do you understand?"

"Yes, but I did not mean for you to get hurt—," she starts to say.

"I don't care what you meant, I will not keep you if I can't trust you, are we clear?" he shouts back, as he painfully unstring her

She doesn't have to say a word. Mashaun is sure she won't let him down again. For days he leaves Dalistra unstung, telling them he doesn't have the strength to use the bow yet.

The road gets narrower as it winds its way through the valleys and into the higher passes, and they wonder if they have missed the side road, but Wilmer keeps going and they follow. After a couple of weeks or so on the road, they come to a narrow path heading off the road. It is not much more than an opening through the trees. Around noon several days later, the path disappears in a meadow. A thick group of trees and brambles climbing about 15 feet up the trees blocks the other side. When Wilmer reaches the edge of the brambles, they open up, revealing a path. They follow close behind Wilmer as the hedge opens in front and closes behind them, blocking any retreat. Soon the brambles open up into a clearing where trees line the edge. The village is a huge round open space surrounded by the thick bramble wall with scores of buildings scattered around the clearing.

Smoke rises from different buildings, and the smell of freshly cooked pastries fills the air. An elderly gentleman without any weapons approaches the group, closing the distance with spring in his step. His gray hair hangs to his shoulders, framing his weathered face with a well-trimmed matching beard. His forest-green tunic has a blue circle with a green triangle like a child's simple Christmas tree. Between the triangle and the circle are two sapphire eyes, one on each side. The old man greets Wilmer and the teamster like old friends who haven't seen each other for a long time. They take the wagon to a two-story circular stone building in the center of the compound. Wilmer introduces Llewellyn, the lord of Myelikkan. After introductions around, Llewellyn asks Mashaun if he wants the village healer to look at his shoulder. Mashaun thanks him but tells Llewellyn he's fine. Llewellyn nods and asks them to follow his men as two men-at-arms lead the four to a single-story tree trunk with a window on each side of a door, looking out onto the center of village. Inside there is a sitting room with a fireplace with some chairs. Two archways lead to other rooms with two beds each. The furniture is grown from an old redwood. A two-story, circular cut-stone building dominates the center of the open area is viewed from their window.

After dropping off the wagon at the circular building, Wilmer returns to take the four on a stroll around the village. The people they meet are friendly; several offer them delicious pastries and other foods. They stop by the healer who insists on looking at Mashaun's wound. The stitching and bandaging impress him. He is even more impressed when Mai tells him it's her work. Before they leave, he request her to work with him. Wilmer nods as they walk out the door. The two-story circular building doesn't have any windows and is a stark contrast from the other buildings made of wood. They are all summoned to the stone building, the four of them enjoy sleeping on a bed—a hard one but a bed nonetheless. With a crackling fire never needing more wood and is always at the same height. Feeling safe and secure in their new surroundings they all get a full night rest.

The next morning, a rap on the door awakens them. A young couple introduces themselves as Aellan and Aioles. They tell the group to follow as they take a tour around the village in the morning before their meeting with Llewellyn. They lead the group to a small plot of land outside the village but inside the wall. Aellan explains they are responsible for any food they want to eat, growing it on the plot in front of them. Mashaun gazes at the barren ground and asks what they will do until the plants are ready to harvest. Aellan tells them there will be plenty of fruits and vegetables in the morning, and make sure they pick it daily. Berg studies the village wall and figures it should run right behind the house where they are standing, but there is the garden.

They spend the rest of the morning touring the compound, stopping at a feed store where Aioles speaks to the owner who gives him a pouch. She tells the group she will plant the garden for them and leaves. Aellan continues the tour, showing them the bathhouse with heated baths, the butcher, grocers, bakers, chandlers, weapon masters of all types, and the practice fields while explaining the rules of Myelikkan. Everybody is assigned a job best suited for them and as long as they work, they can stay. Anyone who can swing a sword or use a bow takes turns on guard duty and patrol. The tour ends around noon at the center building with Wilmer waiting at the door.

From the front door, a walkway extends to an equilateral triangle. The top of the triangle is at the far end of the garden with the closest edge dividing the garden in half. Between each side of the triangle and the circle's edge are two bushes of red flowers lined on the short side like eyebrows. Around the triangle and the walkway are various short flowers and ponds of clear water. They enter an elegant room with a long table filled with a variety of food, surrounded by high back chairs. Wilmer motions for everybody to have a seat. Shortly, Llewellyn enters the room, taking the chair at the end of the table.

During the meal, Llewellyn explains he is responsible for the area because of his close relationship with the elves to the north. He keeps a eye out for any incursions from the eastward side of the mountains and tries to stop them if possible. He tells them the purpose of the tour is to show what Myelikkan can offer. Then he adds they are free to leave anytime. He asks if they are willing to do their share of the work, in exchange, they can stay and train. They all nod in agreement.

The group spends time in the garden. Most of the food in the garden is familiar with some strange-looking plant but they taste good nonetheless. Along one edge of the garden is a line of fruit trees. The opposite edge has some wheat-like stalks. Corn stalks line the back edge. At first, the two pick all the food only to find what they picked regrows, and they end up taking the extra to the farmers' market where people trade different foods. The innkeeper doesn't have a garden and does his shopping for the inn every morning at the farmers' market. They soon learn to pick only what they need for the day. Every day, someone takes wheat and corn to the mill in the morning, and by afternoon, they pick up some bread at the bakery. The inns receive any leftovers every afternoon.

The Emertree Inn is the most popular place in Myelikkan and is the second largest building, second only to the stone building in the middle. Grown like all the buildings, it is the only other two-story structure inside the walls, from the table and chair to the stairs leading to the second floor. Along one wall is a raised platform area where they have entertainment when available. The other wall has a kitchen area where they serve a variety of drinks, with a room in the back for the preparation of food. The inn does not serve any meat to the delight of many of its customers. Anyone who desires meat dishes goes to the Orion Inn which is attached to the butcher shop.

On the opposite side of the compound is the third largest building. The Orion Inn and the butcher are the only two places where meat can be gotten, usually brought in by patrols or individuals. Mashaun finds the name strange since he can't find Orion in the night skies. The inside has a woodsier feel to it with different animal heads grown from the walls, making it popular with the guards. The meals tend to be stews, roasts and steaks, and the drinks are strong.

The next few days, someone different shows up at the door in the morning, taking one of them to find out their interest and abilities so they can find the best position for them in the village. First is Mashaun. They test him with the bow and sword before accepting him into the guards. They will help him improve his skills, and he will learn about the different animals, races, and other creatures known to be in the area. Mai expresses interest in medicine so they test her with the village healer who immediately recognizes her skill. She spends a lot of time studying and practicing the healing arts. The doctor also realizes while she can teach Mai, he can also learn a thing or two from her. Berg ends up in the Hall of Records which is located in the circular building. Like Mai, he will also not be spending time on guard duty as he works with the recorder, categorizing reports and sightings.

Abigail is the hardest one to place. She is lousy with the bow and sword. The sight of blood still makes her sick. They try her out in the bakery, the chandler, the record room, but she fails at all of them. She goes through one position after another, never lasting longer than a few days. Everybody almost gives up on her when one evening, a small group is playing some instruments, and she gets up and starts singing with them. She has found her place in the village. At first, she sings songs from home, but no one can understand. Abigail spends the next few days learning songs in the local language and they help her learn the harp. They allow her to play her ballads. While Mashaun likes them, he disapproves of her embellishing their story.

The days turn into weeks. The evergreen treetops turn white with the cover of snow. However, there is no snow on the ground within the village. Word of Abigail's melodic voice travels quickly around, and they play almost every night in one of the taverns. While her voice is sweet and clear, most of the guys show up because of her enticing outfits which are unique here. Many of the women gossip about her, and some even accuse her of being a harlot, but she doesn't care. After all, it's only a dream. Berg spends a lot of time with the records of past events. Even when he isn't working, he spends long hours reading about the history and the different animals and beasts, along with some research for Mashaun. He is also the only one of the four who is learning how to read and write the new language.

Mai spends her mornings studying with the doctor and her afternoons with either the butcher or the apothecary. Sometimes she disagrees with them, having vigorous debates over which method is better. She often wins. Mashaun's double sword mastery improves daily with the help of a trainer. Even without Dalistra's help, his skill with the bow is already respectable, consistently hitting the target center. At first,

Dalistra believes he is still mad at her, but soon, she understands he wants to practice for the times she can't or won't help him. Knowing she is in control, while in Mashaun's hands.

Mashaun works with a carpenter and a chandler to make a couple of sets of cross-country skis so he can go skiing, something he enjoys. After he finishes with the skis, the townsfolk inquisitively stare at him carrying the skis to his home. When people ask him what they are, he tries to explain but they shake their heads. After the skis are finished, he goes for a stroll outside the wall to see if there are any patches of snow to try out his new skis. As he goes through the brambles, the snow covers his head as the brambles shift to let him pass, sending a chill down the back of his neck. The brambles open to the ground covered in white, nearly two feet of snow with a hard crust. Without a second thought, he rushes back to grab his skis, acting like a child on Christmas morning. As curious eyes follow him leaveing the compound with his skis to explore the surrounding area. The silence is broken—only the scraping sound of the skis sliding across the snow and the occasional *kerplop* of the snow falling from the trees can be heard. During his trips, he often stops to relish the solitude of the moment. Dalistra doesn't understand the need for so much time alone in the wilderness, but since it makes him more relaxed, she gives him his quiet time.

He frequently asks if any of the group wants to join him, but they always decline even though they do not like him going on his own, especially Mai. They are all from the warmer climates and do not like the snow. They are happy the snow doesn't fall in town. While his idea of fun is the solitude of the wilderness, theirs is going to the inn. Sometimes they even dress up where Mai wears her fancy dress. She likes how the townsfolk treat her differently; they are more polite and see her more than he healer.

Mashaun doesn't tell them about the oversize cougar-like animal following him from a distance. He doesn't tell anybody for fear they may decide to hunt it down. He enjoys watching the oversized animal move effortlessly through the naked trees as it shadows his every move but never advances. He scrutinize how it moves, studying every step, trying to learn how to walk in silence like a cat. Once, he asked Dalistra about the tawny animal, and she tells him it is larger than a normal *tsov daj* but she will not help him shoot it. Mashaun mocks her; he does not intend to shoot such a marvelous-looking animal unless it attacks.

Once, Wilmer joined him on the second set of skis. After he gets used to them, they move silently over the frozen snow. When the two of them are together, it is like a class. Wilmer asks Mashaun different questions, and he will name different tracks and sounds. Many of the tracks are similar to the ones he is used to seeing when he was hunting back home in the States. But there are a few he doesn't recognize, including a huge footprint resembling a humanoid but is twice the size of his own. Wilmer tells him it is a mountain giant. They are taller than three men and five times as strong. They are found much farther north, so it is surprising there is one down here. When they return, they report their find to Llewellyn who is a little surprised but says little else.

Chapter 12

STAFFS AND MOONS

http://thesilaprophecy.com/magic/

THEY HAVE ONLY BEEN AT Myelikkan for a month when Berg tells everyone he has a surprise for them. He tells them to pack for the night because they're not coming back until morning, much to the disdain of the girls who do not want to go. In the early afternoon, he takes them out of the village and heads south for a few hours before going to a long, narrow canyon. He study his notes before turning left, following the canyon rim until they come upon a rock tower ruins. A tower grown directly from the cliff is about six yards across and about 40 yards tall. Inside the tower is a mess with only the door remaining barely hanging on its hinges. The first floor are littered with leaves and animal nests, with a winding stair around the wall. Berg takes them to the second, then the third floor. He leads them to the top floor where they have a spectacular view of the surrounding area.

To the east, the mountain drops down a steep cliff into a huge expanse of evergreen trees with patches of naked trees dotting the landscape. At the edge of the horizon, the tip of a mountain peak aligns with the setting sun. At the bottom of the canyon on the south is a stream flowing from somewhere in the west, snaking its way along the canyon floor next to a road running the length of the canyon, and disappearing under the eastern forest canopy. In the distance, a sizable river winds its way through the forest. The other side of the canyon is only an arrow shot, and it is at least five times as deep while stretching to the west beyond sight. Dalistra tells Mashaun they can hit a target on the opposite canyon wall. During the spring thaw, the canyon floor fills with water, and the so-called road would be a river, making the road passable only in the summer and fall, prior to the first snow.

They find it interesting but are confused as to why he told them they would have to spend the night.

"I'm not through," he tells them. What he wants to show them is a small crescent harmony moon peeking over the Khusari Sea horizon to the west, and the life quarter moon almost at its apex. Turning his attention east, he points at an ice gibbous moon, a few hours from disappearing from view. Facing North, he points with his hands. Explaining to them that according to the shadows, he is facing North, assuming we are in the northern hemisphere. On Earth the sun rises on my right or in the East and sets in the West on my left side. But, here it is the apposite. Abigail blankly stares and asks Berg why they are looking at the sun setting in the east. He says the planet has a retrograde spin to it. She smiles, not knowing what he said.

Berg recognizes the blank gaze from his years of teaching. It usually means they do not have a clue of what he said. Berg realizes he will have to explain it to them. He begins by reminding them the sun and the moon rise in the east and sets in the west, to which they agree. He tells them here, it is backward; they rise in the west and set in the east. Suddenly, Mai gets the I-get-it as her eyse light up, as everything comes into focus for her. Abigail understands the explanation shortly after. Mashaun is glad they understand, and Berg continues with his story.

Berg asks them how many staffs there are and what colors they are; they all answer red, yellow, and blue.

"Exactly," he replies before telling them according to some ancient writings he found, there is a connection between them. He tells them according to the scriptures, there are three moons in orbit, and each staff has a connection with the matching-color moon. Mai asks if they go through the same cycles as Earth does. For the first time, she is admitting this is not a dream. Berg explains each has a different orbit and on rare occasions, the three align.

Each moon orbits at a different speed and this part of the world uses the yellow moon, also known as Xania, to determine time. From what he found out, it takes the it about thirty-four days to make one cycle, and it makes thirteen cycles for a year. Mai and Abigail shake their heads in confusion until he explains one month is about thirty-four days long while the year has thirteen months.

By this time, the Harmony moon known as Xania is high above the horizon as the blue moon, Dasjin starts to descend to the eastern horizon. Berg points out the three moons are on course to realign sometime in the next few years. When Mashaun asks when, Berg says they will align again in the year twenty-seven hundred and the world will go through a major change.

Next, Berg points to a group of stars with a bright star in the middle, telling them they use that star for navigation similar to our ancient seafarers who use the North Star. Mashaun thanks Berg for the information. He understands the world better, and he will need to find whatever they use as a sextant when they are in a city. It is late when Berg finishes his story, and they all settle down for the night. Mashaun gazes at the stars and the moons for some time before drifting off to sleep.

Chapter 13

THE PATROL

AFTER SEVERAL WEEKS, MASHAUN RECEIVES word it is his turn to go on patrol which lasts for several weeks. Mai does not want him to go. They have been sleeping together for some time, and she likes having his body next to hers, much to Dalistra's displeasure. She only keeps her anger in check because she understands the need for physical contact, and is something she can't give. He spends time every week rubbing Dalistra down with bow wax, and she finds almost sensual. They have long talks in the forest. He treats her like a member of the team, and she does not want to jeopardize the relationship. It has been a long time since she has had any human contact. Not since they ripped her spirit from the body and forced it into the bow.

He goes to the patrol house where he is given warm clothes—a white fur cloak with matching boots and snowshoes. They always go on patrol in groups of five. Besides Mashaun, there is Aioles, the young man who showed them around the compound the first day. He wears leather armor without a helmet, carries a sword and a shield, with a bow over his shoulder. Next to show up is Darnel, who in his mid-twenties, wearing a leather breastplate, carrying a crossbow and a longsword. A woman similarly dressed accompanies him, carrying only a bow. She introduces herself as Tera. Last is a man in his early thirties. He has a light chain and carries a sword and a shield, introducing himself as Shad. With his gruff voice, Mashaun can tell he is in charge. They all focus on Mashaun's skis with curiosity and wonder. Shad tells him the skis should stay home, but Wilmer overrides the order, telling Shad the skis go. Shad finds it unusual Wilmer countermanded him but accepts the order. They leave

118

the house, heading across the courtyard and through the brambles with Shad in the lead followed by Darnel, Aioles, Tera and Mashaun.

Before trekking across the windswept snow, everyone puts on their snowshoes, except for Mashaun, who puts on his skis as the rest stare with bewilderment. It is the first time on snowshoes for Tera and Darnel, and it takes a while for them to walk with enlarged shoes as they clumsily shuffle across the hardened snow. They are amazed as Mashaun gently slides on the snow, and Shad soon appoints him as the front scout, wishing they all had skis.

Excitement fills them as they leave the village, looking forward to practicing their skills. Like Mashaun, this is also Tera's first patrol, and they set off with anticipation. They continue to head in a northwesterly direction for the day, and even though a blanket of snow covers the ground, they make good time. Their furs are remarkably warm in the cold winter air. At nightfall, they set up camp, and Shad tells everybody if they run into any of the eastern creatures, Mashaun will return and bring reinforcements. They will shadow their movements, but not engage, reminding them they are scouts and not fighters. They try to argue the point but he is unmovable with his command. They don't like it, but they accept it. They also realize Mashaun can travel much faster on the skis than in the snowshoes they are wearing. Mashaun and Dalistra don't like the plan either, remembering what happened last time the group split up.

The next day, they unbury themselves from a few feet of snow dropped during the night before, making their way to a lookout post. The fresh snow slows their travel as they trudge through it, sinking knee-deep with every step. Even Mashaun sinks in the fresh powder; he still glides through the snow. Early evening they arrive at the lookout post. It is not much—a two-story tree house about 12 feet above the snow. A rope ladder hangs down from the bottom of the tree-house. One by one, they enter the post and find a stove. Gears lay scattered around the floor from the previous patrol. The floor where everybody sleeps is hard but dry. It has no rocks or branches to sleep around but it is quite warm. It has an awesome view of the surrounding forest and a northern ravine cuts east to west. The second floor is a covered observation deck allowing an excellent view in all directions. Shortly, the other patrol arrives back and is ecstatic their relief has arrived. The two groups swap stories before the other group takes off and heads back to Myelikkan in the morning.

Each day, the group patrols a different area before returning to the post without any sightings. During Tera's early morning watch, she is admiring the vibrant red under the fire moon, when she spots some movement through the trees in the ravine. In her haste, she trips as she goes down the stairs waking everybody with a start as she lands face first. She gets up and gives her report as though nothing happened before tending to her bloody nose. Back up at the lookout, there is nothing in the ravine. She hesitantly swears something move but only caught a glance of movement. Shad pushes to find out what she thinks she saw. At last, she says they looked like dogs on two legs. Everybody snickers except Shad, who gets a concerned expression Telling everybody they're going on patrol, he tells them to take enough supplies for two days.

The fresh powder is deep and hampers everybody's movement. Even with snowshoes, they sink up to their knees. Even Mashaun with his oversized skis sinks in the soft snow, but he still moves better than everybody else, especially downhill. He arrives first to find a bunch of wolf tracks in the deep snow. Once the team arrives, they discuss the tracks and congratulate Tera for her spotting them. Mashaun and Shad study the tracks. They cannot find any front paw prints, and they are bigger. From their studies, Shad tells them they probably Tsaub. But it has been many years since anybody saw one on this side of the mountains. They appear to be in single file, making it hard to estimate the size of the pack, but he guesses it to be at least 10. They can pose a threat to the villages below. Shad decides to have a closer to confirm his suspicions. They spend the afternoon following their trail, using the compact snow tracks of the Tsaub to make traveling easier.

It is close to nightfall, and Mashaun gets so far in front of the group they lose sight of him. He comes upon a large group of wolves plowing their way through the snow. He gazes in disbelief as they walk upright like humans. Using the forest as cover, he follows from a distance as they slog through the snow-covered terrain. He counts over twenty Tsaub marching through the snow, carrying spears and two-handed swords, and wearing packs. A few times they stop, put their noses up as if sniffing the air. After they drop over a hill, he spends over an hour following his tracks back to the group, where he reports his findings. Shad strokes his chin before telling them they are Tsaub and dangerous. He tells the party they need to follow them to see where they are going and stop them if necessary. Following the plan, he sends Mashaun back to the village in the morning who does not want to wait, but Shad insists, telling him they all need a night's sleep as they make a cold camp.

Early the next morning, Mashaun heads back to the village while the group continues to follow the trail down the mountains. It takes Mashaun all day and late into the night before reaching Myelikkan. His energy was all spent. The guards take him immediately to see Llewellyn giving him some hot food and drink while he waits. Moments later, Llewellyn and Wilmer arrive to see an exhausted Mashaun covered in melting frozen sweat from sixteen hours of hard skiing. He tells them what they found and the rest of the patrol is going to follow the Tsaub. The two listen intently as Mashaun tells his story, and when Mashaun describes the creatures, Llewellyn shakes his head, muttering "fools" before telling the guard to bring the captain of the guard.

Shortly a middle-aged man about Wilmer's height enters the room, wearing a chain mail suit does not make a sound as he walks. Llewellyn tells the captain to have his most experienced "airborne" ready to leave at first light. He tells Mashaun he can stay, but Mashaun declines. It is his patrol and he needs to go back to them. Mashaun tells them he needs a nap and he will be ready at first light.

Mai is surprised when he walks through the door since he has only been gone for a few days. He quickly summarizes what has happened and lies down to sleep. The morning knock comes way too early, but he is up and ready in a flash. He jumps out of bed and heads out. With his skis in hand, he heads through the brambles to find a group of 20 archers in a line on snowshoes, holding a rope. He shakes his head as he wonders how they are going to keep up on snowshoes. Wilmer is on the other set of skis with the rope tied around his waist. Mashaun takes the lead with Wilmer following close behind. The archers float above the snow in tandem, not offering any resistance as Wilmer pulls them along.

During the day, Wilmer tells Mashaun each archer has an ornamental bracelet splits around the middle. When the two halves line up, the wearer floats. He also tells him it takes a lot of training because one wrong move can send the wearer off in an undesirable direction. Mashaun now understands why they call them the airborne. The group makes camp in the evening. Even though he wants to continue, Mashaun understands the need to stop. Sitting with one of the airborne he gets to view one of the bracelets. The owner tells him each one is slightly different, making them unique. The owner needs to gather the components themselves, and even then, a mage can make them only for one person. The bracelet connects to one person only; however, it can be used as a component for a new one. They are usually handed down from one generation to the next. Hers has been in the family for three generations. The next morning, they awake to a light snowfall as they break camp and hurry down to Mashaun's old path.

By midday, they reach the spot where Mashaun left the patrol. The wind picks up, and with the falling snow, it quickly becomes near whiteout conditions, making it nearly impossible to see the trees, let alone any tracks. The archers on the ropes have problems keeping their orientation in the air. Cautiously, they head down the mountain in the same direction Mashaun had followed a few days before. At nightfall, and there is still no sign of the patrol. All they can do is make camp and discuss the next course of action. The storm passes during the night, leaving the next morning cold. The wind blows the snow around, leaving a glassy, smooth surface, covering everything, including any tracks.

The group decides to continue traveling down the mountain. The thin frozen snow crust offers little resistance as they slide down the slopes, careful not to go too fast for the archers who float like kites on a string, each one getting higher until the last one floats along the treetops. Toward the end of the day, one of the archers suddenly drops, hitting the ground quietly, pulling everybody else down while stopping Wilmer dead in his tracks, and almost knocking him over. The archer puts his finger to his lips, and nobody says a word. He signals seeing some movement up ahead in the brush. One of the archers unties himself from the rope and goes back up to scout ahead moving forward, pushing from one tree to the next like a ball in a pinball game. They wait in silence as the seconds drag into minutes before he returns. He tells them there are about thirty of them well-armed, making camp ahead in a clearing.

They set up a cold camp and prepare to attack once it is dark. Before they leave, Wilmer tells the group Tsaub's are mean and will eat anything, but it is unusual for them to travel this far west. Shortly after dusk, the archers move into their locations using the trees to control their movements, silently gliding through the air like a bird. Mashaun and Wilmer ski down to the camp for their attack—setting up a cross fire on the camp. Dalistra tells Mashaun she does not like the feel. They should attack them hard and fast, and she makes a couple of good points. However, the most compelling argument is her knowledge of them. She remembers them from her childhood when they roamed the lands, raiding and pillaging unchecked; they decimate everything in their path.

When they are in position, Wilmer glimpses a spit over a fire is what appears to be a human body. Thinking it is one of the patrols, he lets the first arrow fly, hitting one. Mashaun quickly follows as the other archers send their arrows into the camp from different directions, but they don't fall as easily as humans do, and it takes three or four well-placed shots to kill one. Several charge the two, but the skis make it easy to outdistance them in the deep snow, and the relentless rain of arrows hampers the Tsaubs' movements. They return fire, throwing spears with deadly accuracy, hitting and killing several archers who remain floating in a limp position. The group uses a hit-and-move tactic, effectively keeping their opponent running in circles.

The two on the ground easily stay out of reach from any who tries to charge them, and the trees offer good cover from their spears. The battle rages on for some time before all the creatures lie dead or dying. Wilmer tries to speak to one, but it is like talking to a dog—literally—with growls and whines, then nothing. They find the remains of the patrol's weapons and armor. On the spit is a human cooked, well-done. It appears they cooked him alive. This makes most of the archers sick, and some even vomit.

They salvage what they can and collect their dead before setting the camp ablaze. All 33 Tsaub, the patrol, and eight archers are dead—the worst attack for Myelikkan in over a generation. They wrap the dead in cloth with the spoils of the battle on makeshift sleds and return to camp. No one speaks during the long journey back which takes several days. When they arrive back at the compound, joy turns to tears as they carry the dead into the village. The group goes to the central building to file their reports. They return the dead and their possessions to their families.

Berg categorizes the spoils before the group can divide it. They brought back one head as proof. "Tsaub" Berg tells them questioningly.

When Llewellyn asks him how he knows, Berg gets an ancient book and shows him a sketch with the word "Tsaub" written underneath, and Berg reads what is written.

Chapter 14

LOST AND FOUND

http://thesilaprophecy.com/race/

IT IS CUSTOMARY WHEN A patrol returns with treasure, everything should be recorded in the logbook. Then the members of the patrol choose what they want, in order, starting with the highest rank. Llewellyn starts the dispersion by getting the first choice. The leaders follow, and then the rest of the surviving members. The last are the immediate families of those who did not survive. It continues until everything is gone. In case there is no family, it will be included with the rest of the loot. Usually, the family members will not want the weapons and armor returned, so they are included in the distribution. It may sound cold, but is what Wilmer tells Mashaun. After a couple of days, Berg tells Llewellyn one of the patrol's gear is missing.

After talking to Wilmer and the others, they decide to wait until the current patrol returns. The extended patrols are shortened to a few weeks. They may find the missing member, and it will only be fair to wait before dividing the equipment from the Tsaub. Hope runs high as the village is ablaze with the hope of one of the patrol member may still be alive. After a few hours, there is a speculation is it can be Tera or Darnel. Most bet on Tera, not because of her experience, but because she didn't carry a sword thus she would not be close to the fight.

While asleep, Mashaun has a vision of Tera hiding on the downward side of a tree, shivering and scared, surrounded by snow. He sits straight up in bed in a cold sweat. Barely getting dressed, he runs to the stone structure pounding on the door until a guard opens. He excitedly blurts out he needs to speak with Llewellyn. He knows Tera is alive and where to find her. Llewellyn summons Wilmer, and Mashaun tells him the story. Wilmer listens intently before suggesting the two of them go and check it out. Llewellyn agrees and assigns two of the airborne to go with them. They are on their way in less than an hour, even though it will be several hours before sunrise.

Shortly after sunup, the rescuers pass the returning patrol, trodden through the snow with heads held low. The party doesn't stop to chat but hurries pass, acknowledging them. The little group arrives at the outpost by night and waits until morning to begin the search so they can take advantage of daylight. They start searching for the tree Mashaun saw. They start in the ravine before making their way up to the ridge-line. By the end of the first day, they are exhausted so they choose to make camp on the northern ridge. The night is clear and cold, realizing if they don't find her soon, she would probably freeze to death if she hasn't already.

On the fringe of the usual patrol area, they see a half frozen and barely alive Tera under a tree matching Mashaun's description. They wrap her up in furs and give her some warm drink before slinging her between the airborne and head back to town without resting. With medical skills and magic, they are able to save her. However, frostbite has taken its toll. It takes days before Tera is able to hobble around her room. It will take much longer to get used to missing two toes and a finger due to frostbite. After recovering a bit, she tells Llewellyn, Wilmer, and a few others about what happened the night of the attack.

They had followed them for another day when the tracks showed more than a dozen creatures joining the primary group. The Tsaubs' small

raiding party they were following continued to grow as several small raiding parties joined them. At one point, there must have been close to a hundred. It was hard keeping track of them; there were groups coming and going. Most of the time, the returning groups brought back sacks they dumped into an open area. Most of the time the sacks were full of plunder. But on the third night, they had two bound people in the sacks. There was a lot of howling and dancing in the Tsaub camp.

"We sat there and watched as they tied one to a pole and started to cook him alive. Before anybody knew what was happening, Darnel shot and killed the captive on the spit. Everybody froze, hoping the Tsaub would not be able to locate us. They must have a keen sense of smell because after they put their noses in the air, they started charging in our direction.

"Four against 50 or so isn't much of a battle, so Shad told everyone to scatter. As he shot at the Tsaub, everyone ran in different directions, it was chaotic. We managed to drop a couple of them, hoping it would slow them down, but they fired back with their spears. They were accurate and threw them farther than expected."

She saw Darnel go down with a spear to the back. Afterwards she ran, never seeing any of them again. The snow slowed them down a lot, but they were persistent. They chased her all night through the trees.

When all she heard was her own breathing, she stopped to peek over her shoulder heard a cracking sound and saw a wall of snow heading at her. She scrambled behind the closest tree, falling into the well around it where she curled up and waited. She could feel the cold snow rushing by, covering her with powder. Hearing the tree snap over the roar of the avalanche, she bent over, covering her head. It seemed like hours before it got quiet again.

She found herself in a snow cave with the tree trunk on one side. Using her dagger and bow, she managed to dig through snow next to the tree. She spent the rest of the day and night in her makeshift snow cave, praying it wouldn't collapse and someone would find her.

The next morning, she climbed out to figure out where she was, only to quickly realized she was lost. She would have headed down the mountain except it is where the Tsaub were, and she did not want to run into them again. She made her way up the valley, hoping to find the outpost, but it started to snow. Soon, she was in a whiteout. All she remembers is roaming the mountains and thinking she is going to die. At some point, she went to sleep and woke up here. She is extremely lucky and grateful to be alive, having avoided death three times in the last few weeks.

Chapter 15

THE PRIZE

THE DAY BEFORE THEY ARE to divide the plunder, Mashaun is summoned to the main hall with his bow. There are four people already in the room, waiting for him—Llewellyn, Wilmer, and two others, he does not recognize. They offer him a chair at the end of the table. Llewellyn sits at the other end of the table. To his left sits Wilmer, and to his right an elfin lady introduced as Lidi, Myelikkan's mage. Her wavy long brown hair is a stark contrast to her long forest green robe; her skin is almost bronze in color, leading him to think she is part-elf.

He hangs Dalistra over the side of the chair and sits down, waiting for somebody to tell him why he is there. Shortly, Dalistra says Llewellyn knows about her. The sword hanging on his chair is another one, called Silmara Gensius, an elfin spirit sword from a time before the Thesilans.

"Correct," Llewellyn says as though he can overhear Dalistra. Mashaun jaw almost hits the floor, as Llewellyn grins.

"I don't have to hear Dalistra to know what you are thinking. I have the similar bond with Silmara Gensius. My sword is why I have such a good relationship with the elves to the north," Llewellyn tells him.

"Most spirit weapons will require a quest to prove the person is worthy, has she?" Lidi asks him. Mashaun thinks for a moment before asking Dalistra if it is true. Dalistra remains silent.

"It is usually one of the first things required by a spirit weapon. What did she ask you to do?" Lidi continues. Mashaun thinks about how to answer the question.

"She wanted to go outside and see the sun." he tells them.

"Oh, so she was in a cave, no wonder she was not found before now.

There has to be more to the story. Who or what was your first kill with her?" Llewellyn asks him.

"I don't remember," he says.

The three eye him with disbelief and skepticism.

Wilmer tells him, "Everybody remembers their first. What you say in here will stay here, and Magdalenia will never know."

Mashaun glances at them while wondering if he should tell them, while Dalistra remains silent. In this conversation, he will be on his own. There is a long pause before he tells them he does remember his first kill. It was a person of prominence, and the rest of the details he will keep as a secret. They speak quietly among themselves for a moment before Lidi speaks.

"We are fairly certain it's you who killed Magdalenia's clone, Magda."

The statement catches Mashaun by surprise as he sits there fidigiting, not saying a word. The clone had a name. He thinks. His mannerisms reveal it all and after a brief uncomfortable silence, Llewellyn asks Mashaun how long he has traveled with Dalistra. He tells them a few months. They mutter among themselves before commenting about the same time someone killed Magda. Again, Mashaun stays quiet, realizing he has divulged, what he wanted to keep a secret.

Lidi studies Mashaun for a long time before telling everybody the world will go through a major shift again as they all nod their heads. When Mashaun starts to ask a question, Llewellyn interrupts, telling Mashaun only time will tell.

Lidi asks Mashaun about the dream he had a few days ago, the one where he saw Tera by the tree. She wants to know how often does he have these dreams. Mashaun tells them he has had them for a few months. They study each other as the minutes tick by, before asking if he had these dreams before finding Dalistra. He understands the implication, and it is not something he has even considered. He asks Dalistra if she has anything to do with the dream. She emphatically tells him no. Mashaun tells them according to Dalistra, she is not responsible for the dreams, telling them he has only had six or seven over the last few months. Mashaun can tell they are surprised and want to know about each dream. He doesn't see any harm, so he starts with the dream about

Magda then the bandit leader. Then realizes the dreams started before he found Dalistra, recounting each dream in order as best he can.

As he tells them about the dreams, it becomes clear to him and them as each dream becomes clearer. They listen intently for several hours as he takes them through the dreams until he finishes with the dream about Tera. Lidi asks if he has thought about trying to develop his talent. He never considered it. After mumbling among one another, Lidi tells him if he decides to develop the talent, she will be willing to help. Mashaun acknowledges her before asking if there is anything else. They ask him one more thing—if he ever had any dreams about Magdalenia. He empathically says no.

The night before the choosing, Berg tells Mashaun there is a book and asks him to choose it early. He only says it is important and it may help them return home. The next morning, the dispersing of the treasure proceeds with someone from each family of the slain party members joining.

There is a long table in the middle of the great hall, where Tsaub swords, spears, packs, some clay square with strange markings, some miscellaneous stuff, and the plain book carefully laid out. There are several other tables with the equipment of the slain companions. Each one has their own table with a woodcarving of the lost one with their name carved into the base. For the most part, there are arms and armor along with some supplies, including one of the bracelets on the companions' table.

For a short time, Abigail scans the audience as people examine the equipment thinking they are vultures preying on the dead, and goes to the Inn. She never experienced losing a friend, she leaves the room with teary eyes even though she didn't know those who died.

Onlookers and families fill the great hall. Some want to see what the Tsaub carried while some purchase items from the patrol members afterward. For several hours, people examine the goods while only the ones involved with the distribution can handle any of the items. The Tsaub spears have oblong shafts instead of round. They are about six-feet long, with a barbed bronze tip. There are several swords and bows laid out on the table. None of them stands out, except for a couple of wide scimitars with strange hilts. Without Mashaun asking, Wilmer tells him they are weapons of the Kaovjs, a race far to the south.

Oddly, there are no shields on the table, and when Mashaun thinks about the Tsaub, he doesn't remember them having shields. Next to the swords is a pile of light rope appearing to be spider silk, it is more robust and weighs less than a sword. There are some flint and steel, plain knives, and building equipment. Mashaun thinks the building equipment is an odd item for them to be carrying; when he asks Wilmer about it, he agrees.

Neither one likes finding building tools among the supplies, which probably means they are looking for a place to start a settlement. Wilmer tells Mashaun if they build a settlement on this side of the mountains, it will bring back the dog wars. Mashaun doesn't say a thing but makes a mental note to find out what he can about them later. Finally, the drum sounds and Llewellyn says it is time to begin. After everybody takes their seats, he explains the rules and the order before starting.

Llewellyn starts the round robin by choosing one of the big Tsaub swords, followed by Wilmer, then Mashaun, Tera, and the rest. It takes all morning for the tables to be empty. Mashaun gets the book, Kaovjs swords, some leather armor, a backpack, and some miscellaneous stuff including the rope. Berg is ecstatic when Mashaun chooses the book first and is eager to start translating it. Mashaun offers the group the first choice of prizes before giving it to Wilmer to sell. He will leave for Shen Sherin in a few days and will be gone for about a month. Mashaun asked Wilmer to check on Kazimir and the twins while he is there.

Chapter 16

SNOW TRAINING

LLEWELLYN PUTS MASHAUN IN CHARGE of training the guards on how to make and use the skis. His first class has 10 students. They painstakingly build their skis and practice using them for several days on the snow-covered flat meadow outside the village. Before long, they are weaving through the trees. Then it becomes time to practice with their bows from the skis. They often go into the forest where Mashaun has set up wooden targets, and they practice shooting while on skis. During the first few days, they lose many arrows as they cannot hit the targets. They leave the compound to practice several times a week. Their problem is not shooting, it's being on the skis.

Once when they are skiing through the forest to the targets, Mashaun detects a noise behind him, turning to see one of the students taking aim at the oversized cat. Mashaun quickly scoops up a handful of snow, throws the snowball, and hits the guy on the side of the face, knocking him to the ground. His arrow flies wildly into the air, disappearing into the sky. The tawny cat and Mashaun stare at each other as the minutes ticks past. Mashaun glimpses an intelligence within those green eyes before the cat turns and vanishes into the forest. The guy sits there in the snow as Mashaun approaches, shaking his head in disgust.

"What are you doing?" Mashaun barks at him. The student shrugs his shoulders, not knowing how to answer.

"Are you going to eat it? Was it attacking?" he follows. The guy shakes his head. Dalistra likes hearing his commanding demeanor; it is a lot different from when she first met him.

He thinks this will be a good time for a lesson, making sure everybody understands his rules.

"I only have two rules. One, eat what you kill. Two, do not attack unless they attack first. Remember, you are scouts, not fighters. Your best chance of survival is not in attacking but in remaining hidden. If you need to attack, choose your position wisely, never from the same place more than a few times," he sternly tells the class before telling them about the attack on the bandit camp.

He helps the student up and decides it is time for some fun. He divides them up into two groups on opposite sides of the meadow, each with a flag tied to a tree. The object is simple: retrieve the opponents flag using snowballs and knock the opposing team down. They play in the snow until almost dark. When they return to the village, they are all wet, cold, and tired but they don't care.

Llewellyn summons Mashaun to join him for dinner. His visits have always been pleasant, but a little uncomfortable. He is taken to the usual dining room, where Llewellyn is talking with a woman with short tawny hair. She is a little shorter than Mashaun and moves with grace toward the table. Llewellyn introduces her as Bianca, a good friend. There is a hint of falimiarity about her, but he can't put his finger on it. During the meal, the conversation turns toward the process of his class and if they are ready for a patrol. Mashaun tells them they are ready.

Llewellyn also asks Mashaun about the events of the day. Mashaun gives him a synopsis, not spending any time on the cat incident until Llewellyn specifically asks about it. Mashaun wonders why he is so interested in the cat sighting but tells them about the event in full. Mashaun glances into Bianca green eyes, and her hair is the same color as the cat.

Mashaun shakes his head as he tries to make sense of it. Their eye meet for a moment before Bianca thanks him with her soft voice for hitting the guy with a snowball.

"You're welcome," he simply replies. He says out of habit. Dalistra tells him she is a were-cat. Mashaun takes a moment before muttering the phrase lycanthrope hesitantly. Before he can go any further, Llewellyn announces he is partly correct, except she is a human by night and a cat by day because of a mistake he made many years ago. Therefore, she is stuck in the dual worlds of humans and animals. While the arrow would have hurt her, it probably wouldn't have killed her.

During dinner, he tells a story about how they met in a city while the guards were chasing her. His group offered her safety and protection. Later when they tried to remove the curse, Llewellyn got overanxious and cast a spell on the other side of town. Somehow, the two spells locked her in this state. They have been companions and friends ever since. As Mashaun is leaving, Llewellyn tells him not to tell anybody and to have his class ready to go on patrol in a couple of days. Mashaun acknowledges them and goes home for the night.

They all show up ready to go, looking forward to proving themselves. Mashaun shows up pulling a toboggan with some extra food and supplies. He assigns two to pull it, and they head to the outpost which they make in a day, much to the delight of the current occupants. The other group goes home in the morning, but for now, they swap stories and share a meal. Mashaun gets an update from Opaline, the captain of the group. Opaline tells Mashaun they saw a family of spotted scorpions moving across the ridgeline on the other side a few days ago. She is curious about the skis, asking all kinds of questions about how they work and if she can learn how to use them. Mashaun agrees to teach her when he returns. Mashaun's group will spend the next 10 days going out in groups of five, scouting around for a day and returning at night.

Before going to sleep, Mashaun asks Dalistra about the spotted scorpions. She tells him they are short, plump animals with four legs and a long tail with a set of mandibles on the end. They use their mandibles to break open trees and to cut through corpses for their food. They can whip their tail lightning fast, and she has seen them sever a few legs. They will also use their tail to hold the food in front of them while they eat, opening their small mouths enough to take a whole arm. They are not dangerous, unless harassed or trapped.

Mashaun divides his charges into two groups and goes out for the day to scout around, meeting back at the outpost at night. They are all told not to engage for any reason unless they are attacked. Finally, he tells them if they come across any of the spotted scorpions, they are to go the other direction. Each day, the groups go out to their assigned patrol areas and return during the night. On the fifth day, the guard on duty comes down and tells Mashaun a patrol is returning but something is wrong. Mashaun and the rest go to greet them; they find one of the members, Josiah, broken arm is almost cut in two, along with several cuts and scrapes. After tending to the wounds, Mashaun sits down with each to find out what happened.

The general story is they came across the spotted scorpions on the ridgeline and they all wanted a closer look. They snuck up close enough to see them clearly, and they followed them for some time. When they decided to leave and return to base, one attacked Josiah. They had no choice but to defend him and Josiah was caught by the claw. Then several others came out of the forest along with the large cat. The cat spring at the scorpion with Josiah arm in its claw, knocking it over, forcing it to release him.

"Why did it attack?" Mashaun asks. They don't say anything as they uneasily sit there, looking everywhere but at him. Mashaun knows the answer but wants to hear it from them.

"Who shot first?" he asks firmly. Slowly they point to Josiah. Josiah hangs his head as Mashaun glares at him.

"So you don't follow orders, you don't use cover as your defense, and you were probably saved by probably the same cat you were going to shoot." He sends the entire group back to the village the following morning and reports to Wilmer.

Berg painstakingly tries to translate the book. The writing in the book is an unknown language, and he doesn't think it's Tsaub. Several pages of the book are missing, and others are in terrible condition. But Berg knows in his gut it is valuable. He spends hours cross-referencing the book with other documents in the hall of records, only to match a few words. He often thinks back to the discussion he had with Mashaun about the book. When they looked at it together, Mashaun thought Berg had lost his mind, wanting something that's in such disarray. However, he got it for Berg nonetheless, even though it probably cost him something else. After weeks of poring over scrolls and books both old and new, he finally finds something worthwhile. Berg is so excited he runs out of the room, nearly forgetting to grab the book and forgetting to close the door. He dashes around the village like a chicken with its head cut off, looking for Mashaun. Finding Mai, she tells him Mashaun is on patrol. She wants to know what he is so excited about.

"Not in public," he tells her. He asks her to go with him, almost pulling her off-balance as he drags her back to the hall of records, grabbing Abigail as they pass her. He sits them down and rambles on about Thesila and the wizards while Mai and Abigail sit there bewildered. Finally, the girls calm him down, telling him to start at the beginning and to go slowly.

After some prodding, he gets to the important part of all his work—he found the way to Thesila. The girls are unimpressed. Many people have sought Thesila, all ending in failure.

"The city is a myth," they tell him.

Berg says, "It's not a myth, and we have something none of the others had—this book and Magdalenia's staff. And it is a major key to leaving or waking up, I'm not sure yet."

The girls start to follow his line of thought up to the staff being the key. Berg continues telling them about Thesila and without waiting for an answer tells them the most capable and persuasive mages once ruled city. According to legend, there was a power struggle, and Thesila disappeared. The girls nod their heads in agreement. Berg holds up the book and tells them he has discovered some information about the internal mage war. Several mages escaped the civil war and took gate keys with them.

Thesila has three gates: a red one, a yellow one, and a blue one. And there are three omnipotent wizards—a red, a yellow, and a blue one.

"See the connection?" he says. Mai and Abigail stare at each other as their eyes light up, realizing the importance of what Berg has found. If it is true, there could be many people after the book, including Magdalenia. They ask Berg how they are going to find one of the staffs, before remembering Mashaun hid the red staff. Berg then made a huge leap of faith, telling them if the cave is built by these mages, then perhaps it is also the way home. All three are filled with excitement at the prospect of returning home.

When Mashaun returns from a patrol, the three enthusiastically greet him at the gate, literally dragging him to their residence where they tell him the whole story as he sits there quietly listening. Frequently, they all speak at the same time until Berg asks them to quiet down since it is his story to tell. Afterward, they sit there looking at Mashaun, waiting for some sign. He sits there with his hand on his bearded chin, thinking. He questions them about the findings in the book, asking if they believe it to be true. They all affirmatively nod their heads. He tells them it will be smart if they leave in the spring, giving them time to prepare for the trip and giving Berg time to find more information.

The next day, he goes to see Tera. She can tell he leaving them behind is not sitting well with him, but she assures him, he probably would have died if he stayed behind. He disagrees with her, telling her he has been in tight spots before and has always managed to survive. She smiles before telling him she is quitting and going back to the city where she belongs. At first, he says she is better than she thinks, but gets nowhere. Mashaun tries to talk her into staying a while, but she is adamant about leaving when she can travel, and the healer tells her in a few weeks. He asks her to wait until spring when they will also be leaving so they can travel together. She agrees. She asks how did they find her. He sidesteps the question, and she lets it slide.

Next, he goes to visit Wilmer to catch up on the news from Pavvo, Kazimir, and the twins. He finds him in the inn, having a drink. Wilmer offers him a drink as the two talk for hours. Wilmer gives Mashaun a bag filled with green, yellow, blue, and a couple of red jade marbles. He is astonished they made so much from the Tsaub treasure. Mashaun tells Wilmer about Berg's findings while Wilmer listens intently. Wilmer says according to legend, the three mages betrayed the city by leaving the gates open, allowing the city enemies to enter before they closed the gates for the last time, trapping everybody and everything inside. However, myths tend to distort the truth.

Wilmer eyes him before asking if he is going to become a treasure hunter. Mashaun nods negatively, telling him there may be more to the city than fame and fortune. He asks Wilmer to join them, but he declines saying he has too many responsibilities to go treasure hunting again. Wilmer tells him stories about treasure hunts with Llewellyn, adding it was a long time ago.

"Oh so long ago," he says with a far-off stare. "But not anymore." He thanks him for the offer anyhow.

Mashaun asks Wilmer to tell him about some of his adventures, and Mashaun orders a couple more of drinks.

On the last day of Hlon Sheej or Spring Holiday in 2696, the group and Tera are ready to head down the mountain. They agree to take Tera to the city since she is determined to go even if everybody tries to talk her out of quitting, including Wilmer. The days have gotten longer and warmer as spring will soon arrive. The group is anxious to be on their way. They say their goodbyes and leave Myelikkan behind as they make their way down the snowy road. Wilmer goes with them; it will soon be time for the merchants to travel again, and means they will need guards. He will first meet up with Axtel and then check with Pavvo for a job. They have worked for him over the last several seasons and will probably do so again.

Tera spends a lot of time asking Mai questions about where she is from, explaining she is one of the few she has ever seen with red hair and little sparkles on her ears. Mai examines her hair, dawning on her it is the same as when she first arrived. Mai contemplates her answer carefully before telling her where she comes from, everybody has red hair and wears earrings. Tera says it sounds like fun place and wants to visit some time. Not knowing how to answer, Mai nods.

Chapter 17

THE THREAT

THE JOURNEY TO THE GOLDEN Unicorn takes them longer than expected due to the softer snow and the muddy road below the snow line. The road through the forest at the bottom is hard from the lack of rain. The road has some soggy sections from the melting snows running off the mountains. At times, finding a dry spot to sleep is a challenge. The Golden Unicorn is a welcome sight after spending several weeks wading through slushy snow and mud. It sits on a small rise surrounded by a marshland except for its entrance and the road, which act as a dam preventing the snow runoff from getting to the river. Mashaun tells Wilmer he doesn't remember it being in a marsh, and Wilmer tells him it only happens during the spring runoff. When the mountain snows melt, they drain here. Sometimes the streams overflow, flooding this area. It will be dry in a month.

Sivish warmly greets them when they enter the inn, offering them a table with hot soup and a drink. He has barely seen any customers all winter, and they are a welcome sight. He asks the group how long they will stay, and Mashaun tells him just one night. He inquiries about the bands of Tsaub roaming the forest and attacks to the north, knowing nothing crosses the mountains without the people of Myelikkan knowing. They tell Sivish about the group of Tsaub they encountered and they know some got away. Sivish informs them about the rumors of awrks and ogres crossing the mountains to the south. The group stare at him with bewildered eyes. What he is saying starts to sink in. They know about the Tsaub, but the others are a surprise. When the four ask about the awrks and ogres, alarmed, Sivish tells them some recent travelers have told him ogres and awrks have been attacking south of Tenskie.

Mai asks him about the awrks, and he tells them they are human-size, and while they aren't as smart, they are cunning and are always traveling in groups. Sometimes a group will have an ogre as a leader, relying on strength, with the belief might makes right. Ogres tend to be nearly twice as tall with the strength to match. Both can be outsmarted, but don't underestimate them—what they lack in intelligence, they more than make up with tenacity. Then he leaves the group to talk with a couple of warriors who just entered the inn.

They don't say much during the rest of the evening. Tera and Abigail take one room. Abigail adds another verse to her ballad of the strangers. Wilmer and Berg are in another room, while Mai and Mashaun take a third. One by one, they each head off to bed until Mashaun is by himself, enjoying the solitude and the crackling fire. Sivish joins him, cautiously looking around.

In a hushed tone, Sivish tells Mashaun, "You need to stay out of the Shen Sherin. Magdalenia is looking for you, and it would be best if she did not find you."

"Why? Is she still mad I beat her in court?" Mashaun asks him.

Sivish shakes his head. "I think there is more to it than you embarrassing her in court."

Mashaun thanks him for the information and assures Sivish he will stay out of the city. After another mug of elfin wine, he leaves and goes to bed.

The next morning, as they are finishing their morning stew and getting ready to leave, Mashaun tells them to go upstairs to make sure they have not forgotten anything. When they try to argue, his tone gets harsh. They all go check one last time, wondering what's gotten into him. Sivish is surprised by his demeanor, and when he asks him about it, Mashaun tells him Magdalenia will be walking through the door any minute. He prefers if none of them are around for her to see. Sivish is about to ask him how, when Magdalenia enters, slamming the door open, strutting across the room with her patronizing attitude. Sivish recognizes her demeanor and sends the two serving girls to keep everybody upstairs and out of sight.

Everybody scrambles from the room, leaving only Magdalenia, Mashaun, and Sivish, who stands by the bar. One of her guards is standing by the door, with another at the base of the stairs. Magdalenia quickly covers the distance between her and Mashaun, where he politely but nonchalantly offers her a seat. Magdalenia puts her hands on the table before speaking.

"You know where my red staff is, and I want it back," Magdalenia says with a viperous tone.

"I do?" he replies calmly, barely looking up from his stew.

"I know you do, and believe me, I will make your life a living hell if you do not return it," Magdalenia replies.

"When did I supposedly have this staff, and can you discrib it" he asks her, still not looking at her.

"You know what it looks like!" she snarls, getting irritated at his cavalier attitude, slapping the bowl of stew across the room.

"What are you talking about?" he says, making sure he pauses between each word as he stands up, staring into her eyes.

Feeling uncomfortable at his defiance, she leans back. He stands a full head taller, but he leans toward her, showing no fear. Sivish is amazed as Mashaun looks down on Magdalenia, as few have the courage or the foolishness to do so. He is not the same person who was here last fall. Months at Myelikkan have changed him, made him more confident or foolish.

"Look, you miscreant, I know you have my staff. I want it back." She snarls.

"I hope you do get it back…because you are nothing without your crutch," he tells her mockingly.

A surprised Sivish fears Mashaun's brashness will lead to a fight. They stare at each other for several long moments before Magdalenia leans back, looking around the room. All the animals have turned, facing them, ready to pounce if either one of them attacks the other or if she uses any magic.

"We will meet again. I guarantee. And these animals or my brother will not be there to protect you," she growls before turning around and storming out the door.

After she leaves, Sivish joins him, bringing another bowl and something to drink.

"How did you know she was going to walk through the door?" Sivish asks.

"I don't know. Sometimes I dream, and it comes true," he says.

"Do you always make such an impression?" Sivish asks.

"Not always, just with people who piss me off," Mashaun answers.

"Well, Magdalenia is a dangerous enemy," Sivish tells him.

"Yes, I know," Mashaun replies as he's finishing his drink.

"So it is you," Sivish replies.

"What do you mean?" Mashaun questions, looking at him, puzzled.

"Magdalenia used to be a domineering and influential person in Shen Sherin's lower class. But last autumn, she lost her clone, her staff, and then her slaves in a court battle for ownership. Since then, she has been slowly losing power, and the townspeople have quietly spoken of their disdain for her. Not long ago, the people wouldn't dare challenge her. I feel the winds of change blowing, and they will become a torrent before it calms," Sivish tells him.

"According to the stories of old, the prophecy will begin several years before all three moons block out the sun. If the prophecy is fulfilled then the ancients and Thesila will return. The mages will lose much of the control they have over the people."

"What prophecy?"

"The Thesila Prophecy. You have already put things in motion that are beyond your control. You are the bringer of the Prophecy, and I think Magdalenia has figured out, Dalistra and you are the prophecy."

"Wow! One last thing. Who's her brother?" Mashaun asks.

Sivish appears as though he were about to say something when the others come downstairs, peppering Mashaun with lots of questions. The group decides to stay an extra day before leaving for Shen Sherin. All day long, they pelt him with questions. He just tells them he had a visitor. They all ask him who, but he remains tight-lipped, only saying it doesn't concern them. The next morning, he tells them he has something to do and won't be going to the city. He will instead meet them outside Arnbor.

They voice their concerns about him outside the city by himself, but Wilmer and Mashaun remind them he is better equipped to survive in the wilds than in the city. Before they can argue the point further, Mashaun leaves, disappearing into the forest like a ghost in the night. Mai asks Wilmer if he really thinks he will be okay in the forest by himself.

"There are few able to match his skills in the wild." He quickly tells her.

Tera tells them Shen Sherin is her home and they can stay at her house. Abigail is the first to agree as they head down the road.

They continue to the city, each wondering what transpired the previous morning. They are certain it is has to do on why he is hiding in the forest. It is near dark when they approach Shen Sherin. Tera goes first through the pillars, and as she does, one of the guards questioningly speaks her name in disbelief before giving her an hug as Tera face turns flush. The others gawk with bewilderment, and when they escort Tera into the interrogation room, they become even more confused, except Wilmer. The two guards then ask the group to join her.

They enter a room full of laughter, and Tera introduces them to her mother, Kristina, the gate captain. Food and drink are brought into the room as the guards leave. Tera and her mother catch up on the events in the past few years since she left for Myelikkan. They can tell Tera went to study with Llewellyn with her mother's blessings. Kristina is both happy and disappointed Tera has returned. Tera tells her about the training, the living conditions, and her friends including the ones lost on her patrol. Her eyes start to water, realizing she should have left it out for now. Kristina can tell Tera has stopped short of telling her the whole story and starts asking lots of probing questions out of habit.

Kristina is good at asking questions; after all, she is a topnotch interragator. Tera eventually tells her about the Tsaub, sending Mashaun for reinforcements, the ambush, and her surviving the avalanche. With some more prying, she eventually finishes the story by removing her glove, revealing her four-fingered hand while telling her she is lucky to be alive because she is the only survivor of her patrol.

Kristina hugs her for a long time before asking, "How did you survive?"

"They sent a patrol out to find me, and even though I was outside of the patrol area, they still found me because of one exceptional person," Tera tells her. Mai's eyes flash red, realizing Tera is possible competition.

"Who was in charge of the patrol?" Kristina asks.

"Mashaun, the same one who was sent back for help," Tera replies.

The group tries to leave, giving them some privacy, but the guards will not allow it.

"Has he been to the city?" Kristina asks.

Tera thinks for a moment before turning and asking Mai.

There is a short pause as Mai thinks about her answer before replying nervously, "Yes, he has, ma'am."

"When? Spit it out, Mai," Kristina commands.

"Last fall. With Pavvo, ma'am," she finally answers.

Kristina studies at them for a while, and then it is like turning on a lightbulb.

"Is he the one with the red glowing bow?" Kristina asks.

The three of them nod their heads almost in unison. Kristina demeanor changes in a heartbeat, her voice comanding. The guards stance become ridig as she tells them none of this conversation leaves the room if they value their tongues. Then she instructs the guards to take them to her place and tells them to wear their hoods before they leave the room. Puzzled, wanting to know why. She only tells them it is for their own safety. She asks Wilmer what his plans are. He planning to spend the night at Pavvo's.

She nods, sending them on their way, telling Tera to go straight home and take no side trips. Tera asks Mai what all the fuss is about as Mai looks at Tera puzzled, shaking her head.

"But it's a good bet Mashaun knew forcing his decision to remain in the wilds." Mai asks Tera if he is really any safer outside the city. Tera reassures her. His chances of surviving is better than all of them put together.

Wilmer catches a couple of hooded figures taking a little too much interest in their movements out the corner of his eye. Taking a couple of turns, monitoring the two hooded men follow them. Once on the island where Tera lives, he tells her to go and bar the doors. His firm tone tells her not to argue. Wilmer leaves them just a block from Tera's home, heading down a side street in the other direction.

Kristina lives on one of the inner islands where all the military commanders reside. A modest two-storey building with several small windows overlooks a small courtyard. Tera takes them to a medium-sized room with a fireplace and running water on the second floor. She offers them something to drink, telling them to make themselves comfortable while they wait for her mom. They wonder what is going on. Before they finish their drinks, Kristina walks through the door, making sure all the curtains are drawn.

After getting herself something to drink, she invites the group in the living room before quietly asking them if anything strange happened on the way to the city. They glance at one another, trying to think. Each in turn tells her "no" until Tera mentions Mashaun rudely sending them upstairs at the Golden Unicorn. They had never seen him so demanding and thought it was strange. When Kristina asks what happened afterwards, they tell her when they left the inn, Mashaun said he would rejoin them later before disappearing into the forest. Kristina approvingly nods her head, telling them it was the best thing he could have done.

Kristina tells them she has a theory. The other morning, Magdalenia left town before sunrise and returned about mid-afternoon in a fouler mood. Magdalenia has been obsessed with finding the person responsible for killing her clone and taking her staff, and believe Mashaun is responsible. Kristina believes Magdalenia met with Mashaun at the Golden Unicorn to probably scare him. By the expression on her face when she returned, it didn't go as planned. She asks if any of them saw what happened, and they all shake their heads.

"If Magdalenia believes he is responsible, then it puts him and all of you in danger." Tera asks if it included her. Kristina doesn't know.

Puzzled, Mai, Abigail and Berg all reguard the two of them. Before Berg asks what is going on, Kristina tells them for many years, Magdalenia ruled the city from behind the scenes. "Everything—from the merchants to the judges. Nothing went on in the city without her approval or at least her knowledge. Her biggest rival is Pavvo, the same person you came to town with last fall."

The three shake their heads with disbelief. Somehow, they got themselves into the middle of a feud between two powerful players without even knowing it. Tera tells them they will have to be cautious in town., and they will need to avoid other people. But how are they going to get anything done with Magdalenia looking for them?

It has gotten late, and they are tired from the trip as they decide on sleeping arrangements and settle down for the night. Mai finds a spot by the door and sleeps placing her feet against it; she watched Mashaun do it many times. Morning comes without any incident, and Kristina gets ready for work. They eat and prepare to leave when Kristina tells them not to go out. She will have to find a safer place. For now, it will be best if no one is aware they are in town. Hesitantly, they all agree. Shortly after Kristina leaves, they sit around and talk. The sound of breaking glass and footsteps come from upstairs.

Berg and Abigail hide in the kitchen, drawing daggers, while Mai and Tera hide under the stairs. Four masked men sneak down the stairs with short swords drawn. Like cats, they move through the house when one of them points to Abigail's foot sticking out. When he grabs her, Berg slashes his arm. The masked man recoils as another man grabs Berg. Mai and Tera jump from their hiding place. Tera drops one of the masked men by kicking him behind the knee, yelling at them to run. Berg breaks free. Grabbing Abigail, they run out the back but someone grabs their clothes before reaching the door. Tera knocks another one over, and the remaining one follows Berg out the back. Mai and Tera are close behind, knocking the two masked men down, grabbing Berg and Abigail as they dash past two hooded archers.

Chapter 18

HIDE AND SEEK

THE NEXT MORNING, KRISTINA SENDS a guard to bring Pavvo to the room without telling him why. Pavvo is surprised with the request although it sounds more like a command. He accompanies the guard to the interrogation room where Kristina is sitting on a chair. She excuses the guard and tells him they are not to be disturbed for any reason, and no one is to know he is here. The guard nods as he leaves. She offers him a seat before setting up the four cubes.

"What is this about?" Pavvo asks with curiosity.

"Do you remember the spirit bow arriving with your caravan last fall?" Kristina asks in her usual stern manner.

"You mean, Mashaun. Nice, young man and a good person to have on your side," Pavvo replies nonchalantly.

"Yes, he's the one. What do you know about him?" she asks.

Pavvo thinks for a while before answering. "I met the group on the road, and after his help with some bandits, I offered him a guard's position to help replenish the ones I lost. Why?"

"Before I answer, I have a few more questions. Do you think he is the reason Magdalenia has been losing power, putting her in a belligerent mood?" she inquires.

He thinks it is a strange question coming from her. He thinks for a moment before answering. "I don't know, but her mood deteriorated about the time he showed up, didn't it?"

She decides to throw out a couple of stories to see what kind of response she gets.

"Some say she lost her clone and her staff about the same time, shortly before he arrived."

He reguards her question, trying to read her intentions before answering. "Yes, I have heard that," he answers in a neutral tone.

"Do you think he had anything to do with it?" she asks.

"You will have to ask him," he calmly replies.

"I'm asking you," she snaps back. This is not usual for her, and he wonders what has her on edge.

"I don't know…you need to ask him." His tone gets sharper.

"I would if I knew where to find him," she snaps back, sounding frustrated.

"Why?" Pavvo finally asks, realizing there is more here than meets the eye.

She thinks for a moment before replying. "His friends are back in town, they arrived with my daughter."

"Really? I haven't heard that," he responds. She is a little surprised since Wilmer is at his place. But then again, he probably hasn't talked to Wilmer.

Pavvo wonders what her daughter has to do with the questioning, so he decides to change the questions a little.

"Did Wilmer say where he was going when he arrived?" he inquires.

"He said he was going to see you." She sounds a little concerned. "He never made it." He is also concerned.

"Why is your daughter traveling with them? I thought she is studying in Myelikkan," he inquires.

"Yes, she was. But she had a change of heart. But that's not important. Magdalenia will be looking for them if she even suspects they are in town," she tells him with a little worry in her voice.

He nods his head, knowing the next question.

"I have them in a safe place at the moment, but I would like to move them some place safer, like…yours." He agrees and will send some of his men over in the evening to retrieve them. However, Pavvo still wants to know why Tera came back. By doing so, she puts both herself and Kristina in a dangerous position. After some prodding, he gets the truth about why her daughter changed her mind.

With the truth revealed, Pavvo asks the most important question.

"Why was she really there?" he asks her bluntly.

Using her skills, she regards his movements, expressions, and his answers before asking, "Are you still in a quiet feud with Magdalenia?" Pavvo nods.

She quickly follows up by asking, "Have you heard the rumors about the fourth staff, a group working to unseat her?" And again, he nods.

She asks him what he thinks about the group. He sits there for a moment, deciding on whether it is a trap or something else. There is an uncomfortable silence as he mulls over his answer carefully, knowing the wrong answer can be dangerous.

"Why?" he eventually replies.

Now she is defensive. How much should she tell him?

She leans over the table so she can whisper in his ear even though the cube prevents prying eyes and ears. "I have been involved with the movement for some time, but it wasn't until Magdalenia's power started waning the movement started to grow. People feel less afraid of her and have started to openly mock her, even though the movement discourages such actions. There is a growing number of important people noticing Magdalenia is losing control and wants her gone." She asks him to join the movement and she needs an answer before leaving the room.

Pavvo asks her what is involved.

"Right now, we just watch each other's backs. And with Tera back in town, you know I need some help there," she says.

Pavvo doesn't even think before giving him an affirmative nod, and they both smile as Pavvo leaves.

Early in the afternoon, one of the guards nervously tells Kristina she has a visitor. As she glances up from her paperwork, she can tell from his face who it is.

She nods, and the guard lets in Magdalenia. She strolls into the office as if she owns the place, looking around and chuckling quietly.

"So this is what they gave you," she snickers.

"What? It's usually quiet, and I don't have to see your mug," Kristina responds sarcastically.

"Won't you have a seat?" Kristina follows, trying to be polite but it comes out a bit sharp.

"That's okay, I won't be staying long," Magdalenia says caustically.

"Good! I have some real work to do," she retorts.

"I hear your daughter—"

Kristina cut in. "You and your lackeys stay away from her, or I will personally make sure you end up like your clone." She stands up, leaning forward with her hands on the desk.

Magdalenia just chuckles. "Is that a threat?"

"No, that is a promise!" she says.

Chuckling, Magdalenia replies, "Foolish woman, I'm not here about Tera, I forced her to leave the city in disgrace, I got what I wanted. I want the others who came in with her. I know they are friends with the troublemaker, Mashaun. And I have a score to settle with him."

"Yes you did and everybody know it now, but you will find her stronger than before. I don't know where they are, and if I did, I wouldn't tell you!" she says spitefully.

"Oh yes, I forgot how much you are not a team player," Magdalenia replies mockingly.

"Only with the likes of you," Kristina shoots back.

"My, my, such anger. You really should get it under control. You know I will find them, and when I do, I will have my revenge," she says in a cool, mocking voice.

"My, my, anger! Trust me, you haven't seen me angry yet," Kristina replies.

"I know they are not at your place. I checked," Magdalenia says, waiting for a sign. However, Kristina is known for keeping her cards close to her chest. With deadpan eyes and a poker face she stares at Magdalenia.

"If I find out you or your thugs have entered my place, I will have them brought up on charges and hung, maybe not in that order," Kristina shoots back.

"Now, now, I don't need to send anybody there. I just watch my crystal pool. You didn't think those cheap magic wards could keep me out, did you?" Magdalenia says with a wicked smile.

Since Magdalenia's clone was killed and her staff went missing, her powers have slowly diminished. However, she hasn't been able to use her crystal ball as much for some time, not since she lost the staff. Otherwise, she can use it to find Mashaun herself.

151

"I see. Guess I will have them upgraded," Kristina responds with a warm, fake smile.

"It won't work, but you can try. It's your money," Magdalenia says as she strolls out the door.

Is she telling the truth or baiting her? Kristina isn't sure. She quickly writes a letter telling Pavvo the kids may have left the house and Magdalenia visited her. One by one, she calls in four of her guards, sending three of them to the Synhom three markets with a blank piece of paper in an envelope. She calls in Neil, one of her most trusted guards, and he has a thing for Tera. They have worked together ever since he got back from Myelikkan several years ago. She gives him the letter for Pavvo and tells him it is imperative Pavvo gets it yesterday and nobody should know. Neil nods and head into town.

Using all the magic Magdalenia can muster, she peers into her bowl of vision and scans the four leaving Kristina's. She can only focus on one and chooses Neil because of her familiarity with him from previous scrying. It's a simple task of following him to see where he goes, provided her magic can hold out. She has also sent several of her henchmen to tail them as backup. If she concentrates too hard, he may feel her watching him. Most people don't have the knowhow to lose a magic tail even if they are aware of magic scrying.

Neil neck hairs stand on end, like he is being watched and suspects he has several tails. He also knows there are many ways to follow a person, but his years of training in Myelikkan and his experience have taught him how to shake all kinds of tails. Neil leads them to the Sidusia market, where there are lots of people and shops with canopies. Magdalenia suspects Neil is heading to Pavvo's, so she concentrates her vision on the other end of the market where he will leave if he goes to Pavvo's, trusting her minions to keep him in sight. She waits there long enough for him to have made his way through the market. Looking back at the market, she can't find him. Her magic fades, losing her target. If she weren't so tired, she would be irritated.

Once under the cover of the canopies, Neil puts his hood up. He spends a short while meandering around the market. Shortly he heads out toward the weapons island then circles to another island, where he loses his shadows. After concluding the tails are gone, he continues on his mission. He uses overhangs and canopies to hide from the prying eyes in the sky and doubles back to make sure he doesn't have any unwanted guest following. He makes his way through one of the merchant islands, where he runs into Tera and her friends. Tera gives him a hug thankful to see a friendly and introduces him to Mai, Abigail and Berg.

"It is nice to meet you but I can't talk right now. We will have to catch up later, I have an errand to run." Neil tells them nervously glancing around.

"Why the hurry?"

"I am on an errand for your mother."

"Will you tell her not to worry, we are all safe."

Surprised at her request, "Does your mother know your back in town?"

"Yes, we saw her yesterday. We were supposed to stay home today, but it is too crowded so we came to the market."

"Your mother had a visit from Magdalenia, and she was not in a good mood when she left."

Tera wrinkles her brow, with a tremor in her voice, tells the group they need to return to the gatehouse. Neil is a little confused until Tera tells him what happened at the house.

He tells them it will be better if they stay together and tells them to follow. After talking among themselves, they eventually agree and head to one of the bridge to Kukab, only to find Magdalenia's men already there. They try to double back only to find her men are searching the market, apparently looking for someone.

Zigzagging down alleys and side streets they make their way to the bridge to Oralub island. Finding it also crowded with Magdalenia's lackeys. They continue to the Eposiaj bridge and choose to make a run for the bridge leading to the stables. Neil tells them to stay close as they use the crowd for cover. There are two of her men at the first bridge as Neil readies to draw his short sword. They wait for a crowd to cross the bridge, blending in with them as they pass the guards, making sure they keep their heads down. They are halfway across the bridge when someone yells "Tera". Not thinking, she looks up, and they see her.

The chase is on; they cross into the stable area with Magdalenia's men in close pursuit. Several others quickly join them as they weave among the stables and shops. Neil cuts some of the canopies' ropes, trying to slow them down. They make it to the next bridge, leading to Treasib island, where there are several others waiting. Mai takes a few marbles out and tosses them in the air yelling something about a yellow marble. drawing attention to the green and blue. Abigail follows suit, but before realizing what she had in her hand, she throws them into the air. Someone yells something about a red one.

Fighting and shouting behind them distracts the two men at the bridge. Neil hits one with his body, knocking him over the railing, and then swings around, catching the other one upside his head. The group runs across the bridge and hurries to the next one. The bridge to Cheberin is the longest one in the city at hundred and fifty feet across, trying to make it across before the pursuers catch them. They make a beeline shot to the bridge and find only the island guards at each end of the bridge. They race across onto the Cheberin island, the island of magic merchants. where Pavvo has more influence than Magdalenia. Catching their breath as they continue down the narrow street. They only have one more bridge to cross, leading to Hulyci island, where only the wealthiest people who are not nobles live. There is a gate and three island guards. The ranking guard asks them to state the business. Neil tells them he is on an errand for Kristina and hands them the letter. Seeing her seal on the outside, the guards step aside to their relief. They cross the bridge and Neil takes them to Pavvo's.

Neil tells Pavvo's guard he has a letter from Kristina for Pavvo. The guard opens the gate and lets them pass. Pavvo greets them at the door and is a little surprised to see Tera and the group. He invites them to join him in the den where he reads the letter. Turning his gaze on them and he shakes his head.

"You didn't do what you were told," he says. Tera tells him about the masked men and the attack shortly after Kristina left for work. Pavvo thinks to himself, she is getting desperate to attack a member of the royal guard's house in broad daylight and wonders why she did not attack under the cover of darkness.

He asks Neil, "Do you know what is in the letter?" Neil tells him no.

"Thank you. Return to Kristina and tell her all is well, and send some guards to her house. Oh yes, tell her she is invited to dinner tonight around sunset." Neil nods and leaves.

Pavvo continues, "Apparently, she would like me to check on you at her house. However, circumstances have changed, and things have gotten more volatile than I thought."

Kristina is relieved and furious when she receives the news. The guards don't find any bodies, instead there is a broken upstairs window, torn clothing, stuff knocked over and a blood trail leading out the back door, to a pool, but no bodies.

Chapter 19

THE TRUTH

AFTER WORK, SHE HURRIES OVER to Pavvo's mansion. She is shown into a foyer dwarfing her office, filled with statues, and expensive paintings. Tera greets her and shows her into the living room, where Mai, Abigail, and Berg sit talking. They tell Kristina about their run-in with Magdalenia's men. They continue telling her how Neil helped them escape. They also tell her about Mai's idea of throwing some money on the ground to create a riot. Before they can finish the story, there is another knock on the door. They glance one another, then the door, wondering who else is coming.

A guard shows Kazimir, Ericka, and Elina into the room. Kazimir is wearing a bespoken tunic with a symbol of the house of Pavvo, signifying he works for him. Ericka and Elina wear matching robes with the same symbol. They are ecstatic to see them, exchanging hugs. They ask about Mashaun and are saddened when told, he chose to stay out of the city, but they understand.

Wilmer comes into the room, telling everybody dinner is ready. They enter a room with a long dining table, ornate chandlears hanging from gold leaf painted ceiling. There are five chairs to a side and one at each end. Pavvo stands at the other end of the table, inviting them to have a seat. After everyone sits, Pavvo sits at one end of the table with Toni seated on his right and Wilmer on his left. Next to Wilmer sit Mai, Berg, Abigail, and Tera; across them are Kazimir, Ericka, Elina, and Kristina. The servers bring roast pig, exotic vegetables, and some fine elfin wine to wash it down. They are amazed with the fixings, saying they don't remember ever having such a delicious meal. Wilmer and Toni make sure to keep the conversation lighthearted even though there are no jugglers or singers. In fact, there is no one except for the occasional servers.

After, the servants remove the dishes and bring a fruit dish. The servers retire for the night as Wilmer closes all the doors and shutters the windows. Kristina courousity gets the better of her, but Pavvo puts her mind to rest with a few soft words. Pavvo clears his voice, and everyone turns their eyes toward him. He glances around the room as Toni walks around, drawing glyphs on the walls and doors. As she does this, each glyph glows, and soon there is a silver radiance covering the walls and the ceiling. Ericka and Elina are amazed at her power and studies Toni every movement, intently. When Toni returns to her seat, Pavvo begins to speak. Magdalenia watches as Toni writes the glyphs, realizing what she is doing, letting out a howl as her pool goes blank yet again.

"Magdalenia would like to eliminate of each of you for different reasons, and that is what binds you together this night. Magdalenia and I have had a quiet feud for many years, and it has been kept in the shadows until Mashaun challenged her in court, around the time she lost her staff and clone. The king showing up at Kazimir's trial—his first public appearance in several years—has her scared. Since then, her power has been waning, and her grip on the government has been slowly slipping away. Like a cornered animal, she is becoming more desperate. Her people attack the townsfolk, and even members of the royal guard are attacked during the day. I suspect by morning, several of her people will turn up dead because you got away," he says, looking at Mai.

"The staff increases a person's natural ability to channel magic, allowing them to wield phenomenal power. However, side effects are paranoia, delusions, and addiction. The longer an individual uses it, the more magic they comand, and so do the side effects. The ancients understood and separated the disk of power from the staffs, hoping to stop the addiction, but all it did was slow it down. Magdalenia received Mother's staff and she quietly gave me the disk. Each has its own magic, but as a set, they work together, allowing the channeling of unbelievable power."

They all sit there, stunned by the revelation yet they know there is more to come. Before any has a chance to speak, he continues.

"Several years after she gave them to us, they went on a ride in the country and never returned. That was about 30 years ago. For a while, we worked well together, but the staff seemed to change her quicker than expected. After a while, she wanted to deal in slaves, and I did not. We had a major fight about it and went our different ways. That is when we found out we felt each other's pain. In other words if she is responsible for me getting hurt, she will feel the same pain, and if I am responsible for her pain, I will feel the same pain. I understand why she wanted to deal in slaves. She is looking for the stranger needed to put in motion, the Thesila prophecy. A prophecy will find a way, no matter what you do to stop it. Since then, we haven't spoken much. Actually, we usually avoid each other."

Berg speaks up, asking about the clone and the staff. "If they become paranoid, then why did the clone have the staff? Wouldn't she guard it with her life?"

They shake their heads in unison as they turn toward Pavvo for an answer. He just shrugs his shoulders, admitting he has no answer.

"So far, she has left my people alone. And you being here, she will rightly conclude you are under my protection. However, that does not extend outside of the city wall, nor do I know how long the truce will last. She will not openly attack me for fear will I attack her. That is the curse our dear old Mother placed on us." Everybody eyes fixed on Pavvo with bewilderment. "Yes, she I am her adopted brother." He stops to let it sink in as they stare at him in disbelief.

"I am also from a different world like you," he says, looking at Mai, Berg, Abigail, and Kazimir. "Like you, I escaped the cave and was picked up by a merchant. He had his wife and daughter, Magdalenia, who was a little older. We were traveling north of Tenskie when a bunch of bandits attacked. I saw firsthand the power of the red staff in the hands of a true mage, her mother, Madeline. I wanted to be a mage just like her, but only people with one of the Thesila bloodlines have a chance to tap into the magic. Her husband, William, took me under his wing and taught me everything about the business. On Earth, I lived on the streets in New York, and here, I had a chance to change everything, and I did."

The group continues to listen in disbelief while wondering why he is revealing it to them. Kristina and Tera eye each other then everyone else, realizing they are not from here, except for the twins.

"What do you mean 'not from this world?'" Kristina asks, confused. Mai explains the cave and how they really live in another world, and they think this is only a dream. Kristina and Tera listen with disbelief, adamantly telling Mai this is not a dream, this is my world.

Pavvo continues. "It is not a dream, off-worlders are brought her to help keep the races alive. Off-worlders are needed. During their high emotional states, like anger, fear, love, and admiration, they release something into the air. Local women absorb it and are able to become pregnant. But the effects last for a very short time. Back to my story."

I became part of the family. Magdalenia and I would go shopping and come home with lots of stuff, some by her magic, but most by my negotiations. Soon we were buying goods only to turn around and sell it one island over for a profit. Like most families, we got into some fights; I mean some knockdown, drag-out fights. Finally, Mother had enough and put a spell on us—we would feel each other's physical pain. After the spell was cast, she told us to go ahead and hit each other. We did, and it hurt. We never hit each other again, and if anybody else hits either one of us, the other also feels it." They all stare at one another in amazement before Kristina speaks.

"Why did you agree to help bring her down then?"

He grins. "Sis has had the position of city mage far too long and needs to turn the reins over to someone younger. The problem is only a person with Thesila blood coursing through their veins can use the staff, and she has no children any more."

"You mean she actually had a child? What happened to him or her? How long has she been in power?" Mai asks.

"I will tell you later about her son." Tera whispers to her.

"Mother gave her the staff forty years ago, when she was twenty-five. And she has been in power ever since," he tells them, shocking everybody. Magdalenia appears to be in her mid-thirties. Pavvo tells them she uses magic so no one will challenge her because of her age. That is the real reason for the clone—to keep everybody guessing. They sit there in silence, trying to understand what they just heard.

"They want to remove Magdalenia. But if they hurt her, then they hurt you. With all the help you have given to numerous businesses just getting started, it is not fair." Kristina says.

He thanks Kristina for her kind words as he picks up a small box off the floor and puts it on the table. Standing up, he opens the box to reveal a disk made of red jade embedded in a golden amulet hanging from a gold chain.

"Very few people know about the second half of the staff. I don't think Magdalenia even aware of it. All I really know is it allows the user to channel the ancient magic and she told me to keep the two separate. I don't know why," he tells them.

Pavvo explains only someone with a Thesila lineage can access the amulet's power, and since he is not Thesilan, he keeps the box hidden for safekeeping. Even if the person cannot access its power, it will still act as a protective shield from magic. He slowly walks around the table with the amulet.

"I have decided to give the amulet to one of you for safekeeping, provided you take it out of the city so my dear sister can not find it." As he passes by the twins, the amulet glows slightly to the surprise of everybody, including Pavvo and Toni.

He slowly moves it toward Ericka then Elina to see who has the stronger glow. While the disk glows next to both of them, it quickly becomes apparent Elina has a brighter glow. Pavvo hangs the amulet around Elina's neck, where it glows a bright red before fading back to its normal color.

"You two have the potential of becoming more powerful than Magdalenia, that why she is so mad losing the two of you. You have Thesilan blood."

Elina tells them she can feel the power of the amulet flowing through her already. "So this is why she kept us as slaves. We were the next in line for the staff, but we are not from Thesila, we are from Tenskie." The twins eye each other with disbelief. The test showed them have some magical power, but to be more powerful than Magdalenia, scares them. They will have to leave the city, the only real place they know, and neither of them likes to travel. Mai tells the twins they will be leaving in a couple of days, and it will be better if they stay inside and out of sight until then. Although they don't like it, they know is the best thing to do so they agree.

Pavvo tells them they shouldn't wait and leave before sunup. Turning to Wilmer, he asks him to retrieve some food from the storage and meet him in his study. He asks Kristina to open the gate for one of his wagons before sunrise but she should not let anybody else know. She asks him about his plan, but he tells her it is better if she doesn't know. Agreeing, Kristina and Tera head home with a few of Pavvo's guards escorting them. Pavvo also tells Elina she should keep the amulet in the box so it won't attract any undue attention. It won't take long for Magdalenia feel the magic. The staff and the amulet are connected and will want to be joined. After a few days, they should be far enough away she can wear it.

Kazimir relieves the gate guard in the middle of his shift allowing him eat. When Mai, Abigail, Ericka, Elina, and Berg leave with their hoods over their faces, Kazimir tells them to keep next to the buildings and to be cautious of the city night guards, you don't know which ones are in her pocket. The twins know this city well and lead them through some of the backstreets and alleys, making the rest of the group uncomfortable. Several times, they have to remain hidden or make a detour to avoid the night travelers. It takes some time for them to make it across the islands, but they eventually make it to the Munthiv gate leading to the mainland where Kristina is waiting for them. She sends the guards on patrol, leaving her the only one at the gate. Quickly and quietly, the group slips through the gate only to find Tera on the other side. Tera tells them she is coming along. Mai starts to argue, but Berg quietly tells them this is not the time or the place for an argument. The group heads down the road, using whatever they can find for cover. The night sky begins to fade into day as they pass through the town and are finally in the forest, heading south.

At sunrise, three wagons leave Pavvo's mansion and go to his warehouse. Wilmer is driving one while Kazimir rides on a different one. Once at the warehouse, Kazimir hides under the tarp covering one of the wagons. They all leave about the same time, each turning a different direction. Magdalenia studies the three wagons through her dish of clairvoyance and chooses to follow Wilmer to the east. Wilmer goes to the Golden Unicorn and spends a couple of days before returning to the city. One wagon goes north to Silvaneth, where it delivers some supplies before returning. The last wagon goes south with Kazimir hiding under the tarp. After a few hours, Kazimir joins the teamster up front.

Mashaun heads into the forest, following the river down to Shen Sherin village at the crossroads. The villagers don't pay any attention to him as he makes his way through the village backstreets to the bridge. He mingles with the crowd to cross the bridge only to disappear in the village and then the forest. Dalistra remains exceptionally quiet during the entire time as though there is another spirit device nearby. Once in the forest, she tells him someone, probably Magdalenia, was magically searching, and the best way to stay hidden is not to say anything. Using the forest as cover, they make their way across the entrance to the merchant camp where he recognizes the tunic of Magdalenia on several soldiers just north of the encampment. He moves back toward the city beyond the guards' sight, hoping to catch Mai before Magdalenia's men can see them.

Chapter 20

RETURN TO THE CAVE

MAI, ABIGAIL, TERA, BERG, AND the twins head down the southern road for several hours when they come across Mashaun on the edge of the forest. He motions them off the road, and they join him in the forest. Without saying anything, he leads them away from the edge before a joyous reunion. Before anyone can say a thing, Mashaun asks the group why Tera and the twins are with them. They spend the next hour or so filling him in on the important events over the last few days as Mashaun listens intently. Mai secretly hopes he will send Tera back. She is a little jealous of her, and Dalistra is jealous of both but understands there is nothing she can do about it, for now. Mashaun and Tera have spent time in the woods together, and he saved her life. Tera is competition, and Mai is uncomfortable with the commonalities the two enjoy, she already dislikes the bow, feeling there is an unnatural connection between the two.

Mashaun tells them a second bow is a welcome addition, and he understands why the twins need to leave the city. Mashaun informs them he has seen some of Magdalenia's people nosing around outside the merchant camp. It's not safe here, and they need move. An empty wagon rumble down the road and even from a distance, they can tell it's Kazimir. The wagon stops next to them as he jumps down, giving Mashaun a huge hug which embarrasses him. After spending some time on small talk, Kazimir tells them he's not going. This surprises everybody except Mashaun who stops him in midsentence.

"Yes, I know. You have a family now and you are happy here," he says.

Kazimir looks at him as if to ask how he knew. Mashaun will only say he saw this exact conversation. The others stare at Mashaun with disbelief. They didn't even know despite being in the city for a couple of days. Mashaun says he doesn't have to go and wishes him and his family the best. Mai tries to talk Kazimir into coming along just to the cave, but he is adamant about not going, telling Mai she doesn't have to worry about the twins. Berg asks Kazimir if he got the item. Kazimir hands Mashaun a wooden box about the size of a small laptop with a two-piece sextant, a notebook, and a pen inside. Mashaun thanks the two of them as they all say their goodbyes and part ways. Mashaun suspects they will meet again; however, the rest will not.

With Mai on his left, Mashaun leads the group through the forest. Mashaun asks Tera to bring up the rear because of her wilderness experience. In the middle are the twins, then Berg and Abigail. In the evenings, Abigail plays the harp and Mai shares stories around the campfire. Everyone listens except Mashaun, who spends most evenings on the fringe of the firelight looking into the forest or gazing at the stars, jotting down coordinates he obtains from the sextant. Sometimes, Mai or Tera join him and try to start a conversation, but his answers are always cordial but short. Whenever Tera is near Mashaun, Mai keeps a close eye on them but doesn't do anything. Dalistra actually thinks it's quite comical now Mai is jealous. Sometimes, Mai gets snappy at Tera only to be told it is not necessary because Mai and Mashaun still share the same fur. It takes several weeks to reach the meadow only to find a band of awrks has set up a small village. They're about the same height as Mai, with rough gray skin. Their oversized heads have two protruding horns, with a small round ball on top. They have oversized flat feet with hands to match at the end of stubby limbs.

They move away from the meadow and set up a cold camp hidden among the thick undergrowth. Mashaun and Tera study their movements from sunup to sundown. Both agree there are around 20 awrks with a semi-permanent log-and-mud building in the middle surrounded by a half dozen small tents. They have crude bows, clubs, and spears. The group discusses its options; waiting is not one of them. Tera and Mashaun propose to draw their attention away from the cave entrance, but the group dismisses it fast. Ericka and Elina tells them they can make it to the cave unnoticed, one at a time, and it will take some time. they have to hold their hands, and creep along the wall without making a sound. It will be hard but they can do it. After some discussion, they agree to start after sunset with Mashaun going first.

They move to where the forest meets the cliff, and they creep along the cliff face with a snails pace. Elina mutters something, and they move away from the group. Then Ericka takes Tera's hand, only to have Mai grab her and and disappear. The rest remain hidden while scanning the area as they seem to fade into the wall. Once close to the cave, Mashaun starts to drag his hand along the wall, feeling for the entrance. When they find the entrance, Mashaun goes inside to make sure it is safe while Elina returns for the next person.

Mashaun keeps a watchful eye on the awrks as each member of the group makes their way along the cliff, taking half the night for everybody to arrive at the cave. Mai goes straight to the pool to clean up; the other girls join as they arrive. Berg examines the room and finds some dried blood on the beds and the floor in addition to some bones scattered around. This makes Mashaun uncomfortable, but after searching, he finds the cave empty. Once the girls are done, Mai leads them into the weapons room while Mashaun and Berg quickly bathe before joining the girls.

Once the guys arrive in the room, Mashaun retrieves the staff and hands it to Ericka. The staff begins to glow red, and the twins feel the amulet and staff tugging at each other like opposite ends of two magnets. She takes the staff out to the dome room to examine it. The tip of the staff is not round but actually has 10 unequal sides, While studying the tip, she examines the symbols on the beds and the similarities between the two. She places the staff tip in the middle figure, and it matches, as the other symbols begin to glow. Quietly she calls Mashaun, not wanting to let go of the staff.

All of them go running with weapons ready, only to find her holding the staff has the tip buried into the symbol. Berg tells her to pull it out, and as she does, the symbol becomes solid while all five symbols continue to slightly glow. Ericka understands why the clone had the staff; it is needed to activate the magic on the beds.

"If that is the case, can we go home using the beds?" Mai asks. Everybody glances at each other, shrugging their shoulders. The questions start flowing but they don't have answers. Berg pulls out the book and tries to find references. They decide to sleep in the weapons room tonight for safety reasons. The twins sleep on opposite sides of the room with their new toys next to them.

A piercing scream and the sound of metal clanging on rocks awaken them. Mashaun and Tera grab their bows and head to the dome room, only to stop short of the wall, seeing a half dozen awrks and a man fighting. He moves like a cat, both quick and agile, managing to snap one of the awrk's necks with his bare hands. Mashaun and Tera start shooting through the walls, dropping one after another. It breaks the other awrks' concentration, and the man manages to take out another one. But as he does, he takes a club to the back of his head and drops. The pair continues to fly arrows, and before long, all six lie dead on the stone floor. Everybody rushes out of hiding to help the man, but he is gone. Ericka finds one bed is messed up, and the symbols are no longer glowing. She realizes she has made the bed bring him, but why.

The bodies of the awrks lie in a pool of black blood, but there is no red blood anywhere. They quickly pull the arrows and put swords in the holes before returning to their hiding place, careful not to step in any blood. Back in hiding, they discuss about not finding the man even though they clearly saw one fighting. They come to the same conclusion as they listen to a group of awrks coming into the cave. They speak in an unintelligible language as they study their dead companions. All the awrks step aside, allowing one to move freely to the bodies. It is dressed in a robe of some kind with a necklace of teeth around his neck. He walks using a staff with a glowing tip lighting up the chamber.

From their hiding place, they witness as one of the awrks pulls a sword and studies it before replacing his with the sword in hand. Shortly they strip the bodies and carry them off to the water room before leaving the cave. After the they leave, the group searchs the dome room for any clues as to what happened; they find none. They conclude the dead were dropped into the stream, letting the current pull them through the hole under the rock wall.

During the search, Berg asks if anyone has seen Abigail. shaking their heads, they search the rooms. All they see are her clothes inside the water room doorway, with a couple of slashes and some black blood; there is no red blood or body. They conclude awrks found her hiding in the water room; she didn't stand a chance against them. They will all miss her, but they can't hang around. Berg takes her loss the hardest, feeling he failed her. As he starts to charge out the cave, Mai grabs him and Berg swings around almost hitting her, but she is quick and dodges the blow. This allows Ericka to stop his next attack before he realizes what he is doing. Ericka tells him he should be mad at her. After all, it was her actions and not Mai's that brought the man and the awrks killing him and Abigail. After calming down, Berg apologies before telling them according to the book, there is a passage leading up to a guard room, and they all fan out looking for the mysterious ladder as Tera keeps an eye on the awrks' camp.

Mashaun finds some translucent steps by the waterfall leading up to the ceiling. He climbs the steps into the ceiling, coming out at a landing. An archway leads left and the right, with the ladder continuing up. The archway on the right leads to a rectangular room with four cylinders made of some type of metal appearing to be small pipes and oar-like grips on one side, with each one mounted on the top half of a rock ball along one wall. As he approaches the wall, it begins to fade, overlooking the meadow with the awrks' village some sixty feet below. When Mashaun accidentally bumps one of the tubes, it moves easily, noticing all four tubes move surprisingly easily in unison. After looking around, he concludes this used to be a guard post for the cave. It has a good view of the surrounding area, with the four cannons acting in unison. One or two people can operate it easily. The other archway has an identical room.

Berg goes to work decoding the characters and images on the map, finding it hard to concentrate since Abigail's disappearance. Mai pushes Berg through the map to his surprise. Turning around, the map is more complete with different characters. He is still making notes when Mashaun returns from the guard post. Berg shouts with excitement which brings everybody running into the weapons room, telling him to be quiet. After they calm him down, he tells them about the two different maps and this is an outpost for Thesila. He believes the map will lead them to the city. His shout of excitement brings in some of the awrks who look around a little befuddled before leaving. Berg apologizes for being so loud. Mashaun tells him it is okay. They apparently don't know about this room.

It is late afternoon when Mashaun shows them the new room, and they each take turns trying out the canons. Ericka is playing around with them, and they don't make a sound as a ball of energy shoots out toward the building, the four hitting so close they are a straight line instead of four balls. She jumps back startled, as does everybody else. When they peek at the meadow, the central structure and several tents are gone, repoaced by piles of ash and a burnt spot. The awrks run around in different directions. Berg wants her to repeat everything she just did, including every thought, but nothing happens. Again, Ericka goes over everything she did step by step, and nothing happens. They try repeatedly with no results. Finally, Elina asks her if she thought in Thesilan. Ericka slaps her forehead. Again, four balls of energy explode on the ground, leveling the rest of the awrks' village. What few awrks can stand soon disappear into the forest.

The group spends the evening in the weapons room, discussing their options. Berg needs some more time with the maps, and Mashaun wants to climb the ladder to see where it ends. After a short discussion, they decide Mashaun and Mai will climb the ladder while Berg and Tera will stay in the cave with the twins. Berg will work on the map while the girls stand guard in case the awrks return. During the night, there is a noise, like someone dragging a foot in the cave. They follow its movements around the cave until it goes into the water room. Mashaun swords and Tera with her bow, cautiously go into the water room and find nothing.

The next morning, they find food on the table on the other side of the room. At first, they are hesitant, but they remember there was food laid out for them the first time they were here. They enjoy a meal before going on to their separate tasks. Berg uses some old cloth to draw out the maps so he can carry them. The twins go to separate attack rooms scanning the area while Tera guards the cave entrance. Mashaun and Mai climb the ladder, with Mashaun going first.

Berg makes a copy of the maps onto several different pieces of cloth before laying them on one of the beds to study. He rotates them, rearranges them, and even tries to imagine them on top of one another, but he still is confused. Using the book, he continues to hunt for clues to decode the maps. However, every answer only leads to more questions. Not knowing the language, he asks Ericka to come down. Elina wants to go down also, but the pull of the staff and the disk is getting stronger, so they stay away from each other. With Tera at the entrance and one in the perch, the cave is safe.

It doesn't take long for Ericka to notice the writing on the second map is backward. She goes to read the map from the inside of the weapons room and a symbol in the lower right corner is not on the map catches her attention. When she asks Berg about it, he tells her it wasn't there earlier. Ericka returns to study the other map. As she leaves the room, Berg watches the symbol slowly fades until it's gone. He calls Ericka back into the room. As she approaches, the symbol reappears. This time there is more of the symbol, and they figure there has to be a connection with the staff. They both call for Elina to join them. Standing between them, Berg can feel the attraction of the two. Then, a second and a third set of characters appear in the corner.

Studying the symbol and the map, Berg understands it is not a map of the land but instructions on how to find the map. Asking the twins to follow, he goes to the middle of the room and starts examining the center of the floor. In the center of the room is a small geometric hole matching the bottom of the staff. He asks Ericka to place the staff into the hole, which she does with some reluctance. Nothing happens. As he thinks about it, the sun starts to peek through the hole in the ceiling.

They stare both bewildered and amazed as the sunbeam makes it way down the wall, across the floor to the staff. There is still nothing. Berg runs into the room, gets a small polished shield, and places it on the staff, angling it, bouncing the sunlight toward the map. Elina and Berg run to the map, noticing the wall alters the beam as it shines on the back wall, revealing a detailed map with major cities including Thesilay, Thesilau, Thesilar, and Thesila. Each contains blurry numbers with a different format from the numbers Mashaun has been recording every night. Written down on one side of the map are short descriptions of each city.

Shen Sherin: Where the river braids into the sea, a strong fortress stands, among the tall weeds, is the best hope of man.

Chanvin Lake: The water boils; the air is foul, for those who toil may run afoul.

Thesilar: Hidden under the mountain high, ancient people locked in chains can only watch the world pass by, for in these forbidden halls magic still reigns.

Thesila: In the dead fire mountain lies the city of gold, with three becoming one...

The two of them start to write everything down when it suddenly stops. They ask Ericka what has happened as they find her tired, almost ready to collapse. There is something written under the pictures of Thesilau, Thesilay, Twin Rivers, Tenskie, and many others, but they run out of time as they are too blurry to read. Elina returns to the watchtower as Ericka lies down and falls asleep. Berg puts the map down and starts to make notes on it.

Tera sits on the floor by the cave entrance, keeping a vigilant eye on the forest edge in case the awrks come back or Magdalenia's men find them. She enjoys the warmth of the morning sun as it climbs into the sky once again, exposing the meadow with a burned patch in the middle where the building once stood. Late in the afternoon, some movement in the bushes by the road catches her attention. Standing up for a better view, she nocks an arrow and waits.

Chapter 21

UNINVITED GUEST

MASHAUN AND MAI CLIMB PAST the landing and up into a tree in the middle of a forest of evergreens. They scan the area mindful of any movement before stepping out of the tree into the coolness of the early morning. Once out of the tree, they turn and see it is just like all the others—with a small trunk, much smaller than their own width. Mai hangs a piece of brown cloth from a branch about eight feet off the ground before they start to scout the area. The canopy is thick, blocking much of the direct sunlight, and the needles on the ground make a muffled crunch as they walk.

They move in a zigzag pattern away from the tree for several hundred feet before returning. They do this in different directions, being cautious not to step on any sticks and watching for any signs of life in this apparently dead underbrush. Once, Mai steps on a twig, making a loud snap. Freezing, they wait but the forest remains quiet.

It is about midday when rushing water in the distance permeates quiet. Following the sound, they come upon a small clearing with a stream flowing through, then disappearing into a hole as a mist rises, dissipating just above the cave. They rest under the shade just off the clearing, enjoying the sights and sounds. Almost dozing off, they are startled when a muffled clicking noise comes from the sky. They scramble behind the tree and scan the sky and the clearing, trying to see what's behind the noise.

Two insect-like creatures land near the stream. They are a little over six feet tall and twelve-feet long with a segmented body and a pair of translucent wings. They have six legs resembling a praying mantis with two arms ending in claws. Each claw has two fixed points, and one movable part enables them to remove the packs they carry on their chest. On each side of the pack are three javelins and a sword. They seem to communicate by making a clicking sound with their mandibles.

Mashaun asks Dalistra if she is familiar with them. They call themselves Kaovjs. They are mostly peaceful, but they are unable to speak other languages, and most can't speak theirs so they pretty much keep to themselves. She has known several who have tried to speak with them, but she doesn't know of any have succeeded. Mashaun asks her if she can understand them, and she tells him no. Without saying a word, Mai stands up and walks into the clearing, keeping her hand visible to the Kaovjs. The Kaovj's eyes jerk in her direction, but otherwise, they remain motionless, relying on their camouflage as they change color, matching the grass. She gets too close as they jump in different directions, landing at an angle away from her, forcing her to face only one of them while the other stays out of her sight. Mashaun guards her from the shadows as Mai uses slow hand gestures. They slowly begin to move toward her, trying to mimic her actions. Mai moves to the stream where she gets her finger wet and writes on a rock then points to herself. The Kaovjs follow, and after some several attempts, she reaches her hand forward. The Kaovjs do the same, and they shake hands. It is a strange feeling for both—the warm, soft flesh of Mai's hand compared to the cold, hard chitin of the Kaovj's.

The other Kaovjs begin to move toward them slowly as if unsure and cautious. Mashaun steps out of the shadows with his hands in plain sight, showing he has nothing to hide. The two Kaovjs jump up and back, covering about 30 feet, landing with javelins in hand. Everybody freezes for what felt like an eternity before Mai slowly sits down on the nearby rock. She motions everyone to her as she lays out some food as if she were getting ready for a picnic. With reluctant steps, everyone moves closer to her, with one Kaovj getting to her first. She cautiously takes its claw and shakes it before putting Mashaun's hand in the Kaovj's claw. Soon, they are sharing food and using pictures to talk with each other.

Several swordsmen in full chain armor, carrying bows and swords, step out from the bushes on the other side of the meadow. They wear no insignia on their tunics. This worries her as there are only two reasons why they don't have an insignia. They are too well-armed for bandits, making them mercenaries. A couple walk around the black spot, looking at the ground, while several others scan the forest.

After they spend some time examining the burn, one of the men raises his hand, and dozens of archers come out of the woods. They break up into four groups of six, each with two warriors and four archers. After spending a little time searching the forest edge, they line up along the rocks at the edge of the cliff about 12 feet apart. The warriors then throw rocks at the wall, and the archers stand ready with bows drawn. Starting with the group closest to the trees, they listen to rocks bounce off the cliff, then they move behind all the others to the end. The next batch do the same. It is only a matter of time before they find the opening.

Tera runs and gets Berg and Ericka, grabbing all the maps before running toward the weapons room, but changing her mind at the last moment. She drags them to the water room and tells them to climb the ladder quickly, watching the doorway as they scramble up the ladder. There is an explosion outside, followed by some screams and a second explosion. Then it is quiet.

Shortly rocks bounce across the floor and skitter into the cave followed by a volley of arrows flying into the cave. These guys aren't here to take them back; they want them dead. She turns and flies up the ladder to the landing, where she fills in Berg and the twins. Elina leaning on the device mumbling she got a few, but the weapons are just too draining. The twins guard the meadow, but they are both so tired it is all they can do. The enemy find a blind spot where cliff face meets the ground. Tera has her bow ready, and Berg holds a short sword standing by the ladder.

Chain armor rustling echoes in the cave as rocks bouncing off the cave walls. For the most part, Tera can't make out what is said except she thinks Elina and Ericka names were mentioned. They listen to the intruders for some time before it gets quiet. After a while, Tera goes and quietly asks the twins if they see anything; both shake their heads. Are still in the cave, Tera has to know. She cautiously climbs down the ladder, dosen't doesn't see anybody in the water room. She peeks behind the waterfall and in the stream, making sure it's empty. Warily, she peers around the door into the dome room, where several archers stand by the cave door, watching the meadow. She counts five swordsmen and 10 archers as she listens.

One of the swordsmen has his doubts he group has been in the cave, while the obvious leader is sure the group is hiding somewhere in the cave. He tells the men Magdalenia wants her staff, the twins, and Dalistra alive—and in one piece. She doesn't care about the others as long as they end up dead. Tera returns to the landing and informs everybody what she heard. Berg is not happy they showed up. He needs more time to examine the map and it is not going to happen while the cave is in the control of this new threat. They will probably find the weapons room. If they haven't, they will eventually find the ladder. They seem to know what they are doing. Everybody believe they can hold mercenaries off for a while, but if even one makes it to the landing, it will be over. They think about continuing up the ladder, but will lead them into the unknown, trapping them between the unknown above and the professional fighters in the cave.

After lunch, Mai and Mashaun say their goodbyes to the Kaovjs and return to the tree. Mashaun takes the cloth down before stepping into the tree. The two climb down the ladder to where Tera is on guard. Tera informs them on what happened earlier. Afterward, they all form a circle as Mashaun and Mai tell them about the Kaovjs and the forest on top. Berg tells them they need to go up and head north to Thesila by Chanvin Lake. After some discussion, they will leave in the morning and they will take turns watching the ladder during the night.

The next morning, there is a thick blanket of fog, giving the forest an eerie feel they can barely see the next tree as they make their way. Moving one tree at a time, Mashaun chooses a tree a short distance away and ties a piece of cloth on a branch on the opposite side of the tree, wrapping it around the branch six times before tying it into a knot. When he returns to the group, they wonder which way is north.

The forest is deathly quiet as Mashaun listens in vain for any sound. Using the ladder as a reference point, he starts in the same direction of the stream, confident he is heading in the right direction. They stop a few times to listen and to rest. Each time they ask Mashaun where they are going, he will only answer "to a stream." After a while, the group begins to doubt him. They ask him if he is sure, they are going the right way.

"Yes," he responds.

After walking for what the assume are hours, the faint sound of falling water. Getting a bearing on the direction, they finally arrive at the stream, but the fog filters the light giving the landscape a flat misty look. Following the stream, within minutes they find it disappears into the ground, as the sound of it splashing into a deep pool somewhere in the darkness below. They decide to stop and discuss their next course of action. They overhear the sound of huge flapping wings, and an enormous shadow passes near them but the dense fog makes it impossible to see anything.

After a short rest, they continue traveling in the same direction, across the stream and through an open field. The fog begins to lift as the morning becomes afternoon, but it never completely dissipates. By night, they reach a tree line and choose to spend the night just inside the woods. They set parimeter not knowing what creatures roam about, using only two patrols per night. Tera, Elina, and Berg do the early one with Mai, Ericka, and Mashaun two follow. The next morning is cool and damp with a light fog. They can barely make out the trees in the distance, but it is a far cry better than the previous day. After having something to eat, they continue to head deeper into the forest.

They continue for days with the consistent scenery of the forest. It is an old forest with little or no ground cover. The lower branches of the trees are dead like the twigs and sticks cluttering the ground. The only reason they don't make a sound when they walk; is the fog keeps everything damp and bendable. On some days, it is thicker than others. But it is always there, giving a gloomy feel to the woods. Once, loud cry of a hawk pierces the silence. They duck for cover but don't see a thing. A few times, clinking armor, carries over the air, but they can't see anything through the fog. After traveling for a week, the forest ends at a precipice of a cliff. A faint sound of bubbling coming from somewhere below beyond their sight, as the air carries a scent of rotten eggs. They follow the cliff, looking for a way down or around.

They spend the day searching the cliff for a way down but to no avail. Berg is sure it is the Chanvin Lake at the bottom of the cliff. Out of frustration, Berg tells them there has to be a way down, but there is no mention of one. Shortly he finds a path winding along the cliff face, disappearing down in the fog. Everybody stares at him as if he were crazy, but before anybody can say anything, he steps off the cliff and starts walking down a stair-step path. Mai and Mashaun follow closely behind as the unseen path materializes before them, leading down into the mist. Tera wants to follow but can't see the path. In disbelief, she stares in disbelief as the three head down, quickly disappearing in the mist.

Believing Berg is right, Tera steps off the cliff and starts to fall. Mashaun grabs her arm to swing her on the path, but she cannot still not see the trail. Elina manages to grab Tera's other arm but is pulled off-balance, and before she can let go, Elina is pulled over the side of the cliff. The extra weight and the suddenness of Elina's fall jerk Mashaun off the trail, and the three start to fall. Before anyone else can react, they disappear into the mist below.

The remaining three stare in horror as their companions fall out of sight. Forgetting about Ericka, Berg and Mai run down the trail into the mist to reach the bottom. Near the bottom, they pass by several caves about six-feet across and nine-feet tall. The cave walls are six-feet tall before creating a perfect half circle with a three-foot radius. After passing a half dozen tunnels, they reach the bottom, but they are now a long way away from where their friends went over. The floor is solid-rock, with pools of boiling water of various sizes scattered on the landscape. The smell of rotting eggs lingers on the air.

Ericka is left alone looking over the cliff where her sister fell, when from out of the mist, Elina floats back up to the edge of the cliff, stepping on the ground. At first, Ericka is relieved, then surprised. Before she can say a word, Elina tells her she remembered the float spell, and the amulet gave her enough energy to save all three. Tera and Mashaun are on the floor, safe and waiting for the others. Ericka puts her arms around Elina's neck, and the two of them step off the cliff as a bola wraps around their feet, knocking them off-balance, sending them over the cliff where they float gently down to the base. Tera and Mashaun patiently wait for her return. Seeing the bola, they have been found and they move in the same direction as the path.

"You fool, now go get them." Someone yells behind them with the thud of a body hitting the floor.

Mai and Berg double back along the cliff face toward the direction where the three went over the cliff. The smell of rotten eggs makes them nauseous as the fog thickens to the consistency of pea soup, allowing limited visibility. The place has an ere silence, with only the bubbling water echoing off the rock walls. They feel uneasy as neither of them are fighters. And if they run into anything, it can mean trouble. They hurry along in silence not wanting to surprise anybody or anything when humanoid silhouette appears in the distance.

As they cautiously approach, they realize it is not moving. It's a man within a translucent black crystal statue holding his hands up, protecting his face of sheer terror. The statue isn't smooth as they expected. It is pitted and sharp like old snow after being in the sun for a few days. When Mai touches the statue, black powder brushes off in her hand, turning her skin yellow with a slight burning sensation and smelling like burned lard. After Berg pours some water on Mai's hand, they quicken their pace as they move along the wall. A little while later, they see a couple of silhouettes in the distance. Moving closer, they realize it's the other four.

They quietly greet everybody and exchange stories, deciding it is best not to linger in one place more than a moment. They head out, keeping the wall on their right. They walk in a single file with Mashaun in front, followed by Mai, Berg, Elina, Ericka, and Tera in the rear. Soon they pass by a Kaovjs with its wings spread out as if it were trying to fly, a giant human standing 15-feet tall, and a group of awrks. They are all black, crystalline, with some more pitted than the others, and all with the same expression of horror. Mashaun asks Dalistra if she remembers any stories about flesh turning into black crystals covered with ash such as these. She tells him she has never heard of such stories.

The wall has numerous caves identical to the ones Berg and Mai passed on the way down the trail. Six inches off the floor is the first of three rows of caves. The next row up is off-set, with the top row being above the bottom row. There is a narrow path leading from the bottom tunnel, angling up, passing another tunnel, and ending at the top one. The pattern continue around the walls. The pitch-black tunnels run straight back, with smooth sides like the cave. The moisture clings to the walls, turning them black like the statues. Mashaun tosses a pebble down one, and it stops before hitting the back.

The fog begins to fade as night approaches, and the group doesn't like the options of either spending the night in the caves or out in the open. They decide it will be safer in one of the upper caves. One by one, they head up the narrow path with Mashaun and Tera up front, finding the cave has a T intersection about 30 feet back.

Figuring if they are attacked, it has to come from one of two possible ways. It is more defensible, but they really don't want to meet whatever created the statues. They use whatever is available to protect them from the black soot. Even Dalistra feels the burning when the soot touches her.

They awake the following morning to the sound of rain and water cascading down the side of the walls. The light rain dissipates the fog, allowing them to see the silhouette of the distant wall and the floor covered with a sheet of water, with more than a score of statues jetting up out of the water. Some are twice as tall as Mashaun, while others are half their size with some of the crystals broken.

The boiling acidic water which is just a few inches deep removes the fur on their boots as they trudge across the floor. The group uses the path on the wall leading to the caves. Dalistra tells him what each is as they pass by Kaovjs, Tsaubs, awrks, orks, and humans. Some are in small groups, but most stand alone. None of the statues have any weapons, but all have the look of terror, even the Kaovjs. Some of the crystal statues are broken, leaving the inside filled with a yellowish liquid and a acrid oder. It takes several hours to reach the far side of the depression where there are no statues and the water boils, releasing a yellow vapor, filling the air with the foul stench of rotten eggs.

The tunnels continue around the wall even over the lake. The rain keeps the mist down, allowing them to scan the landscape while it also cools the air. Tera, Mai, and Berg take out a foldable cube with one side open. Tera hands hers to Mashaun. Dalistra tells him if he stays in front of them, he won't need any light. He thanks Tera, but tells her he won't need one. She offers it to the twins and Elina accepts it. The cubes are made of tin holding a small candle lasting for a few hours. It has a small handle attached to the back. Tera's cube has a dial with four triangular slots on three sides and with a handle attachment. When Tera finishes unfolding hers, she rotates one of the wheels, and a strong beam of light fills the tunnel. When they ask her about the light cube, she tells them her mother had it for a long time and gave it to her at the gatehouse when they left.

They all light their cubes and head into the dark, moist tunnel. With all the light behind him, Mashaun has no problem seeing. But he thinks there is too much light, so he asks them if they can put out a few. Mai puts hers out, and Tera gives hers to Mai, allowing Tera the freedom to use both hands. After a short bit, the tunnel comes to a T intersection, angling up to the left and down on the right. Mashaun takes them to the right, down the sloping passage only to come to another intersecting passage. Going to the right, they return to a cave overlooking the lake. They spend the entire day wandering the labyrinth of tunnels, occasionally finding a small room about three times the width of the caves. Their boots are nothing more than rags on their feet, and they use some fabric from their clothes to mend them.

Chapter 22

CHANVIN LAKE GUARD

THEY SPEND SEVERAL DAYS IN the maze of caves, occasionally finding their way to an entrance, only to realize they are going around the lake and they seldom drop to ground level. On the third day, the sound of rushing water brings smiles, but it is different from before. Following the sound, they find an entrance. The only way to reach it is to cross the boiling water. On their side is a stream flowing out of a cave and into the lake. The rain dwindles then stops. The mist starts to form on the water. Across the lake, they see a human on the rocky shore skulking. Tera tells them he might be one of the men chasing them. While staring at him in disbelief, they are impressed with Tera's eyesight recognizing the man at such a great distance.

He is wildly running around when a snake-like creature exits one of the lower caves with an overall length of more than 20 feet. It is holding its head up like a cobra and it stands at least eight-feet tall. Two of its four arms wield swords, and the other, two shields. With its tail, it tosses a sword and a shield to the man. Mashaun thinks about shooting it, but Dalistra tells him it isn't worth it. They're over 200 yards away. *We can hit the creature, but to what end?* She is right of course. Reluctantly, the man picks up the sword and shield and prepares to fight. The two trade blows until the man is exhausted. The snake backs off and let the man rest a little, before continuing to press its attack.

They realize the snake is playing with him like a cat with its prey. It goes on for some time until the man gets tired of fighting and throws down his weapon, producing a loud clang reverberating off the basin walls. The snake makes a few more swipes at the man who instinctively backs away. It makes swipes from each side before wrapping its tail around him so he can't move in any direction. Then a black gas engulfs the man. When the gas dissipates, there is another statue to the collection. The snake picks up the weapons and disappears into one of the lower caves.

They want to do something but they are helpless; they can only witness from afar. Tera says she wants to kill the creature, but weapons don't seem to have much affect.

"It's fast for its size, and if it gets into trouble, it can just turn us into statues and it's all over," Mai says.

Mashaun points out the group has an advantage. The snake does not know about them. If they keep to the upper tunnels, they may have a chance since they are higher than the creature. When Dalistra questions him, Mashaun tells her he wants to face it on his terms.

Once across the lake, Tera and Mashaun position themselves in a couple of upper-level tunnels where they a vantage point a shot when it comes out of the cave. Mai, Berg, and the twins are on the floor, talking loudly about the statues, trying to draw the creature out of its hole. They keep moving, not staying bunched up. They continue until the creature slithers out of a tunnel. They split up, heading to different ramps to the upper tunnels. The creature appears ready for battle. Atop the snake's body is a repulsive woman's head with snakelike eyes. Its scales glisten in the waning sunlight. Moving with lightning speed toward Mai as Ericka creates a ball of energy in her hand and hurls it at the snake, briefly engulfing it in a sphere of crackling miniature yellow lightning bolts. The snake turns and heads toward Ericka.

Tera's arrows stick but fall out just as quick. Mashaun's arrow sticks but it doesn't faze the creature. He quickly fires a second arrow but the result is the same. The snake closes in on Ericka when Mashaun jumps to the floor with a yell and shoots again hitting the snake in the shoulder and getting its attention. It turns, charging him with her weapons, ready for battle. With two swords, it attacks with lightning speed. Using the statues as cover, he runs from one to another, taking shots when he can. The statues don't seem to help so he switches to the swords. The snake runs over the statues, turning them into dust. Mashaun can't dodge it

181

forever, with all his bobbing, swerving and dodging, he barely gets any attacks in. When he hits the creature, the swords only bounce off as it grins at him. Dalistra tells him to forget the swords and run.

Mai and Berg charge in for a strike, but its tail always knocks them aside before they are close, almost sending them into the bubbling acrid water. Tera keeps shooting but to no avail. Ericka throws a few more spells before finding refuge in a cave with Elina. She's tired. The group continues their attack but the attacks are useless. It keeps its focus on Mashaun. In desperation, Ericka runs out and hits the creature with the staff, creating a bright flash, and leaving a red burn on the creature.

Seeing the red staff, the snake lets out a bloodcurdling shreek and turns her focus to Ericka. Mashaun hits the snake in the back. This time, it ignores him and chases Ericka around the floor. Ericka and Mashaun crisscross, trying to confuse it long enough for Ericka to make it into the cave system. At one point, Mashaun jumps on its tail, allowing Ericka to hide in one of the caves while the snake shakes him to the ground. Mashaun gets up and continues to use the remaining few statues as cover. The snake continues chasing him around, eventually trapping him by the water's edge. Out of ideas and out of breath, he prepares to make one last feeble attempt as he realizes it has been playing with him, just like what it did with the man before.

He yells at them to run while they have a chance as the creature gets to within a few swords' lengths. Dalistra tells Mashaun to look at its chest. Between her breast hangs a yellow disk amulet similar to Elina's red disk. The creature asks if Mashaun is ready to give up its weapons and admit defeat. Mashaun asks the creature its name, and this surprises her. No one has ever asked her name before.

"My name is Siguredea. What is yours?"

"Mashaun," he says, moving closer.

"Now," Dalistra says. And in one last desperate move, he feints left and swings around like a cat, breaking the chain causing the necklace to drop on the ground. A cloud of yellow mist rises, obscuring everything before dissipating, showing Mashaun a barren landscape with Siguredea in front of him.

The group witness the mist quickly thickening, making it impossible to see more than a sword length away. Only the distant waterfalling into the bubbling water and some faint voices echoing off the walls. Slowly, they feel their way around, quietly calling out, finding one another but not the snake or Mashaun.

Siguredea stares at the surroundings with watery eyeswhile smiles, saying, "I'm home, I am home at last, but this is not right."

What's not right?" Mashaun asks still holding his swords in case Siguredea attacks. The air is putrid and thick. It all he can to do to keep his insides from hurling out.

"The mages trapped me ages ago with a curse. Only someone not from this world could take the amulet freeing me, from this curse." she says, pulling the arrows from her back with her tail. She glancing them then the arrows in his quiver.

"You hit me! I was also told only the Thesilan magic could harm me, and it has not been around for a very long time." she says, handing them back to him.

"What else were you told?" Mashaun asks her.

"Only the Thesilan Queen would free me, but you are not her," she says.

"No, I am not," he replies.

"As her representative, I command the curse to be broken and you may return home." Mashaun tells her.

"Whether you are the queen or Mashaun, I don't care. I am free at last," she says enthusiastically.

"Before I take my leave, I would ask one more question. Where are you from? You don't act, talk, or fight like anyone else," she finally asks.

"I am not from this world," Mashaun says.

Siguredea studies him for some time before saying, "That explains it."

"Explains what?" he replies.

Why you were able to take the talisman, you are not from this world, you speak for the queen, so the prophecy has begun."

"There is one more thing to tell you before I return home. Listen and remember. Behind eyes that cannot see and a mouth that cannot speak lies the tome of a lost queen and the salvation of the land." Siguredea says. A yellow mist engulfs him again, but when it fades, he is back in the pit.

The group scans the the pit for the snake. Mashaun tells them she is gone for good as they ask him what happened. He starts to tell them what happened when an bolt shatters on the stone floor next to him. Tera returns fire at the archers on the cliff. However, the distance is too far, and the group runs into one of the caves. Using the caves' interconnections, the group moves around the pit across the lake.

Someone yells for Mashaun. At first, he does not answer but decides the only way he'll know what they want is to talk to them. *This is a safe place,* he thinks. The person on top of the cliff introduces himself as Rangier before telling them he only wants the twins. Mashaun refuses. Rangier tells them Magdalenia will pay a good price for them, and he will split it. Again, Mashaun refuses, thinking it is a delaying tactic.

They move to a different cave. They see several archers and swordsmen searching the caves. Mashaun, and Tera, drop them with arrow and Ericka impales another with an ice spear, sending the others back into the caves.

"Nice try," Mashaun yells back. "Call your men back and we will let them live." After a time he agrees and four warriors come out of hiding and scale the cliff face with ropes thrown down, disappearing away from the edge.

In the evening, Mashaun tells them about his encounter with Siguredea. They are surprised to find out it has a name and it's from another world also. Berg mumbles how many worlds connect to this one, He tells them about the world he saw and the mage trapped her. Siguredea told him only Dalistra can free her but was surprised to find out his name is Mashaun.

Mashaun asks the group if they have ever heard of Dalistra. Ericka tells them she heard Magdalenia talk about her a few times, mainly telling different people to find her. Elina thinks she heard a reward of five red for her. Berg flips through his book then reads Dalistra is the destroyer and the savior of Thesila. He turns to another section of the book.

"I have put Dalistra in a safe place until the prophecy is ready to reveal itself," he reads. "Dalistra and a stranger will come together and return the ancients and their magic." He tells them it is all the book says about her. This frightens Dalistra for the first time in a long time. She is the prophecy and she doesn't know why and it scares her. Mashaun senses her fear as the group spend the night in the caves.

The next morning is clear, and the smell of rotten eggs is gone. They spot a seven-stone path made of circular rocks in the lake, leading to a cave opening they had not seen earlier. Jumping on the first one, Mashaun finds it unstable, like a piece of wood floating on the water. He runs across them to the cave, almost sinking. They ask Elina about floating them across the water, but she tells them she only learned how to move something up and down. The twins and Berg don't want to go across the stones so scout for another way. Tera ties one end of the rope to an arrow and shoots it into the cave, with Mashaun and Tera on each end. Ericka holds on to Elina as they float, pulling themselves along the rope. Mai runs across the rocks, almost slipping once, finding the bubbling water cooler than expected. Berg floats with Elina, and Tera brings up the rear across the rocks.

This time they choose straight wherever possible. Mashaun leads the way down the darkened passageway past a dozen intersections. The tunnel goes up and down. Sometimes, it also curves. There is no telling night from day inside the seemingly endless tunnel. Once, they stop and take a long break, giving everyone a chance to nap and eat.

After hours of walking, the passage opens into a cavern. The walls have many smaller caves, with massive square pillars down the center covered in ornate carvings. A waterfall hitting deep waters echos in the otherwise silent, darkened grotto. With slow and deliberate steps, they walk to the pillars in the center of the room. They find dozens of pillars around the cavern, each having two archways going through the base, one in each direction. About nine feet up from the floor, each pillar has a sphere slowly glowing brighter as the party approaches them and dims as they walk away. To the surprise of everybody, there is no dirt or even dust on anything. They find the waterfall. It is almost 30-feet high. At the base of the falls is a circular medium-size pond flowing out to the center of the room and disappears under an archway. Mashaun is the first to stick his hand into the water. It tastes clean and cold, like a mountain stream. It is a good place to rest, and after just a few minutes, they fall asleep.

Chapter 23

THESILARS

THE GROUP SLEEPS FOR A long time before the sound of scuttling feet awake them. At first, they don't see a thing. Slowly, the shadows seem to move closer. Gradually Mashaun rises to his feet, grabbing Dalistra, He asks who they are, and why he slept so soundly. She tells him they are the thesilars, and according to legend they disappeared after she became a bow.

"How dangerous are they?" Mashaun wonders. Dalistra doesn't know.

Everybody wakes up. Mashaun whispers to them not to move. Mashaun walks to the shadow which moves away as he advances. He offers a greeting as he moves, hoping someone will step forward. After a moment, one of the shadowy figures moves out and separates from the rest. However, it's hard to tell anything about the shadow except for it's a little taller and thinner. It speaks in Mashaun's head in a language neither Dalistra nor Mashaun understands. Mashaun slowly shakes his head telling them he doesn't understand.

The shadowy figure points at Elina and motions for her to go to him. She rises and walks toward the shadow with slow and methodical steps. As she approaches, the amulet around her neck begins to glow. Slowly, words become visible. She reads them aloud. The words who are you appear in her medallion followed by what do you want. She repeats the phrases and peers at Mashaun with pleading eyes for an answer. Before he can answer, a new message appears. How did you defeat the demon? Again, Elina repeats the words. Mashaun introduces himself and then the rest of the group starting with Elina. He tells them they are travelers who are seeking knowledge.

"What demon?" he asks. The four-armed snake by the lake appears on the disk.

"Oh, you mean Siguredea. It wasn't hard. I just sent her home," Mashaun tells them. The party glare at him with pomposity. From the shadows, there is a low murmur, and the party can feel the tension increase. Elina backs up, and Mashaun steps forward when Elina shout "NO" a couple of times, with fear in her voice. Mashaun reads the sphere to see the word Thesilans appear in red. Puzzled at first, he remembers what Siguredea told him about the wizards binding her there to guard the lake. The shadows start to move around them.

"No!" Elina shouts.

A shadow points to Ericka with the staff and the words mage, deceiver, and murderer appears in the globe. Again, Mashaun says no while holding his hands up. The shadows seem to materialize before them, brandishing long, narrow curved blades and closing in around them, ready for a fight. Mashaun quickly says they are not from this world, and they just want to go home.

"The Thesilans are dead, and they are gone from this world." The shadows stop, and the word demons appear.

"No, we're not demons. We're not Thesilans, we are just people." Mashaun says, shaking his head. The shadows stop moving for a moment before they fade back into the massive blackness of one. Is this true appears. Mashaun and the rest of the group nod their heads.

Your thoughts do not lie.

Apologies.

Greetings.

It has been a long time since anyone has visited us.

Elina repeats the words, and they nod their heads. The shadow introduces herself as Sabinina of Thesilar's crystal-growers caste. Mashaun, in turn, introduces the group to Sabinina.

Sabinina asks about the creature outside, and Elina says it is gone.

"He sent it home." She points at Mashaun, and the shadows nod. The group is excited they found the Thesilans. However, the shadows remind them they are thesilars. The shadows continue asking questions about the outside for some time. Sabinina asks them to follow. The thesilars slowly surround them as Sabinina leads them across the expanse of the cave. Like the waves of an ocean, the shadows flow in and out, sometimes touching one of the party members in a curious way.

Sabinina leads them to a large room off the main cavern with several large circular tables. There are about half dozen chairs on the inside and over a dozen chairs outside each table. At one side of the table is an opening about two chairs wide, allowing passage to the inner chairs. All of it are grown from the rock itself. The light in the room is a little brighter, like a clear night with a full moon. They can clearly see their hosts have large, bat-like ears and noses while their eyes are slightly smaller than normal. The shadows invite each person to sit on the inside of a different table. Cold fruits and vegetables are set down in front of them. Each of them has a sphere placed in front of them translating words both ways.

Until now, their questions are focused on the outside world and their own world. Sabinina tells them they have lived underground for dozens of generations ever since the Thesilan summoned all the rock shapers to the capital. Shortly the demon showed up and trapped them in the caves. For hundreds of years, the three castes made up the Thesilans and lived peacefully together.

"We worked as a team to improve the lives of all—the Thesilar or crystal growers, the Thesilau or water shapers, and the Thesilay or light benders. We would grow the rocks or the holes in the rocks while the water shapers created the waterfall, supplies us with an abundant clean water, and the light benders harnessed the powers of light. They created the light spheres, but they need the sunlight to recharge, and we have not been able to recharge ours."

There used to be four Thesilan cities: Thesilau, the city under the water where the water shapers lived; Thesilar, which is where they are right now, the city under the mountain; Thesilay, the city of light in the desert; and the fourth and most beautiful, Thesila, the city on the mountain, the ruling city of all the lands. It was the most glorious of all the cities, with its crystal edifices reaching toward the sky.

"Even though each city is built for each caste, all lived harmoniously. But slowly we went our own ways, and when the council called all the rock shapers, supposedly to find a way to bring everybody together again, but they never returned. We had no way to leave and have been trapped ever since." When the group realize this is not Thesila, and their hearts sink.

About halfway through the meal, Sabinina leans forward, touching her head to Mashaun, asking about the bow and if all bows can speak with their owners. Before Mashaun can answer, Dalistra tells them not all weapons have the ability to do so. They also choose their partners.

"We are not on our own. We are a team," she says in a stern and almost condescending voice. Her response startles Mashaun.

"I meant no disrespect but when we were sent here, they were trying to make more spirit weapons." Dalistra's tone is mellow, and the two talk about spirit weapons for a long time. When Sabinina leans back, Mashaun still has to use the globe to talk with any of their hosts, understanding by touching his forehead, it becomes a private question.

The meal drags on, and Mashaun is running out of things to talk about while Mai and the twins are talking effortlessly with several different thesilars at once. The problem with using the globes is you can't tell who is talking. Mashaun excuses himself and gets up to leave. Sabinina joins him as he walks out the door. The rest of the group are involved with their conversations with only Elina seeing him leave.

Once outside the room, he enjoys quietness though he can vaguely hear the other conversations. He wonders how he can talk with her without a talking globe.

"Just think and I can understand, just like Dalistra. I know you are a little uncomfortable, but I am sure you trust Dalistra to keep my thoughts straight." Dalistra gives him a firm yes.

Okay, he thinks. *"I have hundreds of questions, let start with where do you grow your food?"* Sabinina tells him it is quite a way, but she's will show him. During the tour, Mashaun asks her, *"Why did you go private to ask me about Dalistra, instead of asking through the globes?"* Sabinina tells him she gets the feeling the others do not know about Dalistra. All he will tell her is it's complicated, and she lets it drop. She leads them down a long tunnel branching into five other tunnels before opening up into a huge room with light coming from the ceiling.

Rows of plants cover the ground. On the far wall, a steady stream cascades down the wall from the ceiling, splashing in a pool on the cave floor. Then the water flows among the plants then out a second hole. Parts of the ceiling have windows where gentle light beams, piercing the darkness as though they are underwater.

"This is just one of many such rooms. But there is not enough light here to charge the globe," Sabinina tells him as they walk through the cavern. She takes him through the garden, showing him the different vegetables between the furrows for water as butterflies flutter about.

"Have you considered getting out through the holes in the roof?" he asks. She lightly chuckles as she tells him the magic barrier lets the light through, but not the water from Upper Chanvin Lake.

Ah, so that explains the filtering light, he thinks, and she says *yes* then apologizes for reading his thoughts.

Back at the meal, Berg asks how the moons and the staffs are connected. The room becomes quiet as a churchyard. The group nervously glances at one another, their hosts, and the door, not knowing what to expect. At the same time, the thesilars become still, and the spheres become cloudy even though Berg and rest of the party know the thesilars are talking among themselves.

Finally, Ericka asks. "What?" They all turn and stare at her before the globes clear up, telling them they will have to let Sabinina tell them since she is the keeper of the past.

After the meal, they show the group to a small round room. There is nothing but the floor, walls, and the ceiling. It will serve as their room during their stay. Mai stares at the opening, asking about a door.

The Thesilar looks at the doorway. *"That is the door."*

Mai shakes her head and thinks of a door closing and the opening. He shakes his head, telling them there is no need for a door here and they are safe.

None of them likes not having a door, especially when there's a thesilar just outside. When the girls want to go to the pool to wash up, the person at the door makes them wait until several thesilars show up to escort them as the caverns are east to loose ones way. But Mai believes there is more. One of the thesilars tells her the real reason is they don't need doors, forgetting they read minds. The four wash up in the pool as the two thesilars stand like statues, almost invisible in the faint light. Once they return, Berg goes to clean up with one of the thesilars. He tries to start up a conversation, but the thesilar's demeanor is opposite from what they showed during the meal. It is quiet and almost cold. When giving him an answer, it is terse and callous. The Thesilar doesn't take him back to the room. Instead, he leads Berg in a different direction. When he tries to protest, he gets a searing pain in his head so he nervously follows his silent guide. They go down several tunnels before it opens up into a dimly lit room with rows and rows of thin stone tablets. The thesilar motions him to enter, which Berg does, asking if he can touch the tablets. The thesilar tells him to be very careful with them as they are the history of the world before the imprisonment. Berg's face beams with excitement and curiosity, hoping he can fill in some of the missing pieces.

The tablets are no thicker than a magazine. They are about one yard by a half yard, leaning on marble-like stands as one will display a decorative plate. Upon close examination, he finds the writing carved through the stone, seeing the stand behind it. He gently picks up the tablet, finding it lighter than expected and easy to hold. He turns it toward one of the light globes so he can clearly see the writing. The letters appear more like foreign symbols. He tries to find some recognizable characters similar to he had studied but to no avail. His excitement soon fades to disappointment as he gently replaces one stone after another. He walks up and down the aisles, passing hundreds if not thousands of tablets, stopping periodically to examine the writing. He hopes to find something recognizable. Disappointed, he leaves with the thesilar, returning to the room where the girls are glad to see him.

Soon after Berg's return, Sabinina shows up with Mashaun. Sabinina asks Berg if he found the annals from the past useful. He thanks her but he shakes his head. She tells them to rest. They will be going outside around sunset. Ericka starts to ask about the staffs and the moons, but Sabinina cuts her off, telling her it will become clear this evening when they go outside. She walks off, looking at the guard as she leaves. Mashaun and Berg spend a few moments sharing to everybody what they saw before resting.

As they lie on the floor, they try not to think of anything for fear it will be overheard. To their surprise, the floor warms up to each of their taste and soon, each of them drifts off to sleep. Ericka intended to stay awake for fear they will take her staff but she succumbs to the warming floor and silence. Before they know it, they wake up to the sound of soft voices and shuffling feet outside. After a meal of fruits and juice, they all head up to the surface. It is a lot shorter than they remember, and they are at the entrance in no time. Mashaun and Tera scan the cliff for archers but don't see any and move out into the open.

Chapter 24

THE NEW EMPRESS

THE ENTIRE PIT IS IN shadow as the steam rises from the lake. Mashaun jumps from rock to rock until he reaches the far shore. Sabinina starts to follow when the rock starts to sink. She jumps back. The rock wobbles and sinks but only partly. berg chuckles at the irony. He jumps and waits and the same thing happens. He continues across the lake with the same result. The acidic boiling water is neutralized when covering the rocks for a short time.

The rest of the group follow shortly as the Thesilars tremor in fear. In a procession they jump on the stones crossing the bubbling lake. This is the first time they notice the Thesilars' eyes have skin grown over the eye sockets, leaving them blind. It is a little uncomfortable staring at the eyeless faces. Sabinina understands their uneasiness. The group senses relief and happiness from the Thesilars as they begin to gather at the shore. Sabinina tells them she has dreamed of this day since she was a child. Smiling, she tells them the previous elders said it was a foolish dream.

The air quickly cools as the sunlight gives way to the darkness before the moons rise in the western sky. Sabinina asks what color the globe and the staff are. Everyone at once said red, and they see the shock on her face.

"What is it?" Mashaun asks.

"That is the staff of the rock shapers, the staff of our ancestors," she replies.

Ericka holds on to the staff even tighter, fearing they may want it back. Sensing her fear, Sabinina tells her none of them can use it because

193

they don't have the ability anymore. Besides, the staff is just a holder for the disk, which is the real power of the mage. Elina begins to back away, clutching her red disk under her shirt.

"What! They are not together?" Sabinina said, surprised. The twins thoughts reveal they are the youngest members of the group and only now realizes they are alike in many ways. They have been quiet and have not drawn any attention to themselves. Suddenly, they are the focus of everybody, including a group of men on the cliff, watching under the cover of night.

"May I have a closer look at the staff?" Sabinina politely asks Ericka.

At first, Ericka refuses. But with some encouragement and assurance from Sabinina nothing will happen, Ericka reluctantly hands the staff to her. She runs her hand up to the basket telling them *It's broken here so the disc could be removed!* She appears puzzled as if she were asking herself, *Why would someone want to remove the disc?* She returns the staff to Ericka.

Shy of its apex, the life crescent moon climbs into the night sky, as the cliff precipice glows crimson advertising the rise of a full fire moon. Sabinina asks to see the disk, and Elina is a little less reluctant to hand it over.

"Yes, this is full of magic," Sabinina says while returning it to Elina. Dalistra tells Mashaun she doesn't like Sabinina's tone when she handed back the disk. As Flalib crest the nearby ridge, the terrain sparkles like red fire flies, as the basin floor turns into an eerie burgundy glow. Their host fade from dark silhouettes to shades of red shadows with cat-like features. The red disk brightens and begins to pulsate in Elina's hands. Sabinina tells Elina to hold the stone up and face the moon if she wants to see some true magic. Elina isn't sure if she is ready for this but does it anyway.

At first, nothing happens. Suddenly a red bolt of lightning shoots out of the disk, arching to Elina and so on until the energy bolt has reached everybody. It cumulates with the caves, glowing red, and then the staff begins to glow and shake. There is a flash of blinding red light with an explosion knocking everybody backwards. Several Thesilars fall into the lake and disappear. The force tears the staff from Ericka's hands, and the disk chain snaps sending it to the basket. The staff spins on its vertical axis appearing as a sphere. Remaining quiet, everyone is on the ground. Elina is the first to regain awareness and quickly grabs the disk to find it is now one with the staff.

One by one, they slowly regain their senses and wonder what happened. Ericka tells Elina she wants her staff back in no uncertain terms. Elina eyes the staff and disk spinning in a complete basket. She likes the power coursing through her body, telling Ericka they had become one and she's keeping it. When Ericka tries to take the staff by force, she finds herself tossed back several yards away. Everyone stares at the altercation in disbelief. After which, Elina appears woozy and needs help standing wanting to rest but is afraid Ericka will try to take it from her again. Realizing she is too weak to do anything about it now.

The Thesilars kneel before their new mage, who by the ancient laws is now their leader. The rest of the group just stand there in amazement except for Berg, who goes and helps Ericka up.

"I suggest we take our leave now. I do not like the direction we are heading." Dalistra says.

Mashaun tries to say something, but Dalistra is insistent.

Just as Mashaun begins gathering up Mai and the others, Elina tells them to stay the night as the Thesilars surround them, making sure they aren't going anywhere. The guards escort them to their room where several thesilars stand outside. They think about escaping, but their heads begin to feel like fire so they drop the idea.

Elina and Sabinina, along with several others, go to a larger room with its own running water and a raised platform for a table with several rock stools around it. On one side is a door leading into a bedroom and another doorway leading into a room with a small toilet. Sabinina and Elina sit at the table along with a couple of others with Elina placing her back to the wall, leaning the staff on her shoulder.

Elina studies the room, enjoying her newfound authority. Moreover, she understands the connection between the moons and mages, thinking Berg is a fool for not seeing it. The disk captures the energy of each moon, and the staff channels it, giving the wielder an immense power. When used under a full moon the two maximize the magic. She also realizes the brightness of the moon determines the power in the disk. She understands how magic works, and now she needs to learn how to control it and not letting it control her like Magdalenia. She lets out a soft chuckle.

Sabinina starts to ask her a question when Elina glares at her. "What?"

"Your Highness, what do we do to the people you showed up with?" Sabinina humbly asks.

Elina thinks for a while, and any thesilar trying to read her thoughts receives a sharp pain their head. Her first thought is to keep them, but it will only lead to problems down the road. She can just kill them, but they save her and she owes them a debt of gratude. What about her older sister? She cannot just kill her. Or can she? No, she can't kill them because that's just not her, and Mashaun did free her from Magdalenia. She entertains the idea of keeping her sister close, but she will not look down on her. She finally makes up her mind.

She asks Sabinina if there is a throne room. With great joy, Sabinina tells her yes, getting up to lead Elina. Elina tells Sabinina she wants her friends in the throne room. Sabinina sends several thesilars to fetch them while Sabinina leads her to a great hall. The throne room is huge with a cathedral-like ceiling, and the walls covered with ornate etchings. She walks into the room, and the figures on the wall seem to come alive and dance as she strolls down the center aisle to the majestic chair at the end. The room brightens up like the rising of a new moon until the entire room is basking in the glow of the red moon.

She tells Sabinina she wants all Thesilars in this room to witness her first command as their new empress. Soon the thesilars enter the room and take their places on the rows of rock benches. The guards lead the group to the front row. There are guards standing at the end of the bench.

"I have a bad feeling about this," Dalistra says again.

"I do, too," Mashaun replies.

The guards at the end tell them to be quiet even though they are only thinking. Soon the hall is filled, with some standing along the walls. Sabinina walks up and stands next to Elina, telling everybody to be quiet. She has the rare honor to introduce their new empress, Elina, the first keeper of the red staff in over 2,000 years. Elina stands up, and all the Thesilars bow their heads. Elina taps the staff, and everybody turns their eyes at her. She scans the room, pleased with the number of subjects who fill the room. The power swell within her and she likes it.

Sabinina gives Elina a long, red leather cloak, draping it over her shoulders. It is just a little short of reaching the ground. It has a black cotton collar lined with dozens of gems and stone rings of red, blue and yellow. She wears a golden tiara filled with a multitude of gems and precious stones. Her staff glows with an eerie red aura surrounding her. She stands for some time, enjoying being the center of attention, before uttering her first unmemorable words as their new empress.

Her speech is short and sweet. None from the group wants to spend much time listening to her rambles but the Thesilars hang on to her every word. Elina asks Mai, Berg, and Mashaun to approach. Several of the thesilars follow them to the landing just a few steps away from the throne. Elina announces they are free to leave so long as they agree not to tell anybody about this place. They all nod in agreement. Mashaun can tell Elina is getting tired and this cannot go much longer. Elina dismisses the three and tells Ericka and Tera to approach. They may leave with Mashaun, never to return, or stay as part of her entourage.

Tera quickly chooses to go with Mashaun. Ericka takes a minute. If she stays, she may be able to retrieve her staff, but being her sister's handmaiden is not something she wants. If she leaves, she will probably never have a chance, but, she decides to leave with Mashaun.

As they walk down the aisle, Mai turns around to see Elina nearly collapsing onto the throne. Sabinina and the Thesilars in her chambers usher everyone out of the room. Six Thesilars escort the group to the entrance. The Thesilars give them some food while reminding them to never return and speak of this place. They cross the rocks and make camp on the far side, wondering how they will leave the pit. But. for now, they rest in one of the caves.

The dawn comes way too early, but they need to find a way up the cliff. After a short time, Berg finds a narrow path leading up the side of the cliff's face and starts walking up. The others rush to where he is, already about 10 feet off the ground, and he points to where the path meets the floor. Mai and Mashaun barely see the path and start to climb when Ericka says she doesn't see anything. The three of them point to the path, and Mashaun even jumps off the trail to the floor, taking her by the arm and leading her to the path. He puts her in front of him as they walk. She stays on the floor, and he begins to climb. Tera stands off and just stares confused, mutters about not seeing the trail. This creates some doubt to others. Mai is the first to drop, then Mashaun. He yells up at Berg saying they're right behind him. Berg continues to the top before turning around, seeing all of them at the bottom.

Berg yells down, asking why they haven't come up the path. Mashaun tells him it vanished right from under them. Berg puts his foot out to step on the path to show them it is still there, as the three of them yell "No!" He starts to walk back down the path when Mai runs directly under him, yelling at him to stop. like a fading dream, it begins to dawn on him there really is no path. He starts to slide and quickly jumps for the edge, catching himself by his arms. After some scrambling, a hand grabs him and pulls him up. There are three warriors with their finger to their lips. He yells back he is okay.

They spend several hours searching for another way up the cliff, and just when it appears hopeless, Mai finds a group of ledges over the lake. She figures with a running start, she can land on the lowest one and jump her way to the top. However, if she misses, she is going to swim in the lake. She will probably be cooked before anyone can save her. *It is simple,* she thinks. *Don't miss.* She doesn't want anyone to ruin it, so she asks Mashaun to take the two girls and search the other side of the pit for a while. Once they are far enough from her, she takes a running leap and lands on the first ledge. Berg watches her jump, landing on an invisible ledge. He runs over to the area just above her to give her some encouragement even though he does not see the ledges. When she gets close to the top, a hand helps her up.

Soon Mai is looking down, telling them about the ledges. The three of them hunt for the ledge but don't see them even though Mai gives them crystal-clear directions. Berg tells Mai the ledges are not there. She has found them because she wanted to find them just like the path he found, but he doesn't know why Ericka and Tera can't see them.

Mashaun and the others spend hours looking for a way up the cliff face as they run out of daylight. None of them wants to be there if Elina comes to the surface. As the shadows begin to cover the floor, Mashaun has an idea. It is a long shot at best. They will go into the caves and he will find the exit. After all, there has to be one, right?

With Ericka holding on to his shirt and Tera holding on to Ericka, they enter the largest of the caves. Using only Mashaun's sense of feel, they make their way down the many endless passages. Mashaun says to himself through the entire time there has to be an exit somewhere. Tera wants to use her light, but Mashaun tells her no. For this to work, they can not see. Time drags in the pitch-black darkness of the cave until he uses his hand to follow the wall. After a moment it isn't the smooth cave wall, but coarse dirt and roots. Continuing up the path, he begins to smell fresh air, and soon they step out of the car-size rock onto the plains a little way from the pit. The moons have started to peek over the distant horizon, and off in the distance, he can see several figures kneeling over something.

They start to approach when several swordsmen and a couple of archers stand up around Berg and Mai. Mashaun tells them to hang back as he approaches the swordsmen. One of them tells him to stop.

"I'm Mashaun. Who is your leader?" Mashaun asks in their language.

"I'm Rangier, and we want the staff and the twins," he returns.

"That's not going to happen. But I'll tell you what, if you want Elina, you can have her. She is in the largest cave across the lake," Mashaun tells him.

"What?" he asks.

"Do you remember the red flash the other night?" Mashaun asks him.

"Yes."

"That was Elina becoming a stronger mage than your Magdalenia. Now if you don't believe me, go find her yourself. By the way, she is also the empress of an entire city," Mashaun tells him. Rangier studies Mashaun for a long time before deciding he is probably telling the truth.

"Well, the second part of the contract is she wants Dalistra and all of you dead," he says after a time.

He turns around to see Berg and Mai step off the cliff and realizes he does not have any bargaining chips.

"Stop before you do something stupid. I want to ask you a question," Mashaun quickly tells him.

"Okay, what do you want to know before you die?" Rangier asks him.

"How many men did you lose to the creature in the pit?" Mashaun asks.

Seeing the expressions on their faces, Mashaun continues, "Not only did we not lose anybody, we vanquished the creature. Do you really think your men can defeat us when you couldn't deal with one snake?" Mashaun says in a factual tone. Rangier doesn't say a word, knowing Mashaun is right. Telling his men to stand down, he approaches Mashaun, wishing to parley. Mashaun agrees, and they meet in the middle. Mai and Berg approach from behind Rangier, startling him as they pass to greet the group.

Mashaun tells Rangier they are free to leave and tell Magdalenia the staff is in the hands of Elina who is now the ruler of the Thesilars. When Rangier asks about Dalistra, Mashaun quickly asks, "Who?" Rangier was told by Magdalenia to bring Dalistra to her alive along with the twins. Mashaun tells Rangier he is not going to have the twins or the staff. He reminds him what happens to people who displease her, and they should travel to a far away land. Rangier takes his men and leave, heading south.

Chapter 25

INTO THE WILDS

THEY TRAVEL FOR SEVERAL HOURS leaving the pit far behind, before bedding down for the night. They are grateful Elina let them have all their gear back, so the only things they lost was time and Elina. Dalistra and Mashaun talk to each other on the journey, wondering what Magdalenia even knows. After the evening meal, Berg studies the map, a little disappointed it was not Thesila. Explaining his mistake, and how they need to head to the mountain in the east.

They awake at the edge of a clearing stretching off to the horizon on the south. The cloudless sky promises hot day. They proceed east into the shade of the forest. For several days, their journey rises in elevation. They find themselves in a narrow canyon with steep walls reaching upward until the clouds engulf them. The wind and mist penetrate their clothes, chilling them to the bone. Patches of snow remain in the shadowy parts of the mountains, providing them with fresh water. Trying to find a decent campsite in the windswept valley is a formidable task at best. However, Mashaun always seem to find a warm spot for the night.

It is about midday when the trail begins a gradual descent winding its way through a valley of rocks and scrubs. They reach a meadow overlooking a long, narrow lake. It stretches down a glacier valley disappearing at the base of some distant mountains. At the headwaters of the lake stands a circular tower atop a cliff with a narrow trail winding up the face. Berg runs up the trail, throwing caution to the wind as he excitedly exclaims "a tower of Arralk" with the rest following close behind.

There is no door as they enter a circular room with a basketball-sized sphere sitting in a stone cage on a tripod in the center. As they approach the sphere, the room warms and a light radiates from the ball. There is an oblong opening in the ceiling across from the door. Mashaun stands in the doorway, scanning the horizon while admiring the evening glow of the setting sun, noticing he does not cast a shadow outside the tower. Ericka runs her hand over a small pictograph on the wall. A set of steps grows from the wall, forcing her to jump back, nearly knocking Mai over. The next two floors are identical to the bottom, except for crosses on the walls for archers and a picture on the floor. When covered, locks the stairs, effectively closing off the floor below.

Around the evening fire, Berg explains the tower of Arralk is one of many marking the borders of the Thesila kingdom. He gives them a brief history lesson on the Thesila kingdom. The towers used to protect and warn the people of any invasion. But the kingdom became too big, and they were unable to protect all its borders. When it started to shrink, the different classes broke away. They built their own cities, fracturing the kingdom into three separate empires. Shortly the distrust between the classes grew to the point of civil war, and that must have been when Thesila summoned all the mages.

Ericka is the only one still awake when Berg finishes his story. Ericka wants to know more, she has Thesilan blood and wants to know her history. As she fires one question after another about the story, Berg can only tell her he doesn't have all the answers and they both drift off to sleep.

They spend several days following the lake down into a dense forest where Mashaun is able to replenish their almost nonexistent supplies and is glad to be down where wildlife is abundant. The rest of them start a fire and wait for Mashaun to return, hopefully with some fresh meat. He is gone for a long time, and the group starts to worry. After all, he really is the only fighter left. Tera is an archer; Mai, the healer; Berg, the scholar; and Ericka is a budding mage but she perceive herself as a servant and even a hindrance. Having spent most of her life as a house slave, she is used to others making decisions for her.

It is after dark when he returns with a couple of rabbit-like animals Ericka offers to cook, which is something she does well. As they relax around the campfire, it is the first time in over a week where they feel comfortable and safe. Ericka finally asks why she couldn't see the path out of the pit. Tera nods her head in agreement. Everyone else just gaze at them, aware everyone is wondering the same thing. None of them has any idea why. They go through some of the possible reasons, but someone always points out a flaw with the line of thought.

"What if it's because we weren't born here?" Berg blurts out excitedly.

After pondering the idea, Mai asks. "What's that got to do with anything?" He can't answer. Ericka tells them she has heard stories about strangers with special skills, and Tera recounts a story about a stranger who could hide in plain sight. They brainstorm for some time on the matter, when Mai mumbles "This has got to be a dream" under her breath.

"What did you say?" Berg asks Mai.

"I said this has got to be a dream, why?" she repeats down trodden.

"I think you might touch on the reason. For us, it is a dream, but for them, this is real," Berg responds. They ponder the idea for a while before they conclude it is the only commonality. But the importance of the statement eludes them.

Tera suggests it's not real for the three of them, and it is for her and Ericka. "If we went to your world, would the roles would be reversed?"

The rest nod their heads in agreement, still not fully understanding how or why it works. They drift off to sleep.

They follow the lake-shore all day, and the only change is it becomes wider, and the bugs are more annoying. They come across a well-worn trail from the forest to the lake-shore. Mashaun and Tera study the trail for some time, trying to discern the different tracks. There are mostly cloven hooves with over-sized cats, dogs, Tsaub, and some shoe prints. Tera recognize the Tsaub's tracks and starts to say something. Tera begin to shake, nervously looks around, as her mind spins replaying the attack in the snow. When Mashaun puts his hand over her mouth, whispering its ok.

He chooses not to tell them about the Tsaub, giving Tera a cold stare. He points out the shoe prints about the same size as his own and she nods. The sun begins to set behind the eastern mountains. They make camp about a hundred feet off the trail. During the evening meal,

Berg pulls out his journal to chronicle the days events. Telling them it was a year ago today they met Pavvo. With disbelief and amazement, they each think back to their encounter with the merchant, and friend. Some wonder about Kazimir and how he is fairing in the city. They will decide on whether to follow the trail or the lake in the morning. Ericka and Berg will take the first patrol. Tera, Mai, and Mashaun will take the last as they settle in for the night.

Shortly before sunrise, strange voices come from the trail. He quickly but quietly wakes everybody, and douses the fire. Mashaun tells them to stay put and moves to where he has a better view of the trail without giving his position away. Soon, a dozen or so, short stocky creatures with various shades of green, gray skin walk casually down the trail. He can't see their feet through the underbrush but they carry crude slings, spears and swords. Sitting atop a scrawny neck are disproportionately bloated heads, allowing them the ability to turn their heads like an owl. Most of them only wear a fur loincloth with a couple wearing fur from the shoulders down.

"Orks? I thought they were all but wiped out!" Dalistra says.

"Apparently not," Mashaun replies.

The Orks stop and smell the air as if trying to catch a scent. Soon several of them head off through the woods straight toward the camp. They go right to the campsite, calling one dressed in a full-length fur. They exchange a few unintelligible words. The Orks fan out and start beating the underbrush, trying to flush them out.

"You can not let the orks find the group! They won't survive long if captured. Orks' are known for being viciously cruel and without mercy," Dalistra tells Mashaun.

"Great, there are a bunch of them and only one of me. I think I should give them a chance to surrender first," he says sarcastically. Then, he thinks of an idea.

He breaks cover and fires an arrow at one of the leaders, hitting him in the chest. The Ork stands there momentarily, not realizing what has happened before crumbling to the ground in a heap, stunning the Orks before they start looking around. During the delay, Mashaun moves to a different place where he launches another arrow at one of the Orks on the trail, dropping it like a sack of bricks. From a different direction,

Tera fires an arrow at one on the trail. This draws all of them to the new attack. Again, he quickly moves, but this time, the high brush muffles his sound and scent. They head in his direction. An arrow whiz by him, hitting an Ork. Swinging around, he spots Tera. He is both upset and glad to see her, and they split up to confuse the Orks.

When the Orks start charging into the woods, Mai wants to go and help, but Berg puts his hand on her shoulder.

"Stay put, is what he told us to do. Besides, the two of them are more than a match," Berg quietly tells her.

Mai lies there with her head in her hands. "This is not real." Berg mouths to Mai to visualize they are under a rock. Mai looks at him for a minute before realizing what he is saying. They put Ericka in the middle, and soon Berg joins her with the vision of them being hidden. He hopes by putting Ericka in the middle, it will hide all of them.

Mashaun finds another spot to hide. After a moment, he drops another one and slips farther away from the camp. He and Tera work well as a team, always managing to cover each other's back. This continues several times. When they almost find him, Dalistra informs him they are near, so he hides in some thick underbrush as one drop with a crash in the brush, drawing their attention toward him. They noisily walk by within a few feet away. When they are a safe distance away, he scrambles to a new place at the base of a tree when one breaks out of the brush. With no time to hide, he draws his sword, but Dalistra tells him to remember Tera's story. At first, it baffles him. But then remembers the ability to hide in plain sight. He backs up to a tree and freezes, visualizing being part of the tree. Tera, being ready to fire, watches as Mashaun fades into the tree. The Ork walks right by, passing less than an arm's length away, unaware their death is so close. Tera shakes her head in bewilderment.

Suddenly, he has a new strategy. He finds a wide tree with low branches to climb and hides in it until they are gone. Tera drops a few more before disappearing into the underbrush, making her way back to the others. The tall grass makes guarding the campsite impossible. Ones appears to be one milling around the area, while others make a litter to carry their dead. It takes some time before the Orks give up the search and return the way they came with their dead. Tera gets back to where she left the rest only to find an unfamiliar rock. Once the Orks are out of sight, Mashaun returns to the group and finds Tera sitting on a rock until Mai gets up, and Tera falls on Ericka. Berg helps them up, with Tera a little embarrassed about landing on Ericka. At first, Ericka is furious at Tera until Mai tells her what happened, making her laugh.

Quiet as a mouse, they walk down the trail for a while without seeing a thing, making sure the Orks don't return with reinforcements. They rest off the trail until around noon, hoping the Orks are long gone by now. Ericka asks what happened. The all stare at each other and swap stories of the near misses, putting the pieces together as to how the Orks missed them. They realize how Mashaun, Mai, and Berg can find trails and ledges that weren't there. Mai asks about living in a dream.

"Let's assume we are living in a dream, and then we are not confined to the same natural laws Tera and Ericka must follow," Berg rationalizes.

"But you have to visualize and believe it to work," Mai follows.

"Yes, that is why the trail disappeared because Ericka didn't see it, and she put the doubt into our minds," Mashaun surmises.

"That explains everything," Berg says excitedly.

Ericka realizes they will have a better chance on their own, but she also realize if she left, she will not survive by herself. Tera can take care of herself, and if they go together, she will have a better chance. But either way, she does not want to leave the group.

They have become family and friends.

"What about me?" Ericka fearfully asks them.

"What about you?" Mashaun asks her, sensing her anxiety. Dalistra doesn't care. However, Ericka and Tera are competition for Mai, and she secretly likes anything the stresses Mai.

"Well, you could have made it out of the pit sooner had it not been for me, and I have nothing to offer the group. Berg, you are smart, one of the smartest people I know. Mai, you are pretty and the best non-magical healer in the land. Mashaun, you wield a bow like no other, and you are at home here." Ericka raises her arms, gesturing toward the forest. "Tera, you also are excellent with a bow, but what do I have to offer? I have been a slave for most of my life. I am thankful to you for giving my sister and I our freedom, but I have nothing to offer you but what I was taught as a slave," Ericka says tearfully.

Mai is quick to put her arms around Ericka. "Are you kidding? You are a better cook than all of us put together and a good, no, the best cook out here, which is worth your weight in gold. But more importantly, I like having someone who can throw balls of energy. You are family." Mashaun, Dalistra, and Berg are surprised to see Mai jump so quickly to Ericka's defense. Besides, you can use magic. None of us can comprehend the power you can and will weild one day.

Even though they haven't seen any Orks since this morning, they set up a cold camp and bed down for the night. Without the fire, the bugs are an annoyance, making it hard to sleep. Otherwise, it is a long, quiet night. After a cold breakfast which Ericka is more than happy to prepare, they head down the trail. It takes only a few hours before they smell burning wood. At first, they think the forest is on fire—it is too strong to be a campfire. They hurriedly run down the trail to see if they can view the source, almost running right into a city of Orks. Mashaun manages to stop them before entering the clearing, forcing them into the tall grasses on the fringe of the tree line.

"*Almost wiped out? It doesn't appear so*" Mashaun thinks. Dalistra is dumbfounded for the first time since he took her out of the cave.

From the ground, they see numerous buildings made of wood and wattle, ranging from one to three storeys tall. The closest one appears to be shorter and newer. The ones behind have several streets leading into the town and a trail becoming a major road. Over the roof of the buildings, something reflects the sunlight somewhere behind the buildings. Mashaun climbs to the top of one of the trees for a better view. From the treetops, Mashaun overlooks rows of buildings and gets a good view at how extensive the town is. There must be 20,000 Orks living there. In the middle is a tower over six storeys tall. The surrounding buildings are only five storeys tall and gradually become shorter until the closest ones are only one storey, forming a pyramid of buildings.

The tallest building has a round, flat dome, similar to a radar dome sparkling in the sun. Within the rows of four-storey buildings are two silver globes on spikes and two more on the outside corners of town. He cannot see the other side of the town but assumes there are two more on the other side of the city. He climbs down and tells the others. They stare with disbelief. One by one, they climb the tree to have a see, and each one is amazed at the structures and organization of the city. Berg tells them it shows a high level of intelligence and sophistication, wanting to talk with them. The rest of the group don't think it is good idea.

They move deeper into the forest before setting up camp for the night. It is going to be a long and cold night again. They take turns watching the city, feeling a bit uneasy being so close to thousands of orks. When the first moon begins to peek over the trees, they stare with disbelief as the city shimmers and fades disappearing in the moonlight, leaving only the clearing. The trail passes through the clearing with a few side trails. There is no smell of burning wood or smoke rising from where the city should be.

They want to go down and see if it is gone or just hidden like the cave when they first arrived—with far off stares from a lifetime ago. They try throwing sticks and rocks, but it's too far away. Mashaun fires an arrow disappearing toward the end of its flight. Just when they think it is safe, a squad of Orks appears on the road and fan out, searching the brush. They scramble back into the forest before each finds a tree to climb with their stuff to spend the night. Tera and Mashaun are ready if the Orks find anybody, but after a short time, they return to the safety of the invisible city. Dalistra tells Mashaun there hiding in plain sight and we thought they were wiped out—they can't be found at night.

The next morning, as the moon fades from the sky, the Ork city reappears. Mashaun finds an animal trail circumventing the city. They can catch glimpses of it as they slowly make their way down the trail. Berg is busy looking at the city when they come across a log lying on the clean trail. A close inspection reveals a series of trip wires should anything go around it—leaving or going over—which will make them visible to anybody in the city.

They backtrack for nearly half an hour before heading deeper into the forest, realizing the Orks are more creative and cunning than they thought. Travel is slow through the thick branches of the willow-like trees grow like unyielding tall bushes, forcing them to retrace their steps and choose a different route many times during the day. By the time the light begins to fade, they are not sure how far the city lies. The thick canopy prevents them from using the star cluster or the sun for directions, casting a solid shadow all day. For several days, they hunt and pick, going forward only to find a thicket, forcing them to backtrack once again. They break out of the forest only to find a clearing with a small city in the middle. Somehow, they are at the other end of the city.

They sit down, tired, dirty and disgusted. They spent days fighting branches, insects, exhaustion, and even their own sanity only to find themselves back at the Ork city. Mashaun sits placing his head in his hands. In all his years of wilderness adventures, this is the first time he has been so turned around, making him frustrated with himself.

As if to add insult to injury, it starts to rain, turning into a downpour, and he just sits there, shaking his head in disbelief. It doesn't take long for them to become cold and wet to the bone, which forces them back into the forest to set up camp. Once the canopy is over them and Mashaun finally gets a fire going, their spirits improve. Tera tells them at least they don't stink anymore, and they moan with a slight chuckle at her attempt to make light of the situation.

The rain stops sometime before sun-up, but the clouds hang just over the trees with the tops of a few taller ones vanishing in the clouds. The choice is simple: follow the road away from the city, and if it takes them back to the lake, then so be it. The muddy road makes movement slow and treacherous with no way to hide their tracks. Over the next few hours, the road narrows, becoming a path then an animal trail. At a shore, they come to several small abandoned buildings next to a river at least a hundred feet across. Nobody thinks much about the river flowing toward the mountains or it's obviously higher than normal, only it offers them some shelter and protection, something they have not had for a long time. With the dark clouds still low, looking as though it will rain again at any moment, the group decides to make camp until the weather breaks. By early afternoon, they find a building most of the roof, and standing walls. Ericka finds an old pier, which collapsed into the river some time ago. There are a couple of boats sitting on the river bottom, their ropes and wood rotting away.

By evening, Mashaun finds some fresh meat while the rest of them put some finishing touches on the shelter. During the meal, Ericka suggests they build a boat and go down the river. Berg unrolls the map on the floor and studies it for a while the others busy themselves. The map is faded, creased and torn from its many months on the road. The best he can tell is hey are still going the right direction, but the river will take them the wrong way. They are all tired of walking and welcome the rest. The next morning, they wake up to a light rain continuing all day, giving the group time to relax. Mashaun doesn't like sitting around—never did—and goes exploring while the others enjoy the downtime in the comfort of the shelter. Berg continues to study the map and the notebook, while Tera and Ericka talk about their homes across the mountains. Mai enjoys the time off and wonders about her friends back home and the test she was supposed to take.

In the early afternoon, Mashaun stumbles across an upside-down boat made of overlapping slats. It has a fifteen-feet bow to stern and three-foot width. Cautiously looking underneath, he finds it dry and in good condition. He wonders how long it has been there, who it belongs to, and if the owners are still around. He hunts around for any tracks or signs to give him a clue but doesn't find any. The rains have washed away any traces of the owners of the boat might have left. Remembering by believing the three of them can see things not there. He returns to camp and brings Ericka back to the boat, asking what does she see. Touching the boat she confirms it's real and they don't have to build one. They smile and rush back to tell the other.

Chapter 26

THE RIVER

Several days later, the rain finally lets up, swelling the river even higher. Now, the boat sits in knee-deep muck and water. It takes an hour to uncover and turn it over. It starts to float right away. They tie it to a nearby tree so the current doesn't take it before they are ready. Attached inside is a curved handle the full length of the boat with a torpedo-like device connected at an angle on one end. The device has runes carved into the wood with a hole running the full length. The boat has a short flat section on the back with a couple of straps looped over the steering shaft, attaching it to the boat while giving it the freedom to swivel. Ericka loads the group's gear into the boat, while Mai, Berg, and Mashaun hunt for a makeshift paddle. They search the forest but there is no decent piece of wood for an oar. Mai is the last to return to the boat, running and flat out yelling at them to go.

Mashaun stands next to the boat with an arrow nocked and drawn, scanning the forest behind Mai to see what is chasing her. While standing on the boat, Tera gets her arrow ready. Berg takes the rudder and tells Ericka to cut the rope once Mai gets in the boat. She takes a small ax and stands ready. Just as Mai gets to the water's edge, a Tsaub comes into view, followed by another one then another. Mashaun and Tera each hit one, but they don't slow down. It takes three shots before the Tsaub drops. The others continue charging while throwing spears. There are at least 10 of them barreling down on the boat only a few dozen yards away when Mai almost dives into the boat.

"Cut the rope now!" Mai screams as she tries to swing herself into the boat.

Ericka cuts the rope with the first cut, and it starts to float out into the river.

"Mashaun, jump in!" Berg yells as Ericka helps Mai into the boat. Mashaun sends another arrow flying before turning around, tossing Dalistra and her quiver in the boat. With Mashaun pushing it farther out into the river, the water is up past his waist, and he can barely hold on to the side when one of the Tsaub's spears hits next to his hands, forcing him to let go and sending him under the boat. Tera returns fire, hitting another Tsaub. Without thinking, Ericka picks up Dalistra and shoots at the Tsaub to the surprise of Mai and Berg. The Tsaub finds an arrow from Dalistra through its head. Mai and Berg scan the riverbank for Mashaun while Ericka and Tera continue to shoot at the Tsaub.

Mashaun breaks the surface of the water, spitting and sputtering looking for the boat. Finding it a dozen yards away from him being chased down river by the Tsaubs. He stands in chest-deep water, watching the boat and Dalistra drift away when a floating tree runs into him, knocking him off his feet. Trapped in tree branches, bouncing, turning and spinning down river at the mercy of its current. With a loud splash, the tree rolls, sending Mashaun under the water and up the other side. He has lost sight of the boat, but he can tell Dalistra is in Ericka's hands, shooting Tsaubs.

Soon the Tsaubs quit chasing the boat, and the group stops shooting. They put the bows down to join the search for Mashaun in the debris-filled river.

"*Where are you?*" Dalistra asks, searching for Mashaun's thoughts.

"*Dalistra, is that you?*" he asks weakly. Dalistra can tell he is nearly out of range and is moving away.

"*You're alive!*" Dalistra is ecstatic, and then she recomposes herself.

"*Yes, but I'm trapped in a tree branch floating down the river.*"

"*Who else knows what I can do?*" Dalistra inquires.

"*No one,*" he responds.

Dalistra is in a bind. Mashaun treats her like part of the team, never just as an object. Unless one of them picks her up, she is helpless to show them the part of the river where Mashaun is.

"*I helped Ericka drop several Tsaub and found something out about her,*" Dalistra tells Mashaun, trying to keep his spirits up.

"*Yes, I can feel you,*" he excitedly tells her.

"*Her magic is impressive. She can be the grand wizard, a rainbow, or even a diamond wizard.*" Dalistra tells him.

"*I suspected the same. Look at her sister.*"

"*No, you do not understand,*" Dalistra insists.

"*That can wait, I am kind of busy right now,*" Mashaun tells her as the cold water begins to sap his strength. Somehow, he needs to free himself and crawl to upside of the tree and out of the water.

"*You have to return. Otherwise they will give me to Ericka, and she grips like I am going to fly away. She does not know how to treat me,*" Dalistra says tearfully.

"*You're not going to get rid of me that easily,*" Mashaun half-jokingly says.

From the boat, they look and yell for Mashaun, but only the sounds of a rushing river and the splashing of the boat catches their ears.

Mashaun calms down and visualizes the tree rolling allowing putting him on top, and out of the water. As he envisioned the tree rolls putting him in the cool air. Without the force of the water to hold him, he manages to free himself and find a way to the trunk, where the branches are thinner and he can see the boat in the distance. He curses himself for not spending more time learning how to swim. He can swim a few laps in a pool, but trying to swim to the boat will be suicide. He does the next best thing: he yells at the boat. They are too far away and the sound of the rushing river is almost deafening.

Dalistra can see the boat through his eyes, but unless someone touches her, she cannot show them where he is. Mashaun keeps an eye on the boat drifting farther and farther away until it disappears around a bend in the river. Soon he can no longer sense Dalistra. As night is beginning to set in, and heavy clouds loom overhead hiding the moons, mean the night will be dark and cold. Crawling back into the branches, he holds on throughout the night, too tired to stay awake, and too cold to fall asleep, doing whatever he can to stay awake.

The rudder is useless in the river without oars. Still, they take turns at the helm not knowing why. Ericka takes the helm, and the boat surges forward. She turns the rudder, and the boat turns. She discovers if she lifts the torpedo, it pushes the nose down, slowing the boat. When she puts it deeper in the water, the front lifts up, increasing the speed of the boat.

"This is great!" Ericka says with excitement. As she sharply turns the boat upriver, Mai falls on Dalistra and gets a flash of a tree floating in the water. But it is dark, and unless the tree runs into the boat, they probably won't see it. Despite the darkness, they still scan the waters. They decide to make camp on the far riverbank before continuing in the morning.

During the night, the tree suddenly stops, knocking Mashaun off before swinging around, leaving him floundering in the river. He swims to what he hopes is the shore just a little way off, only to find he can stand and wade onshore. He is unsure about which side of the river he is on, but he needs to dry out and build a fire for warmth before he slips any deeper into hypothermia. Taking an inventory of his possessions, he finds the flint and steel. This brightens up his spirits. He builds a fire for warmth. He searches for Dalistra, but she is still out of range. For now, he is safe and warm as he huddles around the fire.

As the suns rays light up the distance eastern mountains only a few high clouds remain. Mashaun heads downriver, hoping to find something. His morning walk allows him time to reflect. The dependence on Dalistra troubles him, but she is needed to finish the quest. Still Dalistra helps him to stay away from the enemy. But, if he runs into trouble, he still has his swords. He stays next to the river but just inside the trees so he can see anybody before they can see him. He barely senses Dalistra and hopes someone picks her up so they will see each other's location.

Mai wakes up first, rushing everybody in the boat to search for Mashaun and before getting anything to eat. With Ericka at the helm, they go back upriver not far from shore, looking for anything. By late morning, they head downriver. Ericka has discovered the faster the boat travels, the more tired she gets. Shortly after noon, Berg points at some movement in the trees. Mai picks up Dalistra without thinking. Dalistra and Mai are uncomfortable.

"What am I doing? I'm a healer, not a warrior. She thinks as she tries to nock an arrow. *However, it is kill or be killed.* She shakily holds Dalistra, ready to shoot with Tera standing by her side. Ericka turns the boat in the direction of the movement. Berg searches the river for obstacles while the girls scan the shoreline.

Mashaun can sense Dalistra getting closer and the tight, nervous grip on her.

"What do you see?" Mashaun asks her. Dalistra wants to use Mai's eyes secretly but is afraid of what may happen if Mai discovers her secret.

"They have spotted something onshore and are going to check it out." Dalistra tells him.

Mashaun scans the river but does not see the boat. If Dalistra can talk, they must be close.

"I don't see you, but you are close," Mashaun tells her.

"No! It is not him. Turn the boat!" Mai shouts. Ericka quickly turns the boat back into the river, dipping the tip deeper in the water as a few spears are thrown, falling short of the boat.

"How did you know?" Tera asks Mai.

"I don't know. I saw a flash of Mashaun looking over the river, and we weren't there," she tells them.

"What else did you see?" Berg asks her.

"Trees and the river," she says. Looking around, it all the same.

Dalistra realizes her connection with Mashaun is getting weaker, and they need to turn the boat around.

"Back, we must go back up the other side," Mai says, first questioning herself. But she quickly boosts her confidence.

Ericka does as Mai says, with everyone looking for Mashaun on the shore.

Mashaun spots a small boat appear from around a bend downriver.

Dalistra also spots the boat and her excitement flows to Mai.

Mai drops Dalistra on the floor, staring at it both puzzled and afraid.

"What?" Berg asks.

"Mashaun is up there, on the bank," Mai tells him, trembling.

"How do you know. Did the bow tell you?" Berg asks a little sarcastically.

"Yes. I saw the boat from his eyes," she says, backing away from Dalistra. Everyone just stares at her as if she is crazy until she points to the spot where Mashaun is standing.

A short time later, they see a lone figure standing on the riverbank, waving at them. Mai is first to jump out of the boat to give Mashaun a bear hug and a kiss. Berg, Tera, and Ericka are also delighted to see him though the other two girls refrain from kissing him. Mashaun gently picks up Dalistra, rubbing her limbs as the others regard with bewilderment.

"What? I am rather attached to this bow," he says offhandedly.

The river is still too treacherous for night travel, and they set up camp, exchanging stories around the campfire. After they eat and relax, Mai tells Mashaun about seeing the boat from this spot and other strange happenings when they were looking for him. Mashaun can feel Dalistra's embarrassment as she tells him it was the excitement of the moment. Mashaun thinks for a minute. The group has gotten out of a lot of scrapes, but it just not safe for them to know the whole story.

"You remember the pit when you saw the trail and the ledges but they weren't really there?" he asks Mai. She nods affirmatively.

"Well, don't you think it is the same?" She shakes her head.

"No. The bow told me you were not at the first place, and then it showed me where you were. There is something going on with you and the bow."

"This is a dream world, and strange things happen."

"I guess that's it," she says, convincing herself it's the bow and not just some wishful thinking. She doesn't understand why he's keeping it a secret from them. You don't need to know how to read minds to see Mai is a little disappointed. Nevertheless, Dalistra tells him it is for the best. *Maybe.* But keeping her a secret after all they've gone through together is tearing his insides apart.

The river subsides a little, putting the boat on a patch of mud. It takes them over an hour to move the boat into the water enoughto float before continuing downstream. For days, they travel downriver as it snakes its way through the forest, collecting the water from other tributaries, stopping only at night. Under a cloudless sky, the reflection off the river not only makes it hotter but also turns their skin red and sore. They stretch a canopy across the boat. The forest slowly gives way to plains stretching on forever. By the fifth day, a wooden palisade comes into view. Civilization, at last. But after the last city, they want to make sure it is safe.

There is no sign of life, but it appears well maintained. As they approach, arrows suddenly fly over the wall. Ericka sharply turns the boat out to the middle and downstream but not fast enough as Berg takes an arrow in the leg. Mai gets him under the canopy while the archers search for a targets. Even Dalistra can't find anything or anybody. Berg is lucky the arrow didn't hit anything major, but he will have problems getting around for a while.

Ericka rounds a bend in the river, revealing a wall of stone. Similar to Shen Sherin, it stands towering over the water's edge reaching up 40 feet. Ericka studies the confluence of two major rivers, splashing and swirling, creating a chaotic landscape up ahead, plotting a way through. It will be a rough ride if they stay their course as she turn the boat toward the river center, but the current catches the little boat, taking them down along the wall.

Chapter 27

TWIN RIVERS

THE BOAT ROUNDS THE CORNER of the wall to where the two rivers converge. They expect the ride to become rough when an open gate forces the boat into a city. The gate closes, and the waters become calm. They are trapped in a docking area, for better or worse. There are a couple of warriors, a dockhand, and a man standing on the dock with shoulder-length golden hair, bronze skin and dark-blue eyes. He is about the same height as Ericka, wearing a shirt and pants made from some unknown fabric. Mai shows them Berg's leg which still has the arrow, and the man says something to one of the dockhands who takes off running only to return shortly with a small flat-bottomed boat and a couple of men. They load Berg on the boat and move off without any means of movement similar to their own boat. Mai tries to go with him, but one of the warriors stops her.

"He is my patient, and I should be with him," she tries to argue, but they don't understand her and will not let her on the boat.

They load them on a second boat. There are three benches across the boat with three guards and a steersman. It soon becomes clear there are no roads here, and the sole means of travel is by boat. Mashaun sits back and enjoys the ride, figuring if they were going to kill them, they would already be dead. Dalistra agrees with him. The girls do not like the situation, and Mai is especially not happy because she doesn't know where they took Berg. They don't understand why Mashaun appears unconcerned as they proceed down the waterway.

All the buildings seem to grow from the ground, including the steps leading up to the doors. The three-storey buildings cast their shadows over the canal as their boat makes its way to an area in front of a plain building of white stone with inlays of gold. The men help them out of the boat and escort them inside. A different man gives them each a bag for their weapons before it is sealed shut. Much to Mashaun's delight, they allow them to keep their weapons after the seal is in place. They march them into an throne room with frescoes in rich colors line the red copper walls. At the far end on a pedestal is a golden chair adorned with a sphere in the middle of a triangle, and a circle at each corner. Are they in Thesila? They each whisper.

An elderly man and woman enter the room, and all the guards bow as they approach the throne. One of the guards hits Mashaun behind one knee, dropping him to his knees where he stays. Dalistra tells him to hold his tongue, as they let the girls remain standing but with their heads bowed. They help him up. When the couple is sitting on the throne next to each other, one of the guards speaks in hush voices as the guard keeps pointing to them. The old man waves the him off and says something. They glance at one another again before shrugging their shoulders. He repeats his words, and again they shrug their shoulders.

"It is an ancient language. He wants to know who you are and where you are from, repeat what I say exactly." Dalistra tell him.

Mashaun's first attempt brings curious gazes from the couple and the guards.

"No, not like that," Dalistra tells him.

The girls glance at him strangely. "What? How?"

One of the guards says something and goes to slap Ericka, but the queen snaps at the guard. He backs away, bowing.

Mashaun's second attempt is more successful. "My lords, I am Mashaun from distant lands." he says, bowing.

"These are my companions Mai, Ericka, Tera, and your doctor has Berg," he continues.

"No, they are called a healer. What is a doctor?" Dalistra asks Mashaun.

The term got a puzzling look from everyone else except Mai.

"It will help the argument," he tells Dalistra.

"A doctor is like your healer," he tells them, and they nod in agreement.

They question him for some time. Mashaun often mispronounces the words, and he is sure his sentences are clumsy at best, sometimes to the laughter of everyone. After some time, they are taken to see Berg. He is sitting upright and is glad to see them, telling them he has tried to talk with them but they can't understand each other. The girls twitch one eye with a questing glare. Asking Mashaun how he understood them. Berg studies him inquisitively.

"You can understand them?" Berg asks.

"A little," he replies, but the girls shake their heads.

"A little? You were able to answer all the questions, I think. You know more than a little," Mai states.

Mashaun starts to say he studied it at Myelikkan but Berg will know better. He probably has studied more languages than the rest of the group combined. He tries to change the subject, but when they do not let it drop, he tells them "Later." The guard asks them to follow him though they don't really have a choice. They are led to a third-floor room not far from where they have Berg.

The room has a single window overlooking a canal about ten feet across allowing two narrow boats to pass. The room itself has a small round wooden table with four chairs, a basin with a pump for some water and a couple of feather beds. Mai is the first to lie in the bed, almost disappearing into the soft mattress.

"Oh, I had almost forgotten how good this feels," Mai says as she squirms in the bed.

"Okay, how do you understand them? I'm from here and speak ancient Thesilan and I didn't understand them," Ericka nonchalantly asks Mashaun with a biting tone, leaning against the wall. Mai sits up as the other two turn and stares at him. He can feel their penetrating stares as he thinks about how to answer the question. Dalistra keeps telling him not to say anything about her.

"It is the bow? Right." Ericka flatly blurts out. This shocks both Mashaun and Dalistra. Saying it more as a joke, Ericka realizes that's right by the surprise on his face. There is a long, uneasy silence as they each consider what was just said.

"That's why the bow glowed red at Shen Sherin, isn't it?" Mai asks him coldly. He nods his head, like a little boy caught in a lie.

"You can't tell anyone. No one must know about Dalistra, promise me!" Mashaun frightfully tells them. They all agree. Mai is upset he did not tell her after all this time. She isn't sure if she should be mad at him or hurt.

Berg stares Mashaun for a while before realizing. "Dalistra, the same Dalistra Magdalenia is looking for, the princess mentioned in the prophecy, the—"

Mashaun interrupts, "Yes, the very same one…" He stops when a knock on the door breaks the tension in the room. A dumpy short woman with graying long, blond hair wearing a loose fitting off-shoulder dress enters the room. She says something and turns around to walk out the door. Mashaun gets Dalistra, but she stops him and points at their weapons before saying something. Dalistra tells Mashaun all the weapons are to stay here. Mashaun starts to pick up Dalistra when the woman shakes her finger before curling her forefinger. The party leaves their weapons on the table and follow her.

She leads them to a boat, which takes them to a bathhouse, where they each have a servant helping them with a bath while someone takes their clothes. They are given a clean set of clothes, and the girls each have a long ballroom gown. This takes Mashaun by surprise, thinking they look gorgeous. They step into the boat with some help and find themselves at the palace again.

In the center of the room, the tables form a U with Berg already seated. They seat the group on the same side as Berg. When the king and queen enter, everybody stands including them, bowing their heads and waiting for everybody else to sit down. The king claps his hands, and the food comes in one after another. Most of it is fish or shellfish, along with aquatic plants. There is a lot. During the meal, they have jugglers, acrobats, dancers, and other performances in the middle of the U.

After they eat their fill and the entertainment stops, a rather lanky older man stands in the middle of the U and faces the four.

"Your ability to speak our language is, let's say, needs some work," he says, and the crowd chuckles.

"However, you did try, and we give you credit for that." The crowd gives its approval by bowing their heads. He then introduces each one in both languages, starting with Mai, Tera, Ericka, Berg, and Mashaun, each standing in turn.

"You are no doubt wondering why we're holding this grand feast in your honor," he continues. Actually, they didn't know it is in their honor, and they wonder why.

"It has been many years since any human has visited us, and we would like to learn more about what has happened in the last 50 years," he says. Looking at them, he clears his throat and continues. "Oops, how about the 10 years." He realizes they are all somewhere between their teens and mid-thirties.

They all glance at one another, wondering who is going to speak. They all stare at Mashaun.

"No way," he tells them. He is at home in the wilderness, but not in front of crowds. Just as Berg starts to hobble to his feet, Tera puts her hand on his shoulder and stands up. She tells them about Shen Sherin, Magdalenia, and the slave trade, which draws a gasp from the crowd. She follows with the meeting of the city of Thesilar and the crystal growers, the invisible city, which brings murmurs from the crowd. Everybody focuses on the king. He raises his hand, and everybody leaves except for the group. Looking around, they notice the guards seem tense and nervous, barring the doors after everybody else has left. The king wants to know more about the invisible city but is disappointed when Tera tells him they went around it, spending days lost in the forest before finding the dock where they got the boat.

The group neverously glances around as the king's court hangs its heads before telling Tera the king sent an envoy to the city but they never returned. When they saw your boat, they were hoping for some good news. Berg realizes the city guards think they are the emissaries from the city, which is probably why they opened the gate and forced them into the city. Tera continues with the attack from the Tsaub, nearly losing Mashaun. She tells them his envoy most likely didn't make it to the city. She tells them about the attack where Berg caught the arrow.

"The Awrks," the translator tells her.

"Awrks? I know about the Orks, but what are Awrks?" Tera asks.

"The Orks and the Awrks have been fighting for many years for control of the area. The Orks are friendlier and are excellent craftsmen. We traded with them for many years. The warlike Awrks have made it all but impossible to travel upriver. It was an Awrk arrow in Berg's leg," the translator tells Tera.

Tera thinking back to the Awrks at the cave. So much time has passed, a lifetime ago they found themselves strangers in a strange land.

"You're obviously not here to set up a trade route, so why are you here?" he asks her.

"We merely wish to resupply and continue on our way," Tera says politely.

The king asks through the translator, "Where are you heading?"

"Your Highness, we are seeking the city of Thesila," she tells them. They all gasp, negatively shaking their heads in silence. "Not for the riches, which are supposed to be there and are probably long gone. We wish to visit the ancient sites of Thesilar, Thesilau, Thesilay, and Thesila. We are historians, and we have already been to Thesilar."

They ask her for the real reason why they are going to Thesila if not for the riches. Tera repeats the same story several times, trying to convince them the real reason but to no avail. She needs a new tactic and decides to sidestep the answer. She asks the translator how he learned her language. This brings a hush to the room as the guards take a few steps closer until the king waves his hand, stopping them, before giving an affirmative nod to the translator.

"I have been here for nearly a hundred years. I woke up in a cave and was sold to a merchant. I used to be a translator, and it didn't take me long to learn their language, so I was given to the lord Kavelan, who became king some 50 years ago. Okay, I answered your question. So will you answer mine? Why are you really going to Thesila?" he asks, ending his monologue.

Tera asks each one to stand and tell the king where each was born in their native tongue and asks the translator to tell each of them where they are from, and he agrees. He has a little problem with Berg. However, he thinks Berg is from Africa. He guesses Mai is from the Philippines. Mashaun is from America while Ericka and Tera are from here.

"You have proven what you say is true. We have heard we can return to our world from the city," Tera tells him.

"I know why you are seeking the cities, but that's an old wives' tale. In any case, the hook-billed dragons guard the entrance. Several of our people have tried, but none has returned. It is a foolish quest, it will kill all of you, should you proceed." he tells Tera.

"Maybe yes, maybe no. But in either case, we are still going. All we ask is to replenish our supplies and be on our way, and from the sounds of it, you know where the entrance is. We would be most grateful if you could tell direct us to the entrance," she says humbly.

After he translates her story, the room is deathly quiet, like a cemetery on a moonless night. They wait for some kind of reaction from the king. After a few tense moments, the king finally says something before standing and leaving the room with the queen and the advisers following.

"Yes, you will get your supplies, and I will show you where it is on one condition," the translator tells them.

"Yes...what do you mean 'I will show you'?" Tera says hesitantly.

"I'm going with you. The king is dying, and he gave me my freedom some time ago. I would like to return home also," he says pleadingly.

It takes them by surprise, but they have no choice but to agree. He introduces himself as Alandra and looks forward to going home after being here for a hundred years. He agrees to meet in the morning to replenish whatever supplies they need before leaving. He politely begs them not to leave without him before almost running out the door with excitement.

The group returns to their quarters where the guard leaves them without saying a word. They sit down at the table to discuss their new travel companion. They don't want him but they know there isn't much of a choice. They tell Tera she has handled herself well in the king's presence. She informs them it is not her first time in a royal court, reminding everyone who her mother is. Several hours later, Alandra surprises them by showing up and offering to take them out to eat, which they gladly accept not knowing when the next good meal will be.

He takes them to an posh resturant overlooking the wall across the fork in the river. They can feel all eyes are on them and people whispering as they find a table by an easterly window. Alandra points to a tiny peak backed by a golden sky.

"That's where we are going," he says as they gaze at it for a long time. They are so close yet so far from finally going home.

"How long will it take to get to the entrance?" Mai asks Alandra.

"It will take a few days before we arrive at the trail, then we face the guards, and from there, I don't know," he says in a hushed tone.

"Why so quiet?" Berg asks.

"We receive so few strangers they're not trusted, and I am sure word has spread, I will be leaving with you. This city is slowly dying. Just look around at all the children you don't see. How many have you seen since your arrival?" he asks them.

"None? With all the travel we have done, none. Not one child here or in the crystal growers' city. Why?" Mai says.

"But there are children in Shen Sherin, and my home of Tenskie," Ericka says.

The others think for a moment and then nod their heads in agreement. They stop talking when the servant comes to take their order. Alandra gives her a round cylinder about the size of the pen with a gold band around one end. The servant puts the pen-like object in a slab about the size of a business card twice as thick as the pen device. She touches a few places on the blank slate before returning it to Alandra. They watch in amazement.

"Yes. We are quite advanced here inside the wall, which is one reason why we don't trust outsiders," he tells the group.

"I'm afraid the advancement does not apply to our weapons. Once we are on our way, I will tell you more," he continues quietly.

They are careful of the small talk during the meal, always conscientious of others trying to listen to the conversation. They head back to their room, and Mashaun asks Alandra to stay with them so they can leave early. He just wants to keep an eye on him. Like the townspeople, he doesn't trust him either. Alandra shows Mashaun a way to the roof where he takes a reading with the sextant, recording the numbers in his notebook before recording it on Berg's map. Alandra stares with curiosity, as Mashaun takes his usual sleeping spot with his feet at the door. They all tell Alandra that is Mashaun's sleeping spot so they are not surprised during the night. More than once, it has prevented a surprise attack. Alandra just nods his head and finds a corner.

Chapter 28

THESILA

EARLY THE NEXT MORNING, THEY eat before going to several stores for their supplies and swinging by Alandra's place to pick up some personal supplies and a rucksack. At the boat, Alandra has to turn over his pay stick and couple of strange metal devices before they will allow him in the boat. They gently push them away from the dock before Ericka takes the helm and steers them out another gate into the torrential river. Just as the boat reaches the gate, someone on the dock starts frantically yelling at them, and Alandra nervously tells them to go as the current catches the little boat, sending it quickly downriver.

Once in the river with no one following, Mashaun asks Alandra. "What is that all about?" Alandra pulls out a little metal disk, telling them it has information about the city and the world. He plans to take it back home to write about his life here. Dalistra tells Mashaun he's lying. She can tell by his voice. Mashaun nods his head affirmatively, letting it drop for now while keeping an eye on him. The others listen to the whole conversation, and they don't buy his story either. Although it sounds true enough, they really can't tell.

During the monotonous journey downriver, Alandra tells them sometime in the distant past, a woman of superior intelligence arrived in the city as a slave. According to the story, she bought her freedom by teaching the townspeople how to make the devices. She showed them many new gadgets making life easier. She also used her feminine charm to manipulate the townsfolk. Some of the elders didn't like her methods and banished her by putting her on a raft and sending her downriver during a heavy rain.

"I understand they were going to destroy all she had done, but some townspeople hid the devices until all the elders had died before revealing some of her stuff survived. Some of her inventions is so advanced most can't begin to understand the workings. One of her little toys almost destroyed the city, since then they don't trust outsiders."

Alandra ask Mashaun where's he really from. Mashaun tells him the United States. Alandra gives him a blank stare. Going down the line, Mashaun tells him Africa, South America, and the Philippines, but he gets the same blank stare. Being a little sarcastic, he says "Earth" to which he receives the same puzzled face. When Mashaun asks him about his answers in the throne room, Alandra tells him he is a natural linguist. He knew where they were from because he had heard those words before.

Frustrated, Mashaun pulls out some marbles, puts a yellow one down, and says it's the sun. Then he puts a couple of pebbles down before placing a green ball down saying it's the Earth. Alandra's face lights up as he changes the yellow one for a red one and removes one of the pebbles, telling them the red is the star and the green is home. They study each others systems with disbelief and amazment at once.

Berg almost shouting with excitement.

"You know what this means! The portals connect to different worlds. But why?" he says. They are silent as they each ponders the implications of such a discovery.

The river grows as other streams filter in. Meandering through the plains under the glaring sun. The hours turn into days before the river flows into a fresh water sea, where the distant shore fades into the horizon. Alandra tells them to follow the northern shoreline for a couple of days and they will see the entrance to Thesila and the two stone statues. By early afternoon of the second day, they go to a cove ending in a rock cliff, but Alandra tells them it actually turns.

Ericka heads up the cove through a narrow passageway with an archway on the left, leading to a small bay. At the other end is a rock road disappearing up a narrow canyon. On each side of the path are two statues of hook-billed dragons made of blue stone, about twice the size of a horse. A cross between a lizard and a centaur, with bearlike claws for feet and an eagle beak for a mouth.

The creatures stare out across the bay with their catlike eyes, which seem to follow the little boat while Ericka maneuvers around the bay, looking for a good spot to land other than in front of the dragons. Ericka point to the statues, piles of bones lay neatly stacked around the stone figures. Worried, they peer into the water where dozens of small boats lie broken on the bottom. Strange fish about four feet long dart arong the wrecks. Not liking the feel of it, Ericka quickly turns the boat away from the dragons while Mai observes them moving toward the water with slow, meticulous steps. One of the dragons scoops up a ball of water and hurls it at the boat like a rock as Mai yells at Ericka to turn. She whips the little boat as the water boulder hits the lake they're in, soaking them. Ericka zigzags the boat while heading back into the bay, but the entrance is gone. It must be an illusion, but if she guesses wrong, the boat will crash into the rocks, and they will end up in water.

The golems hurls another ball of water, falling short of the boat. Ericka keeps the boat out of range for now, but they need a plan. The archer's fire arrows bouncing off the statues at the water's edge. Fifty foot sheer cliffs surround the bay reminding them of Shen Sherin. The rain of water from the splashes is filling the boat with water, as they bail.

"Nobody says a word. Ericka, bring me next to that rock." Mashaun says sternly.

She gets the boat next to the cliff, and Mashaun jumps to the cliff, grabbing hold of a shelf only he can see. Alandra starts to say something, but Mai quickly covers his mouth and tells him "Don't say it" in no uncertain terms. Berg and Mai begin to see the rocks as he climbs, yelling some encouragement, and even pointing to handholds and a small shelf so he can rest about halfway up. Alandra and Tera follow his every movement, with amazement as he seemingly grabs on to air. Ericka keeps the boat moving in a random direction as the golems continue to hurl water rocks. Each one gets closer until one lands next to the boat, almost capsizing it. The climb is slow and strenuous, but Mashaun makes it to the top only to find it is narrow path. The cliff circles the bay with no rock or trees to the rope off. The other side drops down into another bay.

Looking over the other side, he finds a thick tree stump sticking out. He ties the rope to before throwing the other end down to the water. Alandra wants to be next, but he is no match for Berg and Mai. While arguing, a boulder hits near the boat again. Mai is on the rope, heading up the cliff as Ericka swerves the boat away, leaving Mai with only the water beneath her. One by one, they climb the cliff with Tera, Alandra, then Berg. The last to clim is Ericka. When she lets go to grab the rope, the boat starts to drift toward the golems, which is something she had not noticed before. Within minutes, the little boat sinks, joining the other boats at the bottom of the cove. She briefly thinks about all those who went down with their boats.

They proceed down the narrow path overlooking the bay and the two golems have moved back to their original positions. They can see dozens of ships in all manners and sizes resting on the bottom. They try to find theirs, but it's impossible among the carnage. When they pass the golems, the ridge begins to widen, easing the tensions of walking on such a narrow trail as it turns into a grassy area sloping down away from the canyon trail. It narrows to just a few yards across on the other side a grassy hill also sloping away from the trail. They feel open and exposed as they travel along the ridge, ever vigilant for an air attack which they are sure will come. The ridge ends at another cliff, the trail below opening into a octagonal area.

To the left are two blue columns carved into the cliff face with a matching archway carved into the mountain with a shimmering blue door. Heading back toward the golems is a shimmering gold door while to the right is a shimmering red door. Straight ahead is a barber-pole column with a door oscillating the three colors.

They will never make it down before nightfall so they make camp near the cliff with two groups on patrol. Alandra will be with Mashaun, much to his protest, not so much as being with Mashaun, just on having guard duty. The girls tell him they have to take turns, why should he be any different. His reply is feeble at best, trying to argue he is not a fighter. Mai and Berg scornfully stare at him as Alandra realizes it is a bad argument. There are really only two warriors in the entire group, and Alandra reluctantly agrees, trying to be with Tera. But Tera refuses to be with him as she likes partnering with Mai; it gives them time for girl talk.

During the early morning hours, Ericka awakens Mashaun, telling him she heard the flapping of wings but can't see anything with only crescent moons up. He scans the sky for a while but doesn't see anything and only silence fill the air. Just as he goes back to sleep, the sound of wind rushing over a pair of wings crosses the dark sky. While they can pinpoint the sound, they can't see anything in the skies. Ericka wakes everybody else. it passes by several times, as the turbulence from its wings moves light stuff around. But they still can't see a thing, scaring Alandra the most although the creature never attacks.

The sun begins to chase the night away and the sounds of the creature also vanishes. They listen to it fade into the distance never glimpsing it, leaving them shaky and tired. The only way down is using the rope, but they don't want to leave the rope. Mashaun has a grasp on this whole belief thing and tells them not to worry about it as he belays the rope while the others climb down to the clearing. He visualizes a trail down, and soon there is the trail to the floor by the yellow arch. They tell Alandra not to say a word as he stares in amazement at Mashaun walking down a make-believe path shaking his head with disbelief. When he asks someone about Mashaun's trick, Mai tells him it is something he can do.

Alandra is the first to the rainbow arch, receiving a mind-numbing jolt when he tries to walk through it. While Mashaun is looking for a way to climb up the cliff, Mai taps him on the shoulder, telling him to turn around where there is a knight wearing a heavy armor made of light. He is a little taller than Mashaun, wielding an ornate bastard sword with a duel head hookbill dragon heads. His other hand has a kite shield with magical symbols around the Thesila crest.

Dalsistra trys to contain her excitement, as Mashaun tells them to settle down so he can focus.

Mashaun tells everybody to split up as they circle the knight. Dalistra tells him is a guardian, and to enter the city, it must be defeated. She is confused why there is a guardian at the city entrance. Mashaun and Tera both shoot an arrow, Tera's pass right through it as if it is just an illusion, as Mashaun's bounces off the shield. Ericka hits it with an energy ball exploding on contact, getting its attention as it turns to face her. With its back to Mashaun, Mashaun takes out his swords and charges, only to have them slice through the knight like air. The guardian hits him with the shield, sending him sailing through the air and landing on the other side of the arch. knocking Dalistra across the clearing, and Siguredea's amulet ends up lying on his shoulder, visible to all.

Not fully understanding what just happened, he painfully stands up. The amulet dangles outside his clothes, and the knight kneels on one knee, bowing his head before fading away. He brushes off as the others hesitantly walk under the arch. Tera gently hands him a shaken Dalistra. Ericka is the first to ask him why he has kept the yellow disk a secret, and he didn't realize it was of any importance. When they ask him where he got it, he tells them about being on Siguredea's world, and she gave it to him.

Ericka wants the amulet. As the only magic user, but he doesn't want the same thing to happen to her like her sister. It takes prodding by everyone else, but he gives her the amulet. The amulet begins to glow and pulsate as he hands it to her. As she puts it around her neck, it becomes bright gold then fades into its yellow color. Ericka can feel the magic from the disk coursing through her. She reveals in the power moving through her body smiling all the while.

The last time Dalistra was in Thesila, the streets were teeming with people. Looking upon the emptiness, it hits her. Everything and everybody she knew are gone—all her friends, the royal court, and her family have vanished ages ago. For the first time, a mournful mood sets in as Mashaun feels her sadness and wants to say something to cheer her up. But what do you tell someone who realizes everything and everyone they know is gone?

Dalistra remembers how she and her friends would play in the city streets. She remembers the royal court, formal balls and the happy times. They are now gone. Unknowingly, Mashaun gets a glimpse of her life. He thinks maybe he should have let Sivish perform the ritual to set her free, when Dalistra interjects.

"*That…is…not…going…to…happen until Magdalenia is dead,*" she says.

Going through the shimmering light, they walk out of the door, looking at a huge open area near the top of the mountain where they are astonish at its magnificence and splendor. Rumors say it disappeared thousands of years ago, but you wouldn't know it by looking at the buildings—glistening rock spires laced with stained-glass windows reaching toward the sky. Each side of the cut-stone road has multilevel buildings extending out from a cliff made of grown walls from different types of polished marble.

Each building door appears to be a wall of light, but when they try to enter, they run into something solid without any visible means of opening. The walls are smooth with streaks of lights upon close inspection seem to pulsate in veins embedded within the rock. One by one, they try the doors and the windows only to find them impenetrable until Berg closes his eyes and walks through an open door in his mind.

He finds himself in a modest living room with tables and chairs of grown rock. There are paintings on the walls with a bookcase in one corner. A door leads into what a cooking and dining area while along one wall, a set of stairs rises to a second floor. Soon Mai, Alandra, Mashaun, and even Ericka enter the room. All of them are amazed at the vibrant colors and the cleanliness of the place. Upstairs are three bedrooms and a toilet with running water and a shower. There is a square section on the floor with a hole beneath with a circle of holes in the ceiling. Curious, Mai walks under the holes, and water comes down like a rainstorm, soaking her clothes almost instantly. Startled, she jumps out with shock, looking like a drowned rat.

"Oh, that's cold," she exclaims.

On the wall just outside of the shower is a vertical set of symbols. Berg can't make them out, but he suspects it has something to do with the water temperature. There is also an oval-shaped hole behind a fancy partition, similar to the cave. They leave the room and continue exploring the rest of the house. The bedrooms are all about the same—a rock bed, a table, and a chair, with shelves stacked up along one wall, with silk and cotton clothes hanging on hooks in a small alcove on one wall. Each of the bedrooms has a window overlooking a street below, which hasn't dawned on them before. They can see out but do not remember seeing in. As night falls, they decide the house is better than being on the streets so they choose their spots, settling in for the night.

During the night, Mashaun hears the water running and sneaks into the bathroom, with Dalistra ready to shoot to see what's going on, only to find Ericka taking a shower. She lets out a scream as they both embarrassingly glance at each other before Mashaun turns and secretly smiles, apologizing. He stops the others from coming down the hall, telling them everything is okay and he accidentally startled Ericka taking a shower. Alandra wants to make sure, but he can tell by the stare of the other girls it would be a mistake. Mai jealously asks him if he liked what he saw as she walks by.

Ericka tells them the water has to be on for the symbols to work, and all they do is slide their hand up or down for the water temperature and side to side for the water flow. One by one, the girls take a shower while the others make sure the guys don't try to peek. Afterward, the guys take their showers.

The morning sun reflects off the tops of the buildings giving the city a surreal rainbow effect. They continue up what appears to be the central road. They pass by numerous side streets and into a once market area. The canopies still brightly colored, in the windless city. Ghostly figures turn to follow the group. they glance up a half dozen roads leading from the market, trying to decide on which one to take when Berg starts walking up one. They just follow him, not asking why. After a short time, it ends at a majestic building carved into the mountain face. Streams of red, blue, and yellow lights shoot in every direction, crisscrossing over the entire front of the building. Up a dozen steps, two gigantic ornately carved arch doors stand just a few feet away from them.

Cautiously, they approach and open the doors with ease. Without a creak or groan, they enter into the largest and most magnificent room they have ever seen. Several doors are along each wall, and on the back wall are two sets of double doors with ornate carvings of gold, silver, and precious gemstones. About two-thirds from the front door are two crystal pillars filled with a vacillating light in a rainbow of colors flanking an oval stone dais sits in the middle of the room.

Dalistra remembers the first time she was allowed here. The room was full of people as they watched the new prince of Thesila accept the crown from his father. He had passed the rite of passage, signifying to all he was no longer a boy. He was their prince and next in line for the throne. Only forteen at the time, she remembers holding her father's hand as she watched the gem-encrusted crown of light placed on the prince's head. It was later that day when she learned about the arranged marriage to the young prince. It was the last time she talked with her father as sadness fills her. A few years later, they were officially decreed as a couple. She spent the next few years living in the palace, learning how to be a queen.

It was a spring day when she went riding outside of the city with her guards. they were ambushed and she was kidnapped. Surrounded by six masked people wearing the different color robes, She remembers her spirit being ripped from her body and forced into the bow. Bringing such sadness, tears roll down Mashaun's cheeks, as he senses her memories.

For a long moment, they just stand there in awe until an apparition appears in front of them, inquisitively looking them over. It motions them to follow before turning and going through the right back door. Berg is the first to follow, being the most curious. The rest trail behind with Mashaun pulling up the rear. The phantom leads them down several long passageways before stopping in front of a shimmering door. Pointing at Ericka and Tera, he shakes his finger side to side. He also points at the gear and the weapons, again shaking his finger. He glides through the door with Berg and Mai quick to follow. Alandra is a little more hesitant, but he soon enters the room.

"Will you be okay for a while by yourself?" Mashaun asks them, knowing he will be returning, if not the others.

"Yes, we will be fine. Don't worry about us. I actually feel safe here, almost like home," Ericka tells him quietly as she brushes her hands as if to say go already.

Tera asks if he is coming back, and he just shrugs his shoulders, telling her he plans to.

He puts his gear on the floor and hands Dalistra to Tera, telling her to take care of Dalistra if he doesn't return. Tera can feel an immense sadness from the bow but thinks it is just her own feelings.

Berg, Mai, and Alandra are in a enormous room with hundreds of beds lined up in neat rows, looking like a cemetery stretched out into the darkness. The specter leads them past rows upon rows of beds in varying sizes, each with a different set of symbols carved into the base. Few beds have ghostlike images of humans, awrks, Tsaub, elves, dwarfs, giants, and more sleeping with some of the symbols glowing.

They come across a bed with Berg-like image and the figure motions for him to lie down. Berg shakes Mashaun's hand and thanks him for the adventure before taking his place on the bed. He slowly becomes one with the image and sleepily says he can see his bedroom as he falls asleep. He merges with the image then slowly fades away. Soon they go to Mai's bed. She gives Mashaun a hug and a kiss before whispering in his ear she will find him again. He tells her his websites with his name. She promises to call him as she hands him her last earring. She lies down and slowly fades away. The figure motions for Mashaun and Alandra to lie down on their respective beds. Sitting on the bed Alandra stares at Mashaun for a short while as his eyes become droopy.

"I assume you are not going home," Alandra says. Mashaun shakes his head.

"For me, this is now my home."

"I thought not. I need to tell you something before I return home. I lied back at the city…I didn't tell them where you were really from because they would have not let you leave. Over the years, I have learned the beds bring new life to this world, and without them, the world slowly dies. Cities without outsiders will disappear. So beware of what you say." As Alandra, slowly drifts asleep, Mashaun puts his feet on the bed and watches him fade away, turning the bed back to a plain slab as the symbols on the side fade until they are just etchings on the stone. Picking up the metal disc, Mashaun turns to walk away.

The specter points at the bed for Mashaun. He negatively shakes his head and starts walking back the way he came. The figure blocks his path and points to the bed. Again, Mashaun shakes his head, trying to go around. The figure gets in front of him again, pointing at the bed. It continues for some time until he remembers the doors. He just closes his eyes while walking forward, until he hears Tera, Ericka and Dalistra yelling he's back.

"Where are the others?" they ask Mashaun.

"They went home," he tells them emphatically.

"Oh, aren't you going home also?" they ask.

"No, I live in a city, and I am not a city person. This place is more my home. Come on, let's leave this place." They divide the rucksacks and head down the hallway only to find the specter in front of them. The phantom stares at Mashaun before giving him an affirmative nod and a smile, bowing his head before fading away.

"What was that about?" Ericka asks.

"You are the one foretold in the Thesila prophecy." Tera says, handing Dalistra back to Mashaun.

"Yes! I knew it. I knew you would not leave me here alone!" exclaims Dalistra, almost yelling in Mashaun's mind.

Ouch, Mashaun thinks.

"Sorry, I am just so excited," she says.

"What do you say we go back to the house and decide where to go next? and you can tell me about the Thesila prophecy," Mashaun says as they walk down the hall.

Chapter 29

HOME

http://thesilaprophecy.com/Book2/

Abigail wakes up with a jerk in a cold sweat. She is exhausted. Her blankets are tangled up as if she tossed and turned all night. She vaguely remembers fighting two ugly monsters with swords, and just before one of them hits her, she woke up. Looking around, she finds herself in her room at her parents' house. Her stuffed animals are scattered around the room and her schoolbooks are still on the desk. She hears lawn mowers outside and realizes it is Saturday.

Dad always mows the lawn on Saturday, but not today. She jumps into the shower, really enjoying the feeling of soap and warm water on her body. She starts to sing some songs. Stopping, she tries to remember where she heard them but to no avail, and sings them repeatedly. Soon her mother knocks on the door and tells her to hurry up, reminding her they are going to her aunt Kerena's wedding. She is not the only one who needs a shower. The wedding. How could she forget about the wedding? Quickly she finishes getting dressed before heading into the living room, giving both her parents a big hug. Surprised, they both stare at her then glance at each other before asking what that was about.

"Just because," she says, and they let it drop. Her mother has made her a vegetarian omelet for breakfast. She savors every bite as though it has been ages since she had a home-cooked meal, as the rest of the family gets ready for the wedding.

During the long drive, Abigail keeps humming the tune of songs, writing down the lyrics she remembers. When Abigail's mother asks her about the songs she is humming, she is at a loss for an answer. She finally tells her it came to her in a dream. Fortunately, her mother doesn't ask anything else about the dream. She vaguely remembers parts, but they are disjointed and don't make any sense. The only thing she really remembers is some ugly thing swinging a sword at her right before she woke up.

Her mother tells her she should talk to Kerena's new husband, Jack. After all, he has his own band. Abigail forgot about that. She will bring it up after they return from their honeymoon. Over the next few days, she plays the songs with a guitar, but it just is not the same. She buys a small harp. She tries recalling the music and the words while learning the instrument.

Berg awakes in a soft bed covered in a light-blue blanket. The smell of bacon and eggs permeates the air. He hears his children's laughter over a cartoon on television. Is he home? Or is this just another dream? He sits up in bed and scanning around at the room he recognizes as a smile covers his face. He did it, Mashaun really did it. Remembering the stone floor in the dream. He tries to hold on to the last remembrance of the dream, grabbing his notebook beside the bed. He jots down what little he can remember. He mainly remembers the symbols intrigued by him, with some names and places as they slowly fade from his memory.

His wife call the kids for breakfast. He quickly puts on some clothes and joins them at the table, remembering it is not normal for him to do this—he plans to make a change. He was up late the previous night, so everybody is pleasantly surprised when he joins them at the table. They ask when he is going to work. He thinks for a short while, realizing it is Saturday. He tells them he is not going. His family is shocked but delighted.

After breakfast, he gives his wife and his children hugs and kisses before helping with the dishes to his wife's pleasant surprise. Afterwards, he tells them he is going to take a shower and then they are going to spend the whole day together at the amusement park. His daughters run around, yelling and screaming with laughter as his wife gazes at him with a puzzled expression, but a happy one.

"You're not the same man I slept with last night," she tells him as she gets the girls ready.

The whole family is surprised by how affectionate he is during the day, which is not like him. Berg takes them out to dinner at a fancy restaurant. When they're home, he and his wife send the kids to bed and snuggle on the sofa. She lies there curled in his arm, enjoying the moment. It has been a long time since they just sat and enjoyed each other's company. Finally, she asks him about the change in his demeanor. He starts to tell her about the dream but finds all he can remember are disjointed and fragmented. They don't make any sense, even after he gets his notes from the morning. She peers at him with her soft brown eyes and tells him it doesn't matter because it must have been a good dream. It brought back the man she married, and missed.

Mai opens her eyes to the four bland walls of her dorm room as she sits up, making her head spin. She glances at her purple nightgown, and sadness slowly begins to creep over her as she faintly remembers the dream. Before taking a shower, she looks at her cell phone and realizes her test is in an hour.

All those months and I didn't miss the test. Damn, she thinks. She stands in the shower absorbing every precious minute, eventhough she isn't any dirtier than normal this morning. She remembers the shock of an icy shower before the end of the dream. After the test, she goes to the library to research dreams and their meanings. She is disappointed there are no books describing the meaning behind her dream.

She looks up the only name she can remember, Mashaun, and finds several in the internet. She tries to remember more but can't. The more she thinks about the dream, the more she remembers and the happier she becomes. But it fades as the day wears on. She feverishly writes down everything she can remember. Sometimes, what she writes doesn't make any sense. She finds sometimes when writing, something sparks more of the dream.

Reading her notes, she has a feeling there is more, but there is something missing. Somehow, she and the others ended up in another world where they lived for a while but wondered how is it possible. She remembers Mashaun and her feelings for him but wonders if he remembers her or thinks she's just a crazy woman. The next few days, she spends her free time learning about clairvoyance, astral travel, and parallel worlds.

She shares her thoughts with her friend, and they tell her it's just a dream. Still, they cannot deny she has changed. She is no longer a pure pacifist and actually tells them there is a time and place for killing. She is also more vocal about her ideas—a much better student in general. Some of her friends don't like the new Mai so they drift apart. She reads her notes each night, hoping it will send her back to that dream world with Mashaun. But she always wakes frustrated without any new memories, only the fading idea of her dream man.

As the days turn into weeks and weeks into months, they all slowly forget the dream itself while some of the ideas and attitudes they brought from it become part of their new lives. Each of them eventually search for the stone, but none are found.

Thank you for reading *Thesila Prophecy* and I hope you enjoyed the story. Please return to where you purchased it and give an honest review.

Purchase on Amazon:
    Go to the product detail page for the item on Amazon.com.
    Click **Write a customer review** in the Customer Reviews section.
    Click **Submit**.

Find Robert on the following:

http://www.thesilaprophecy.com

https://www.facebook.com/AuthorRMRumble

For a behind the scene at: https://youtu.be/PoK1sapAmSQ

https://www.patreon.com/RobertR

https://www.instagram.com/authorrobertrumble/

Thank you.
Robert Rumble